David Ralph
programmes as well as two acclaimed novels featuring
Detective Sergeant Vic Cromer. He lives in Dorset.

Also by David Ralph Martin

I'm Coming to Get You
Arm and a Leg

David Ralph Martin

DEAD MAN'S SLAUGHTER

ST. ALBERT PUBLIC LIBRARY
5 ST. ANNE STREET
ST. ALBERT, ALBERTA T8N 3Z9

ARROW

Published in the United Kingdom in 2001 by
Arrow Books

1 3 5 7 9 10 8 6 4 2

Copyright © David Ralph Martin 2001

The right of David Ralph Martin to be identified as the author
of this work has been asserted by him in accordance
with the Copyright, Designs and Patents Act, 1988

This book is sold subject to the condition that it shall not,
by way of trade or otherwise, be lent, resold, hired out,
or otherwise circulated without the publisher's prior consent
in any form of binding or cover other than that in which it is
published and without a similar condition including this
condition being imposed on the subsequent purchaser

First published in the United Kingdom in 2000
by William Heinemann

Arrow Books
The Random House Group Limited
20 Vauxhall Bridge Road, London, SW1V 2SA

Random House Australia (Pty) Limited
20 Alfred Street, Milsons Point, Sydney
New South Wales 2061, Australia

Random House New Zealand Limited
18 Poland Road, Glenfield,
Auckland 10, New Zealand

Random House (Pty) Limited
Endulini, 5a Jubilee Road
Parktown 2193, South Africa

The Random House Group Limited Reg. No. 954009

www.randomhouse.co.uk

A CIP catalogue record for this book
is available from the British Library

Papers used by Random House are natural,
recyclable products made from wood grown in sustainable forests.
The manufacturing processes conform to
the environmental regulations of the country of origin

Printed and bound in Germany by
Elsnerdruck, Berlin

ISBN 0 09 927865 0

DECEMBER 1999

Ten past eleven on a freezing December night and Rupert Lang, twenty-eight, ex-Bryanston School and Leyhill Open Prison, was sitting in a big white U-Haul van sandwiched between two carloads of Turks watching his last chance slide down the pan.

Five grand for driving a van full of heroin from Bristol to London stuck between two lots of Turks who were too fucking cunning to take the risk for themselves.

Jesus Christ how dumb could you get?

As if, knowing what he knew, they'd let him walk away with a big smile, a cheery farewell and five large ones in his back pocket – he was as good as brown bread already, sliced and toasted.

Oh shit –

And now, only five miles out of Bristol, they were all about to get fucked in spades and he was feeling paralysed.

Oh shit –

Up ahead at the floodlit entrance to the New Severn Crossing the orange and blue lights of a police road-block were pinging off the metal and concrete of the bridge. Instead of racking his brains for a way out, Rupert found himself with his mind stuck in neutral thinking how Christmassy it all looked. Maybe it was the bullet-crease throbbing across the top of his head – maybe it was the general exhaustion of a day and a night that had gone from bad to worse, but he felt he was falling downstairs inside a wardrobe and there was fuck-all he could do about it: the springs of action were lying sprawled and jangled on the floor of his mind as if someone had just kicked his grandfather clock in.

Pity he'd miss Christmas, he thought; he'd miss the Millennium as well: he'd be banged up with all the fucking Turks in the cars in front and behind him for possession and intent to supply God knows how much fucking heroin –

Oh shit –

His last seconds of freedom ticking away and all he could feel were his bowels going hot and runny and loose –

Oh shit –

Now the police, with four dog-handlers, two to each traffic lane, were separating the vehicles into cars and commercials. As the Turks in the Granada in front and the Scorpio behind peeled off into the outside lane, Rupert found himself going for it. There was no thought involved – all he had by way of motivation was an image of police dogs snarling and crawling all over him while he sat there crapping himself.

The next second he was plunging the van down the chalky embankment into a broad unfinished drainage trench. The van nose-dived on to its springs as it hit the bottom – any deeper and it would have gone arse over tit and landed on its fucking roof –

Instead it ploughed into the opposite bank and tried to bulldoze its way up. Rupert kept his foot hard down, held the lever in first with one hand and wrenched at the wheel with the other. The van slewed sideways and began accelerating along the ditch towards a mass of half-buried six-foot concrete drainpipes.

He slammed the gearlever into second and, engine screaming, hit the earth ramp burying the drains at just over thirty.

The van bucked in the air as the front wheels hit three feet of rounded concrete and then – *thank fuck* – the rear wheels went on driving up the earth bank until the whole van was leaping and banging and thrumming and hammering across the tops of the drains and into the ribbed and frozen yard where the dozers and the JCBs and the big yellow six-wheel trucks had been parked up. Rupert switched off his lights – there was enough mercury vapour security lighting in the plant park for him to see – and hurtled through the towering mud-splattered machines in third. The back of the park was surrounded with eight-foot chainlink topped with triple strands of wire and the track narrowed down into a gated V-shaped entrance. Barrelling along about forty, with the back of the van a chaos of cardboard tubes and boxes of Christmas wrapping paper – the cover for the parcel-taped heroin packages beneath – Rupert hit the security gates head-on. One flattened under his wheels and the other, hanging off the passenger mirror, clanged and scraped along the side of the van for at least twenty yards before dropping off, and the thought flitted through his mind that U-Haul weren't going to get much of a van back –

Then he was sliding down the backside of the hill, with the brown chalk turned to thick black Severn mud and the shallow, brightly-lit arch of the New Severn Crossing was sliding sideways across his view through the windscreen.

Holy shit, he'd got the fucking thing sideways and no fucking grip at all.

Helpless, he watched as the van pirouetted right round once, then twice, and finally came to rest with its arse end in a bunch of thin scabby birch trees and its wheels in thick black loam.

Severn Beach, I'm on Severn Beach.

He switched off and listened for signs of pursuit.

Nothing.

No sirens, no clacking and blattering helicopters.

Nothing.

What he needed was a joint, but the van seemed to be full of white fog. Fog you could taste – sour, sharp, bitter. Heroin. One of the packages must have burst open.

He rolled the window down. Thin white dust was sucked out into the cold air. He started the engine, inched the van forward slowly until it was out of the trees and on to a grassed-over tractor track. The grass stood up, spiky-white with frost. Rupert switched off and began to roll himself a fat four-inch joint. His whole body was shivering and trembling uncontrollably like a wet springer spaniel and he made a terrible funnel-shaped bodge-up of the joint.

Fuck it – at least he was free.

Free at last, oh Lord, free at last.

He could feel the hit of the joint moving from his throbbing scalp right the way down to his ankles; slowly his muscles stopped shivering, and as his mind stopped yawing all over the place, his concentration returned, and he realised that he was not only free but he was in sole possession of a large and highly valuable load of heroin – how much he wasn't sure: his mind wasn't up to multiplication and percentages – but it was big.

Oh boy.

The fucking jackpot.

He sucked at the joint and let his mind surf effortlessly along on the rush of what he'd fallen into.

You've fucking earned it, mate. By Christ you've fucking earned it. Through storms of blood and shit to the green fields beyond . . . Fucking right – Sri Lanka here I come.

He needed a piss. A big, long, luxurious piss.

He slid out of the seat – his legs were still a bit glassy-wobbly – and stood, leaning his head on his arm against the van door. Shuddering and thankful as the piss flowed out, glittering, steaming, endless.

Lovely –

Then there was a soft footstep and a colossal, sickening blast of pain in the back of his head as the point of a fireaxe bit into the base of his skull, and, as Rupert turned and slipped down the side of the van through his own spraying blood, he knew he had well and truly missed the Millennium and had lost his chance to see the Thames in flames, on fire from end to end –

Oh shit –

APRIL 2000

I

Senda, a lean brown Jamaican in his forties with a face as lined and scarred as a butcher's block, was a specialist slaughterman by trade and to his way of thinking this was the best of deaths.

Before he began he washed the cattle prods carefully in bleach and near-boiling water, rinsed them under the cold tap and placed them on the drainer. Exchanging the blue kitchen Marigolds for a pair of thin surgical gloves Senda turned to look at the body of the 55-year-old black man on the floor. His hands and ankles were bound with three-inch white tape, his mouth was raw and blistered and his eyes ran with pain.

By the back kitchen door to the yard the blue-overalled Saudi-looking kid driver gave Senda a nod. All clear.

Senda kept his voice quiet and nice, to calm the old black guy. 'You poor rass. You couldn't a known anything, because if you had a known anything you would a told me. You would a been glad, you hear me nah? Ain't no way a man can bear what you been through and keep a quiet mouth, I don't care what sum a money you looking at. Had a been me, bro, I would a howled and bellocked and shouted out, Sweet Jesus, anything you want a know, boss. I would a beg you to end me sufferin'. Instead you denied me and, yeah, you suffer. Now I make it easy on you – OK?'

9

He smiled and knelt down on the man's right to make sure the man could not see the cloth roll of knives at his side. Then he opened the man's shirt. He took out his broad-bladed twelve-inch cutting knife, made an incision between the man's fifth and sixth ribs and twisted the blade sideways to wedge the ribs apart.

Thin sheets of blood scalloped outwards from the incision.

He slid his gloved hand in between the man's ribs, took hold of the rubbery-feeling fist-sized heart in its skein of fat and squeezed. The man tried to writhe away from the pain in his ribs but because none of the nerves in his heart had been severed there was no other pain and he was unaware that he was dying.

In Anatolia, in the yards where Senda had worked as a civilian butcher on the Tuslog Det-8 USAF radar base outside Diyarbakir, the chosen lamb or goat would stand long minutes after death, spilling no blood on fleece or hide, and only falling when its lowering neck drew it down.

Senda increased the pressure. The pulsing stilled and the light in the man's eyes dulled to blue. It was beautiful in its silence, and Senda, as always, felt privileged to have been this death's instrument. He said a brief prayer for the man and asked forgiveness and deliverance for himself. He stood up and away from the body. Already the thin sheets of blood were slowing.

He washed his gloves, and then his hands. He put both sets of gloves and the knives and the cattle prods and their chargers in a zipped leatherette shopping bag, gave it to the Saudi-looking kid driver and motioned him to go. He swilled water round the sink again and when it had gone Senda noticed how waiting-still it was in the small kitchen. He glanced at his watch: 6.58.

By five past seven a woman in a black chador left the house and made for the Bristol City Centre bus stop on Gloucester Road. A black four-litre Ford Explorer eased down the hill slope opposite and drew up by the woman in the chador.

Senda slid into the front passenger seat and held the shopping bag between his knees. A freshly lit joint was offered from the back seat; Lance, thirty-five and built like a heavyweight, leaned forward and put his long Easter Island head on his forearms next to Senda's ear. His voice was deep, morning-rough. 'What 'appen, Sen? What a man say?'

'He ain't say nothin'. Nothin' then and nothin' now,' Senda took a long and thankful drag. 'God rest his soul.'

'The woman?'

'Gone.'

'Shit. You take a look?'

'Mattresses, everythin'. Nothin'.'

The driver, looking clean-cut now in a white shirt, red bow-tie and blazer, said, 'Keep it down at the lights if you would please, Mr Senda.'

Senda held the joint low between the seat and the door. He said to Lance, 'You wouldn't keep a weight like that in you own house, man.'

'Hell of a weight,' said Lance. 'Seventy-three k. Weight of a man.'

Senda calculated in his head. 'More like a woman.'

'That right?'

'Average, yeah.'

'All a same, you got a keep it somewhere, Sen.

Seventy-three k of H. Got a keep it somewhere.'

'Spose he got a slaughter somewhere. Some lock-up he don't tell nobody where. Some nice little steel roller-door somewhere, under some arches somewhere, double steel doors inside, like that. Nice little slaughter.'

'Yeah.'

A pause as they thought it over. Neither believed the guy could have kept his mouth shut, but what else was there to believe?

Senda had failed?

There was no way Lance was ever going to tell Senda that. Yeah, Lance was big and still fast with his hands, but Senda was hard, hard and vicious. Worst thing was you never knew when he was about to go. Senda was like that guy in the Samurai, the quiet hatchet-face guy: one second you didn't even know he'd seen you, the next you was cut in half and you was looking down at you guts lying in a pile and steaming up at you from the dust.

So you didn't say, Senda you just fuck up. But that was why the North London Brothers had sent you and him in the first place: you to stop fights and fuck-ups, protect the Brothers' down payment and help locate the stuff; him because he knew Turks, knew enough a their fucking lingo in case they double-gypped you; and both a you because the Brothers were very low on product and both a you were hard enough and tooled up enough to see all the H got back to Chalk Farm uncut and unfucked up.

So what did you say?

Without it sounding like some fucking suicidal insult?

*

Sometimes Lance wondered how he'd got into this fucking game. Sure, he and Senda made a good payback team, but he'd been in the game long before Senda come over. Time to time he'd trace it back and trace it back, but all he could ever come up with was he was always just too fucking big. Jesus, he was too big when he was born even, practically killed his mother –

As she never stop telling him.

Then at school older kids would give him their sandwiches and he'd say, What's that for, and they'd say, Nothing, Lance. And that was nice, having friends; having people who admired you.

Except next day they'd come up and ask you to hit shit out of some other little fucker.

And you'd eaten all their sandwiches, hadn't you?

Then it was boxing and wrestling, Lance 'Buffalo' Bull, just because he was so fucking big and looked right. Boxing wasn't too bad because he was younger then, but training was fucking hell, man, and wrestling was ten times worse: wearing them fucking great buffalo horns and shortass leopardskin cape like some fuckwit fruit asshole Zulu.

Then having the crap slammed out of you by some hairy-back white piece a lard because you happen to be the black guy.

Well, shit on that, man.

By the time years later Lance figured out a way he could make money out of being big without actually getting hit to shit all the time he was already in the game. Had been ever since school, probably. Maybe it was what he was good at, what he was for, Chrissake.

What he wanted now, age of thirty-five, with nobody else in his line a work looking at making it much over thirty – what he really wanted now was to be one of the guys sitting in the big armchairs with their heavy three-piece funeral suits on telling the rest of the crew what to do.

And the way to do that was you had to do this first. And to do this first, you did not fuck up. Because if you fuck up, you got fucked. No second chance. Too many shit-for-brains waiting to blow you away, step in you shoes.

Holy fuck, maybe even Senda.

So speak to him man to man, sound like you was asking him advice. Yeah, was it. Cool.

'Shit, Sen, somebody got to know. Somebody in this no-no fuckin' town got to know if they sittin' on seventy-three k a shit or not.'

'Yeah.'

'Maybe the Turk know somethin'.'

'Yeah. Maybe.'

Neither Lance nor Senda went much on Turks, Lance because they come from East London and they had this idea black people should pick up the crap and the aggro while they drove off with the profits. All Senda said when he was laid-back and stoned one time was he knew Turks, they was heavy dopeheads and ass-bandits, got no respec' for the black man, and top of that, their human rights was all to shit, so fuck 'em.

So the job had never looked full a promise from the start. Now it was worse: with the old guy saying nothing, they were in the hands of this Shabba guy.

'Hey, Drive.'

The driver was checking him in the mirror. 'Yes, Mr Bull?'

'Where we meetin' the Turk?'

The driver hesitated, glanced down at his

Routeplanner. 'Mister Sabbahatin and his colleagues will rendezvous with us at Severn View Services, here, sir. Fourteen miles out on the M4.'

'What time?'

'Time to be advised by Mr Sabbahatin on arrival, sir.'

'This kid, this local kid, this Richie. He be there? –'

Another hesitation. 'I'm sorry, Mr Bull. I don't have that information at this time.'

'That right?'

'Yes sir.'

Was how the kid spoke, like some fucking mouth-piece. Everything wrapped up nice but telling you shit.

When they came to a junction, the kid got on his mobile and started all that jabber-jabber-jabber in Turkish, Arabic, whatever it was.

'Where's he at, Sen?'

'Sound like he tellin' this Shabba guy what come down back at the house.'

Lance put his head close to Senda and held out a huge hand for the joint. He stuck it in one end of his fist and sucked at the other, making sure to keep his fist in front of his mouth on account of this smartass Saudi-looking kid driver. 'Way I'm thinkin', Sen, the question is where. Question is if they don't know, how we gonna find out. Question is how a fuck we gonna find a dead man's slaughter. With or without the Turks. Because we do this without the Turks, we get this stuff up to the Brothers without the Turks –'

'The Brothers still gotta pay, man. Rule a business. You don' pay you got a fuckin' war.'

'No, Sen, you ain't with me –'

'No, I ain't –'

'We get the stuff to the Brothers, sure, they still

gotta pay – but they got the edge, they got the fuckin' edge, man. Fuckin' Turks can't do a fuckin' thing. We put the Brothers in a bargain-seat, they owe us, man. Owe us big. We get a nice little deal – a nicer little deal an' they watch our backs for us. Way I'm lookin' at the deal –'

'The deal the deal the deal –' Senda sounding pissed off. 'The deal is water till it turn to steel. Y'know? You hear me nah?'

'Yeah, but what I'm saying is if we do it right –'

'Yeah,' said Senda. 'If we do it right. We do it wrong, we got the Turks *an*' the Brothers lookin' to mash us, lass us, leave us for dus'.'

'Always is a If, Sen. Fack is, in this game, no fucker trust no fucker. Why you had this kid driver watchin' you every fuckin' move.'

'Yeah.' Senda turned his head away from the driver. 'One ting in our favour, man.'

'What that, Sen?'

'Down here, these Turk guys stick out more'n we do, man. Mek us look fuckin' normal.'

'Heh heh heh. Seen, man.'

'I *know* Turks,' said Senda. 'I fuckin' live with 'em way back. This Shabba guy, you only got a look at him, he ain't been out on a street for years, man. He one a their big-ups.' Senda sucked his teeth. 'But he ain't *the* big-up, and it his deal, his shout, and he done fuck up, man. He like a woman, man, he got a woman's spite, you can see it in 'im. He don' find this shit, he loss his face, man, loss all respec'.'

'Yeah, you right.'

'I know these fuckers,' said Senda. 'He go back to his other big-ups an' he ain't got this stuff, they ain't gonna say, Well that's too bad, they gonna stick one a

16

their burp-guns up his ass and pull the trigger till it don' shoot no more. He fuckin' dangerous, man because he in a fuckin' corner – you hear me nah?'

'Yeah, I hear you,' said Lance. 'What about the ress of 'em, this kid here, them other fuckers?'

Senda spat a shred of tobacco out the window. 'They jus' Turks, man. Any shit come down they fuckin' gone, man. Fuck 'em.'

'Yeah.' Lance handed the joint back. 'Way I'm thinkin'. Question is when.'

Lance leaned back and looked at the brown mirror-glass office blocks sliding past the big Ford's windows.

Somewhere out there was three and a half million.

2

It was half past seven on a cool blue April morning and Vic Hallam, thirty-eight, Detective Sergeant with Bristol Central CID, was laying out bookie-sized ballpoints and recycled scrap pads around the sectional mahogany table in the Mansion House conference room.

There was a pleasant smell of polish and the sixty-foot room, hung with heavily varnished oils of Bristol ships and shipowners, felt light and airy.

Ordinarily, Vic would have been highly pissed off at having to play desk monitor at this hour of the morning, but what the hell: Ellie, the nurse he lived with, was on earlies at A and E in the Bristol Royal Infirmary, and he didn't go a lot on lying in their empty bed with nothing but her warm oatmeal smell to remind him, so the night before he'd said he'd do it.

'Fuck me,' said Sam Richardson, the abrasive Northern Detective Chief Superintendent who was acting head of CID, 'twenty years in the force and finally Vic fucking Hallam volunteers. Hoo-fucking-ray. Fuck's up now, Vic?'

'Not a lot.' There was, as a matter of fact, quite a lot up, but as far as Sam Richardson was concerned he could stick his fingers up his arse and whistle 'Dixie'.

Sam, built like a lock forward and never one to miss a chance to bully and needle, had stuck his chin out like Mussolini and put his face close to Vic's. Sam had harsh pepper-and-salt hair, a face the colour of fresh veal and a furious herring-gull stare, and when he grinned his lips vanished because his teeth were nearly always clenched.

'This nurse of yours like a bit in the morning, does she? Wearing you out, is she?' It was Sam's way: he pushed and shoved and riled until you lost it and then he'd got you.

Vic smiled back. 'Don't they all?'

'I don't know, Vic, I'm a married man, me.' Sam's face was so close Vic could smell his wine-and-garlic breath. Sometimes when Sam had had a few he would get a cheap laugh out of his CID cronies by referring to his wife as Madam Saddam or Mrs Milosevic; in fact, she was a perfectly pleasant dark-haired woman who was a Liberal councillor and head governor of a school for the disabled. Sam called this school variously Buchenwald, Dachau or Belsen, but never for some reason Auschwitz, so maybe certain things were sacred after all.

Vic had known Sam for years, and at first had put it down to Northern defensiveness and Never Show Weakness; then, after meeting Sam's wife, and seeing them together, he realised Sam was defiantly proud of her, loved her with a dour Northern possessiveness he could never admit – not even to himself, let alone her.

Sex was another thing of course. It always was.

So maybe that was why Sam came on to Vic as jealous: jealous that, in Sam's mind, Vic was for ever getting it and Sam never did. On the other hand, with a fucking heavy control freak like Sam, it was just another lever, just another way of putting you down and keeping you down.

But not for much longer, Sammy baby.

Vic walked round the table with the ashtrays: heavy cut-glass numbers for the police side, anodised tin for the punters. It was all of a piece with holding the meetings in the Mansion House: when the St Pauls community leaders – four black and two white – had turned down the Bridewell and Trinity Road Police Station as too intimidating and Sam had done the same to their suggestion of the Malcolm X Centre for what he called 'security reasons', they had come to a compromise on the Mansion House.

Nominally the home of the incumbent Lord Mayor and Lady Mayoress and set on the edge of 450 acres of open parkland in the whitest and poshest part of Bristol, the Mansion House now earned part of its keep as a conference centre. The fact that the nineteenth-century portraits of Bristol's Merchant Venturers and their vessels were not altogether unrelated to the Slave Trade was neither here nor there to Sam. His attitude was 'Let the buggers look – if it reminds them where they come from or how they got here, so much the better.' The same with the scrap paper and the bookies' ballpoints.

'Black cunts'll only pinch 'em, Vic.'

'Fuck's sake, Sam.'

The lipless grin, seeing he'd got through. 'Sorry, Vic. I forgot you like a bit of black now and again.' Then turning to go, 'You know what they say, don't you?'

'What about, Sam?'

'Shagging before sparrow-fart.'

'What's that, Sam?'

' "Uncle George and Auntie Mabel fainted at the breakfast table. Let this be a solemn warning – never do it in the morning." Cheers, Vic. Don't be late.'

Vic set out twelve 330-ml. bottles of Highland Spring, capped each bottle with a paper cup, lined up twelve metal-framed chairs, and that was it.

No expense spared and let battle commence.

The reason for the last-minute meeting of the Police Liaison Committee was tomorrow's funeral and memorial service for Maelee Thomas in downtown St Pauls. There had already been two meetings, one to discuss the ifs and whys, the St Pauls point being there'd already been two big memorials for police victims, so why not Maelee, and the second to discuss security needs and details.

Late on in the second meeting the leaders of the St Pauls black community had sprung one on them: as well as the service itself in the Lion of Judah they wanted a procession to the church from Westminster Road Community Centre. Westminster Road Community Centre was the old school where Maelee Thomas had been shot, accidentally, during the course of a police drugs raid.

'Fuck me,' Sam Richardson had said to the police group afterwards, 'it won't be a fucking procession, it'll be a fucking march; oil-can bands and blaster vans, hundreds of the buggers jigging about stoned out their fucking trees – it'll open up the whole fucking can of worms all over again and you mark my words there'll be wagon-loads of fucking so-called fucking protesters fucking bussed in – black and white – and we'll end up with another fucking brick-chucking riot – lootings, burnings, God knows what. I say ban it, ban the whole fucking shooting match. Grounds of Public Order.'

When Caroline Coombes, the uniformed community beat inspector for St Pauls, pointed out that if they did ban it there'd be a riot anyway, Sam reluctantly saw sense, agreed to a last-minute meeting 'to bang some fucking heads together' and stormed off home.

After Sam had gone, Caroline, an attractive and thoroughly self-possessed young woman in her early thirties, sought Vic out. Years ago, when she was a probationer and he was a rising young detective, they had had a considerable thing going, but because she put the job before risking dismissal by letting Vic into her knickers, it had never quite reached fruition. As a result, even though Vic had got married in the interim and was now all but divorced and living with Ellie, there was still something there, water not quite under the bridge.

'What d'you think, Vic?'

'One up to you, kid.' The rat part of him wondering if her mouth still tasted as sweet.

Glancing his look aside. 'No, Vic. D'you think Sam's right?'

'Sam exaggerates to cover his arse – so he can say I told you so.' He offered his pack of Marlboro.

'No thanks.'

'Given up?'

'Everything. Booze, everything.'

'Bit of a waste.'

'You know me, Vic. All or nothing. How's Ellie?'

'Fine.'

'Good.' Looking at him to show she wasn't bothered.

To kill the pause, Vic said, 'How many bodies can you put on the street?'

'Twenty, twenty-four. But that's only lining the route. Won't be any good if they start bussing in.'

'They won't.'

Darting him a look. 'D'you know something?'

'All I meant was –'

'Because I'm fed up with your lot –'

'So I see –'

'Never telling anybody anything – playing stupid bloody mind games.'

'Getting a bit paranoid, aren't we?'

'Who wouldn't?' Blue eyes flashing. 'They've been trying to get me off this patch ever since I got stuck in over the shootings. Even you know that –'

'Look, Caroline –'

'All a bunch of middle-aged middle-class white males, Vic, just as fascist as they ever were –'

'Listen, Caroline – you're not going to like this, but just listen a minute, will you?'

'Here we go – pat on the head time –'

'All right. What time's the service?'

'Eleven thirty.'

'What time's the march?'

'Not a march it's a procession –'

'When?'

'Eleven.'

'Right. Now if it was five, six in the afternoon on a baking hot summer's day, I'd say yeah, you're right to be worried, you and Sam both.'

'So?'

'Not at that time in the morning. Black or white, no self-respecting fucking anarchist is going to get out of bed before twelve –'

'Jesus Christ, Vic, you're as bad as the rest –'

'And they certainly couldn't organise buses for then – be nobody there.'

'Yeah yeah yeah –'

'Something else you're not going to like.'

'What?'

'The blacks are as bad as we are.'

'Meaning?'

'If this was a young black guy just been shot I'd say yeah, grip your shit because this is it. But it's not a young black guy is it? And he's not just been shot has he?'

She looked as if she'd like to kick him in the scrotum. 'You're saying because she was a young woman –'

'I'm saying the blacks are as bad as we are –'

'Jesus Christ, Vic, am I hearing this?'

'I'm saying the blacks are as bad as we are, as bad as you *think* we are, because they don't give a fuck either. As you well know –'

'Yeah yeah yeah –'

'Women don't count in their world. Young women don't count at all, and young black single mothers like Maelee Thomas count even less.'

'Why?' Chin-up stubborn now. 'Give me one good reason.'

'Because they've served their purpose. Fuck and fly. Jesus Christ, you must have seen enough of it, all the baby-mothers you get to deal with –'

'And you think that's natural, do you? You think because that's what they do, that's what they should do?'

'All I'm saying is if you're a young black dude with no job, no prospects and no hope beyond the next street-corner deal, a woman's a natural-born victim. End of story –'

'So it doesn't matter if she's shot in the stomach and left for dead –'

Losing it, and knowing she was nagging him into losing it, and suddenly not fucking caring: 'Course it fucking matters – but Maelee Thomas is not a fucking hero, is she? She's not a dead fucking hero – because if she was, if she was a bloke, Caroline, there'd have been fucking riots all over the place long since, and not just here –'

'And it's as simple as that, is it?' Smirking at him, egging him on.

'Yes, basically.'

'I see. Thanks.'

To wipe the annoying little smirk off her face, he said, 'Apart from anything else –'

'Apart from anything else, what?' Cold as ice now.

'This may sound brutal –'

'You are brutal. Go on.'

'Apart from anything else, Caroline, Maelee Thomas is past and gone. She's been in a mortuary drawer for the last four months.'

He watched her breathing herself down until she could trust herself to speak. 'And that's what you think?'

'Yes. Basically. Anybody on that march – sorry – procession, will be there out of respect.'

'Not anger?'

'No. Respect and solidarity yes, anger no.'

'And that's why Detective Sergeant Hallam of Central CID thinks there won't be any trouble.'

'Hopes.'

There was a glisten of sweat on her upper lip. She took a tissue from her sleeve and dabbed at her nose. 'I'll try to see where you're coming from, Vic. But don't count on it.' She picked up her document case and a mottled grey box file. Before she left, she said, 'You knew Maelee Thomas, didn't you?'

'Yes. Why?'

'I just wondered.'

Vic stood in the Mansion House conference room, smelling the polish and looking at the dust-motes rise and fall in the early morning sun.

I just wondered.

It was a mistake arguing with them, it was a mistake talking to them, looking at them, even. Once they got your attention you'd already taken their bait when you thought you were just window-shopping. Remembering her nice round arse tick-tocking down the tiles and out through the double doors. And when they banged shut, it was as if they'd banged shut on his prick.

So what was all that about?

You can think yourself as calm and as settled and as loving-faithful as you like – one sniff of a bit of fresh and the rat's up and raving to get out.

Yeah, that was about it.

All it was.

Probably.

As he climbed the Portland stone staircase to the galleried first floor, and then on up the narrow wooden staircase to the second floor CCTV and obbo room, Vic felt his mood lightening. So he'd been stupid to lose it with Caroline, to let her get to him. All it was, she was an inspector, he was a sergeant, he was a man, she was a woman. It was all the same old shit, so fuck it.

Six months, Hallam, and you'll be out.

Jesus Christ it would be like walking out of nick.

Grinning to himself, thinking, basically, Hallam, you don't give a toss.

It was like being out to sea after a rough night's

26

fishing: one sight of the pier-head lights and you forgot all about your wet arse and throwing up and coming back with nothing in the bag but a stinking thawed-out bait box – one sight of land and you didn't give a toss.

Because you'd been enjoying yourself, hadn't you?

And now you were home safe you didn't give a toss.

Because you'd seen the sight of land, the end, the way out. And Sam and all the rest of the grinding, whining, mardy-arsed grisly crew could go and get fucked, black and white alike.

Yeah, that was about it.

Vic Hallam, six foot, straight dark hair, pale grey eyes and a faint fuck-you grin on a face that had suffered the odd dent or two over twenty years in the force, could afford the luxury of this attitude because four months ago, just before Christmas, he had picked up two bullet wounds in the right leg and one in the left. He had also picked up a couple of Commissioners' commendations and the sudden realisation that he was dangerously sodding mortal. Not only that, he also realised that his smugfucker so-called superiors DCI Parnes and DCS Richardson, who had turned up pissed and grinning at his hospital bed to so-say congratulate him, didn't give a rat's left nacker whether he lived or fucking died.

Consequently, but also because he was now living with Ellie, Vic had decided to quit – or, as he told his partner Detective Constable John Cromer: 'I'm going to give it up and go straight, mate. You'll have to save the world on your fucking own.'

Vic reckoned that, come September, all he had to do was keep his nose clean and wait for his divorce from Pat – Trish as she was now calling herself – to finalise, and he'd be on his way: goodbye Bridewell, hello Sunshine.

With a full twenty-year pension and a fair old whack of disability, Vic saw himself somewhere down on the South Coast, Devon, Dorset, nowhere too expensive; bungalow, bicycle, check shirt, woolly hat – and the biggest and fastest charter fishing boat he could afford.

There was a Lochin 33, 250 hp Volvo Penta and a good 15 knots on the plane, he wanted to check out near Weymouth.

Fuck Richardson, fuck his smarmy fat-arsed sidekick Parnesy, fuck that bent bastard Barnard whose fault all this was but he was dead anyway – fuck the meeting, fuck the blacks, fuck the whites, fuck the lot, Caroline fucking Coombes included.

And if Ellie wanted kids, well fuck it, more the merrier. We'll manage. It was what his father always said –

Vic could hear him saying it . . .

He was seven years old and his father was teaching him to fish the Avon below Bathampton Weir, scattering pellets of garlic-soaked bread for ground-bait. 'Cast up, cast away now and come down with 'em.'

The float, made from the spine of a gull's feather and coated with nail varnish, sped like an arrow into the oily flotilla.

'Just the job.' His father's thick red paw of a hand came down sandpaper-rough, and rubbed the back of Vic's sunburned neck. 'Now keep it there, in amongst 'em.'

Vic bending, ducking away, 'Yes dad.'

For most of the year Vic's father was away to sea, chief engineer on one company vessel or another out of Avonmouth and across the 'Western Ocean' – never the Atlantic – bound for South America and the West Indies.

In consequence of these year-long absences, though it was only Vic's mother who realised, it took some time for the pair of them to get used to moving round each other. Although they idolised each other when apart, they didn't seem to understand one another when they were abruptly thrust together: the time-lapse caused a fracture that seemed to take longer to heal each year.

It wasn't just the sight of his father in his mother's bed, or his alarming, strongly built, hairy nakedness, or the metallic machine-oil smell he carried round with him – as though he were still part of the ship and its engines even when he was on his six weeks' summer leave – the truth was Vic found it hard to respond because he couldn't help feeling his father's presence as an embarrassment.

Suddenly he was always there, a grown man on the edge of vision wearing either a panama or, worse, a fieldhand's straw, watching Vic and his friends, kicking the football back into play, fielding longstop, throwing in with a whoof of effort, calling out advice, and, worst of all, being harder and sterner on Vic than he was on the others: trying to pack a year's worth of fatherhood into six weeks.

All Vic felt was that his father was displacing him, like a cuckoo, stealing his friends and his mother and his whole summer holiday away from him.

They got on best when they were on their own, and

the links and bridges between them could repair themselves naturally, in their own time. At Bathampton, with the clear water spending itself endlessly over the big green-haired stone blocks, Vic caught his dad looking at him as if he was burning every small detail of him into his mind in case he never saw him again. The wrenching intensity of that look put Vic off his cast and his line caught on a black and slimy willow branch midstream. His father put his arms round him from behind and quietly guided him this way and that until the line pulled free.

'All she wants is patience, see, boy.'

'Thanks, Dad.'

His father hugged him hard for a long time. Then, in a voice that was going all over the place, he said, 'It's not your mother's fault. Nor mine either. We'll manage, lad, we'll manage.'

The next day Vic was on the train to a place called Timperley south of Manchester. Seven years old, a cardboard suitcase and a canvas toolbag satchel with six sliced Kraft cheese sandwiches and a bottle of Whites' Dandelion and Burdock.

Every lift and loop of the telephone wires catching you, hooking you, dropping you back. The engine punching into the falling night and the steel rails sliding endlessly through your eyes and into your heart, hissing you were nothing-nothing-nothing-nothing-nothing and your face was hot and your hands were cold and everything was leaving you and finally you fainted face down in front of people who all looked as if they thoroughly disliked you, face down into the hot scratchy dust-thick moquette – and then it was Timperley and you were banging your suitcase into your knees along the corridor and stepping-falling

30

down on to the wet platform, jarring your spine with the weight of the suitcase because you'd suddenly remembered you'd left your satchel under your seat and in the dark you'd missed the wooden footboard. Then the train was leaving before you could say anything, its red-lit back-end swaying, and the steel rails going straight through you, hissing and slipping, cold as ice.

Then you were alone, in the dark, in the rain, no mac and your face burning wet and your teeth and arms and legs starting to shiver again. People butting past heads down against the rain and cursing, their feet slapping on the streaming platform, disappearing into scattered ice-blue mercury light without even seeing you.

Nobody else was giving a fuck, so if they didn't, you didn't. If this was how it was, then this was how it was meant to be. But it was a hard lesson for a seven year old.

Or a thirty-eight year old.

Eventually somebody turned up. Some fussed powdery-smelling old lady gassing away like one of them in the snug on Coronation Street. She said she was his Auntie Gwynnie and the buses had gone to pot because of all the rain. She wasn't really his Auntie Gwynnie but by then the rails had passed through his heart and entered his soul.

But they hadn't fucking killed him had they?

So it was all a bit of a fucking joke really wasn't it?

So it wasn't that fucking bad really was it?

And the only honest answer to that was Yes, it fucking was.

Because for ever after that there was always some part of him where it was always dark and raining and the train was leaving and he was so cold and alone and feverish he had to fight for every breath.

Three weeks later after a lifetime of embrocation, cabbage, bacon, fried potatoes and blubbery red hot water bottles, his father and mother came to fetch him. There were a lot of hugs and then a lot of looks, supposed to fly over his head but Vic had learned to catch them years ago, and adult murmurings, and the occasional angry shout or rare burst of laughter after he'd been sent to bed.

And then his mother and father had taken him home. All the way the wires unloosed him, spooled him out, and the rails pulled out of him like teeth. When they got home his mother and father found a glass lighthouse full of different coloured sands in layers tucked under the bottom fabric of Vic's cardboard suitcase. They sent it back to Auntie Gwynnie and Vic felt betrayed all over again.

After that his mother and father stayed together, and when his father was home they seemed happy enough. But his mother seemed lighter, less oppressed, when he wasn't there. Vic never asked and they never told him, but when Vic said he was joining the police force and wanted to get into the CID, neither of them had the faintest idea why. Now, of course, they were both dead, and whether it was hysterectomy or adultery Vic would never know.

3

Because their row was still going on DC John Cromer got out of his fiancée's car without kissing her. 'Thanks for the lift.' No reply. Jesus Christ. He was twenty-four years old, she was twenty-two and she was making his life hell. 'Bye then.'

Louise shoved her white Mazda convertible into gear, gave Cromer one of her you-hurt-me-so-much-you-can-turn-to-shit looks, spun her wheels and snaked off down the Promenade. He thought the way she was driving she was a gift to any parked-up pissed-off traffic patrol. But if she got done that would be his bloody fault as well. What was it with women? What made them keep rows going for fucking ever?

It was two minutes to eight. He crossed out of the darkness of the Avon Gorge and felt the sun on his back. It was a crisp fresh morning. Here and there a spectrum glowing in the dew on the grass and a smell of fresh earth.

Maybe all was not lost. But if it was, fuck it.

The Mansion House was a solidly handsome detached three-storey building with triple bays and quoins in Bath stone with dark red sandstone in-fill. Brightly painted ship-and-castle coats of arms were mounted high on both front and side elevations, and the Lord and Lady Mayoress had their own flagpoles and standards to show whether they were in residence or not, like the Queen.

Cromer and Vic had recce'd the house and its security arrangements the week before: on the ground floor there was a conservatory vivid with green palms, red poinsettia and hanging brass lamps with vast white-glass globes, heated to a temperature of 80°F by undershelf diamond-latticed radiators. The glass roof and windows were dead-locked and alarmed and the steel rafters were studded with smoke detectors and mini-digital colour CCTVs Vic said must have cost half a year's wages.

In the main building, either side of the galleried three-storey entrance hall, there were matching high-ceilinged public rooms, each sixty foot by twenty, one containing the gleaming sectional mahogany conference table almost as long as the room itself, and the other a grand piano and a scattering of repro Georgian and French Empire furniture. The fireplaces were black-and-white polished marble, the walls damasked, the moulded ceilings hung with triple brass chandeliers, and the CCTVs set discreetly beside the green EXIT signs over the ten-foot doors.

Behind the entrance hall, double doors led to a full-sized billiard table in first-class nick with a green silk overhead shade. Beside it, incongruously, stood a nine-gallon steel beer barrel on its own specially constructed oak stand. Vic had taken a look at it and said, 'You can tell Labour got in, can't you?'

Upstairs, off the galleried landing, a carved wooden sign announced the LADIES' POWDER ROOM. While Vic went up to check out the security control room on the third floor, Cromer poked his head round the LADIES' POWDER ROOM door. Two more doors faced him. Behind one lay a set of eight pale blue lavatory cubicles and eight porcelain sinks. Behind the other lay an inch-thick dusky rose-coloured carpet scattered with low boudoir-style chaise-longues and dinky little bow-leg chairs in Regency-striped satin upholstery. Along one long wall was a row of vanity units and gilt rose-lit mirrors. Along the other were cheval mirrors, racks of curved cast-iron coat-pegs, and spindly-legged tables bearing big blue china bowls of shrivelled pot-pourri. Cromer, who came from a respectable Methodist background in the Victorian red-brick East Bristol suburb of Fishponds, found the smell reminded him of the Anne Summers soirées Louise used to hold in her hairdressing salon.

Not any more though: all that was out the window since the engagement.

Then Vic had come back, and the rest of the recce had passed in a vicious but amiable political argument; Vic saying the whole place was a monument to civic corruption, built by the slavers on the backs and the blood of blacks like the rest of fucking Clifton, and Cromer arguing that since the place belonged to the people now and was used for the public good, it didn't matter whether the original money was bad or not. To which Vic had replied that shit stuck and as long as it stuck it stank, and the best thing to do with it was turn it into a drug rehab for dreads and skins to annoy the fucking neighbours.

Now, crossing the green in front of the Mansion House, Cromer remembered the argument and grinned: if only you could argue with women like that. Call each other fascist cunts and stupid socialist jamrags knowing it didn't matter a fuck.

But you couldn't and that was that.

He ducked under the barbered trees surrounding the striped and edge-shaved lawn; nothing much in the way of greenery yet, although the buds and shoots were there, just waiting for a good warm week to burst into leaf like a fucking great green brass band.

'And that's another thing!' she'd screamed. 'Ever since you've been on that CID your language has been unspeakable, you know that? Absolutely vile you are sometimes, *vile*.'

He put up a hand to touch a sticky bud and sniffed its sweet resin smell. It was all so simple when you were a kid, before dick took over and started doing your thinking for you. Now he'd got the black sticky resin all over his fingers. Oh shit, maybe Vic would know the answer.

'Vic!' she'd screamed. 'Don't talk to me about Vic! Vic this, Vic that – you're like a pair of big fat sweaty puffs – why don't you sodding well sod off and marry him?'

Seeing she'd already lost it, he'd said, 'I think he's already spoken for.'

Shortly after that, she'd hit him. Smiling at her while she laid into him with her soft little fists was another mistake, apparently, because he was always trying to put her in the wrong. But that wasn't the start of it, that was just the aggression coming out.

Cromer let himself into the Mansion House through the stable yard and made his way into the downstairs Gents: mahogany, copper, ornate elbow-high porcelain stalls. He turned the squeaky brass tap and tipped the chrome sphere on the wall until both palms filled with green pine-smelling liquid soap.

So where had it started?

Looking into the big mirror above the row of sinks he saw the answer.

The haircut. Three days old and still no better.

Like most coppers, especially when young, Cromer was an optimist. Coppers were like nurses, he thought: you had to have reserves of optimism like you had to have reserves of stamina, so you could take hold of one shitty end after another and still do the job. Vic was an exception of course – but even he was a negative sort of optimist and never gave up.

That was it, thought Cromer. Never give up.

It was as simple as that. You gritted your teeth, locked your jaw and no matter how life slung you about, you bulldogged on and never lost your grip.

But this fucking haircut was fucking close to the edge. From the side, his head looked like a celeriac with an acid-yellow fringe. Three days ago he'd had a decent head of soft mid-brown hair short at the sides but full and wavy on top with nice reddish lights when newly washed, and now he had this grapefruit-coloured abortion.

It had to be deliberate. Had to be.

She'd said that soft dangly floppy bit had irritated her for yonks and anyway she'd had enough of that soppy Hugh Grant look and wanted him a bit more butch and Robson Green. Cromer wasn't convinced but let her get on with it thinking there might be a fuck in it somewhere. But virtually the minute she'd finished snicking and clipping and stood back for a critical look he caught her gnawing her lip and wincing. She couldn't admit it though, couldn't admit the guilt, couldn't admit she'd fucked up.

But she didn't have to live with it day after day, minute after minute, did she?

Without being allowed to fucking mention it.

He knew how bad it was when all Vic said was, 'I see you've had your hair cut then.' No piss-takes, nothing. And that was really fucking serious. But he daren't say anything because that would be kicking her right in the middle of her professional pride. And she couldn't apologise – well, because she couldn't. She was either too fragile or too pigheaded: some mechanism seemed to come down between her and reality so she was always left squeaky clean. Unless she felt like being really fucking dirty – which of late she hadn't.

So the haircut was where it had all started to turn septic.

Then they had gone to Ikea.

And she'd gone hissing-mad then shitfaced with rage and despair over a black lacquered bathroom cabinet he'd bought and she'd hated, going on and on and fucking on, showing him up, until out in the car park he'd cracked and told her he didn't know whether he wanted her or her fucking June wedding any more.

That had shut her up. Worse than if he'd hit or slapped her. Which he never had. Because both of them knew, from the look in each other's eyes, that he wasn't fucking joking.

He watched her collapse from the inside out, like a dynamited tower block.

And of course he'd had to backtrack after that, and say he hadn't meant it. She said it was the cruellest thing anybody had ever said to her, and when she saw that was a line that worked she used it over and over, like an Afrikaner sjambokking a dog.

All it did was drive Cromer further into himself.

38

Once there, in the last private space he had left, he found he could be holding her in his arms, stroking her and murmuring to her, while mentally he was screaming and raving and pouring abuse into the delicate whorls of her ear as if it were nitric acid.

I'm not going to marry you, you stupid ignorant cow even if you are a fucking fully qualified Wella stylist with your own fucking fully-paid-for upstairs salon in Fishponds – there'll be no fucking June wedding for you, d'you hear, you fucking dozy wombat?

All the while calling her darling and lovepuss, and listening to her sniffing, and asking her what the matter was den.

But he still couldn't get a fuck out of her. And that, in all his experience of rows with her and the other two women he'd been serious with, was the bottom line. You either fucked away like fucking maniacs or the row was still on. Rules of the game.

But this was different, different in degree, different in kind: there was no fuck, no row, no war and no peace, just something acidly curdling away between them, turning everything from squeezing toothpaste and slicing bread to giving and getting a lift into a silent and bitter power struggle that looked at the moment to be going on all life long.

Cromer had left most of the black stuff on the roller towel so he pulled it round until it looked clean again, then took his heavy heart upstairs and rang Vic on his mobile to say he was in. Vic said he was still setting up the gear in the control room so could Cromer watch both front and back until he could get down. Cromer said no problem.

Ten past eight. He checked the double doors, the fire alarms, the blinking red lights on the CCTVs, and adjusted the CONFERENCE arrow signs. It was good to be farting about, doing daft little things, the routine took your mind off the rest of it, made you feel safe.

Maybe that was why blokes went to work.

Women, too, to be fair.

Five minutes later another rubble-load of reality hit the skip of his heart. The deep-down difference was that he was basically kind and, like most men, wanted an easy slobby home life like a dog – while she was making herself vicious in order to win every single fucking battle to prop up her fragile and wobbly sense of herself. Yeah, that was about it: if he was a dog then she was a cat. She didn't mind the odd screaming and writhing night on the tiles but she was fucked if she would go at it, well, doggedly, like he wished she would. So that was why they got on the way they did, like cat and dog. She was in the pink-tongued face-licking, titivating, paw behind the ear business, and he was in the shit-sniffing guard-dog business.

But who was the real killer?

Oh fuck it. In the end it was all down to sex. Probably.

Dick rules.

For example – he tried to shake himself out of it, but his mind wouldn't let go now it had its teeth into it – she said she was feeling broody but she wouldn't come across would she? So where was the logic in that?

Three weeks so far; next thing it'd be 'No you can't. I've got the curse.'

Cromer was seriously thinking of taking up masturbation again. Only thing was it made you feel so fucking desolated afterwards you had to eat half a pound of chocolate to get back anywhere near normal.

But – thinking about it seriously, giving it the long-term forecast – if she wasn't putting out before the wedding, keeping the beef curtains firmly closed and pussy-whipping him into submission until he Learned to Obey, became a Craven Servant of the Orifice and Never Bought Things Without Permission – what were his chances afterwards?

Very very slim.

Six weeks to go.

Six weeks to go before the giant blood-red sea anemone slurped him in and sucked him dry; then forty years later spat out a stuttering and apologetic old man with a very shaky right hand.

Perhaps it was just pre-marital tension.

Perhaps – although he doubted it – she was feeling the same tepid uncertainties. But if she was, why was she wearing that terrifying nonstop eighty-mile-an-hour I-hate-you smirk all the time?

Perhaps she'd convinced herself that, just for the wedding, she could grow her fucking virginity again. Not that losing it had been anything to do with Cromer.

Outside, the street gate to the dark back garden creaked. He began to move towards the back door. Past the sixty-seater conference room on his right and the billiard room on his left. Next to the billiard room, the same stone and wrought-iron staircase that led up to the LADIES' POWDER ROOM on the first floor curved and flowed elegantly down to the GENTLEMEN in the semi-basement.

To the left of the staircase a brown and white fleur-de-lys tiled hall led to a rectangle of dazzling April sunshine where he'd wedged open the double doors. It was here, framed in blazing light against the dark and sunken garden, that he first saw her.

4

When she looked up, at the top of the steps, the young woman's face was as pale as a lamp. She held a hand to her cheek and tried to focus through the bright slant of sunlight, peering this way and that to fix on Cromer at the other end of the hall.

Stoned, he thought, twenty past eight in the morning and stoned already.

She began to walk unsteadily towards him, thick cuban heels clacking on the brown and white tiled floor. She was tall and busty: light hazel eyes, straight nose, well-modelled lips, firm round chin, frizzly dark hair pulled back from the perfect oval of her face.

Then it came on him in a rush like being simultaneously knocked down and lifted up by a big curler of a wave and he was shaking all over.

She was beautiful.

With that creamy-gold skin she could be black she could be white she could be Greek, Italian, Lebanese – it didn't fucking matter – she was beautiful.

Pale, pale as a lamp.

Apart from an emerald silk scarf tucked into the V of her jacket, she was dressed head to foot in black. There was a gap between the pinched-in waist and the long shiny skirt: a strip of warm ivory midriff showed a silver navel stud. As she came closer, carrying herself well despite the clumpy T-strap shoes, he saw a glisten of sweat on her upper lip.

42

He stepped out in front of the arrowed CONFERENCE sign. He figured she was at least a couple of years older than he was – twenty-six, maybe twenty-eight even.

'Can I help you, ma'am?'

First she flinched then she seemed to be translating into some other language. 'You a policeman?'

Her voice was breathy and young – as if it hadn't quite caught up with her woman's body – and she spoke with a slight lilt: not unattractive but it set his alarm bells ringing.

He had heard it before, among the white girls who hung out with the black guys in St Pauls. He had a bad moment thinking she was just another City Road scrubber; then, telling himself not to be such a canteen fucking racist, he held out his ID card. 'Detective Constable John Cromer, ma'am, Bristol Central CID.' He clipped the card back on his grey herring-bone sports jacket. 'How can I help you?'

She took her hand away from her cheek. The skin was red and shiny as a Canadian apple, the flesh already swelling, with three distinct fingermarks striping the side of her neck.

'He whacked me, man.' She shook her head slowly. 'Man, he whacked me.'

Cromer looked through the open doors of the main reception and the billiard room for a WPC. There wasn't one.

There never fucking was.

He said, 'Who did?'

She shook her head as if it suddenly didn't matter. 'You got a Ladies?'

He pointed to the sign. 'Up the stairs, left and it's

43

facing you.' For the second time she was looking at him as though her brain had stalled. 'You OK?'

'Yeah. Fine.'

'I'll see if I can find someone to come up and see you.'

'Fine. Great.'

'A WPC —'

Nodding but not comprehending. 'Yeah, right.' She put out a long, slim hand – lilac fingernails, he noticed – and touched him softly on the back of his wrist by way of thanks. To Cromer it felt like the touch of a butterfly's wing – he found himself looking at his wrist for a trace of that powder they had – then as she moved past him he caught a waft of her perfume: jasmine or something.

He watched her haunches start to sway up the stone staircase; and in one single powerful burst of self-illumination, as her buttocks slid smoothly and complicatedly past each other under her black satin skirt, John Cromer understood he was a sexual exile in a sexual desert; and for the first time ever, in his whole entire life, he was looking not at the mirage, but at the real, the bona-fide, one-and-only Promised Land, and holy fuck, was it flowing with milk and honey.

He pulled out his mobile to contact Vic.

'Vic?'

'Hallo?'

'How you doing?'

Vic looked at the fuzzy dark shapes on the monitors. 'Fucked if I know, John. This digital stuff's too clever for me.'

All he wanted to do was tell Vic about her, over and over, but the last vestige of his common sense said No: to speak was to betray.

'Vic, where've you got the cameras?'

'Looking out the fucking windows, where d'you think?'

'What, straight out?' He wondered what her name was.

'Yeah. It's all a big fucking blur, John. Fucking cameras. All the good I'm doing, may as well stick 'em up me arse.'

It ought to be something strange and beautiful, but it would probably be something like Christine or Nicola.

'You know why it's a blur, don't you?'

'Do I fuck.'

'You're auto-focusing on the glass.'

It was amazing he could still think of stuff like that.

'I'm what, John?'

'The cameras. They're on auto-focus.'

'So?'

What was even more amazing was that life, which had seemed so biliously and depressingly fixed and final was now so fucking rich and sweet again – he could feel his whole inside laughing and shaking, brimming and flooding, effervescent with joy.

'If you point them at the glass, Vic, they'll focus on the glass.' Poor old Vic – how he pitied him – how he pitied everybody.

'Don't take the piss, John, I've been a fucking half-hour up here –'

'It's infra-red, Vic.'

'Well there's no need to fucking laugh about it, is there?'

'Who's laughing?'

'You are, you cunt. The fuck you on, anyway?'

'Nothing – listen, Vic – because it's infra-red –'

'Yeah yeah yeah –'

'It hits the glass and bounces straight back at the camera.'

'Because it's infra-red?'

'Right. That's what sets the focal distance.'

'You're the kiddy for this, John, not me. Why don't you get your arse up here?'

'I can't at the moment, Vic.' Pause. 'I will as soon as I can.'

Vic said nothing.

'You can outwit it, Vic.'

'I wouldn't be too sure about that, John.'

'All you have to do is put them close to the window so they're shooting across each other at an obtuse angle –'

'Obtuse? What the fuck's obtuse? I went to Hartcliffe Comprehensive, mate, don't give me fucking obtuse –'

'As parallel as you can get them to the window and still have them pointing out.'

'Right. Hang on.' As Vic shifted the cameras, the monitors magically cleared to hard, jewel-bright digital images of the Promenade and the Gorge. 'Fuck me.'

'Vic –'

'Thanks, mate.'

'Vic, I've got a woman here.'

'I knew there was something.'

'She's been assaulted.'

'Shit.' Vic stared out of the window. Two black guys were coming down the hill from the Observatory, one old, one young. 'She there now?'

'In the Ladies.'

'How bad?' The old guy was wearing a linen suit.

He was in his fifties, lean and dark, with a grizzled grey Haile Selassie beard and hairstyle. The young guy was at least a head taller, looked about six five. Hooded dark grey sweat and brand-new pump-up trainers.

'Whacked across the head.'

'Any blood?'

'Not visible.'

'Think it's sexual?'

'All she said was "He whacked me."'

'And she's in the Ladies now?'

Vic started the right-hand camera on zoom and moved the pan-and-tilt to pick up the two black guys.

'That's right.'

'OK. Now then, John. You want a WPC and a camera.'

The zoom went right in on the black guys' faces. The old guy was Rufus James, community counsellor for St Pauls, funeral director, occasional lay preacher at the Lion of Judah and useful all-round contact. The young guy was his nephew, cousin or something. Colston? No, Granville. Small head, wide shoulders but a light build, nearly all leg, loping spring-heel walk. Yeah, Granville. Played basketball for the Condors. Centre. Guys in the Bridewell team said he was good enough for the South West. As usual Rufus was doing all the talking; Granville was listening and grinning and wagging his head.

'Guess what, Vic.'

'What?'

'I checked. No WPCs. All still down the Bridewell.'

'Shit.'

Now Rufus was waving his arms about, gesturing with a panama which had a black and yellow tie for a hatband. Granville was bent over double laughing.

'Parnesy's got them doing the catering, save fucking money.'

'John, listen.'

'I'm listening.'

'Get the camera and the first aid out the Escort.'

'Right.'

'Talk to her through the door, John. You got that? Through the door.'

'OK.'

'Now, what you say, she's not exactly bleeding to death, is she?'

'Not when I saw her, no.'

'And she's compos mentis, is she?'

'I suppose, yeah.'

'Reasonably compos mentis, then.'

'Right.'

'Right. Now this is what you do. You offer her the camera, say it's evidential, and that if she wants, she can take the pictures of her injuries herself. The same with the first aid kit. You offer it to her, say she can use it herself. Or she can wait till we get some paramedics up here. Got that?'

'Yeah, but Vic –'

'How old is she, John? Under thirty?'

'Yeah.'

'Good-looking?'

Vic listened to Cromer breathing. Even over the phone the kid was transparent.

'Yeah,' said Cromer.

'On a scale of one to ten, how many, John?'

'Fourteen.'

'You cunt.'

'I know.'

'Most dangerous thing known to man, John.'

'I know.'

'A fuckable in distress.'

'I know.'

'You still got a month's probation to go.'

'I know.'

'Don't fuck up now.

'I know.'

'Listen, John. Whatever you do, don't go in the khazi with her.'

'I know.'

'I'm stuck here on this stuff so you're on your own.'

'I know.'

'Cheers, John.'

'Cheers, Vic.'

As Vic put his mobile on standby, a voice said, 'Managed to drag yourself off the nest, then.'

Sam Richardson's bulk all but filled the small doorway. Entering one shoulder first, Sam nodded at Vic's mobile. 'What the fuck was all that about?'

Vic wondered how much he had heard: Sam was well known for ear-holing through half-open doors. 'Cromer. Some woman claims she's been hit, he can't find any WPCs.'

Sam consulted his chunky black-faced Seiko Sports. 'They won't be here while nine. I didn't want 'em here at all. You know what women are like round villains while they're getting the old allo darlin' they're creaming themselves, minute it's over they're complaining sexual fucking harassment. I said best keep 'em out of it, but it's all equality now Vic, and Brother Parnes said he thought they might just catch something we hadn't, and I said, what, like clap, and he said you're not supposed to say things like that any more. "Not supposed to." What a cunt, Vic.'

'Yeah.'

'You could have had his job, you know that?'

'Too late now.'

'He was a sergeant when you were a sergeant.'

'So?'

'You could have made DI like that,' flicking his finger off his thumb. 'But you wouldn't kow-tow, would you? You wouldn't fucking kow-tow.'

'Would you?'

The DCS turned from the monitors to the window. 'You don't have to like it, Vic, you just have to do it. You kiss one arse, you've kissed 'em all. Ask Parnesy, he's Public Bumsucker Number One.' He put his arms behind his back, stuck his chin in the air like Mussolini, and gazed down his nose at the Promenade. 'What them brown jobs doing? Lost their fucking assegais or what?'

'They're coming here.'

'Whose fucking say-so? They weren't here last time.'

'Trinity Road, I suppose.'

'Caroline fucking Coombes?' Sam cocked his head. 'Didn't you used to rod her drains once upon a time?'

'The relationship didn't progress that far, Sam.'

The thought of Vic's failure pleased the DCS no end. 'And all that time I thought you were knobbing it rotten.'

'You know what Thought did, don't you?'

'What?' said Sam, grinning.

'Shit himself, thinking about it.'

Still grinning, Sam eyed the two figures ambling and gesticulating down the Promenade. 'Look at 'em. Walking round as if they owned the fucking place.

Fucking bone idle, the lot of 'em. Fuckers weren't here before, why come here now?' Then, frowning, answering his own question: 'This is what they do, Vic, to fuck us about.'

5

Rufus stopped talking and walking to draw a four-foot equilateral triangle in the air. He pointed to the baseline with his panama. He said one end was Lagos in Africa and the other end was Kingston Jamaica, so what did you get going from Lagos to Kingston?

Granville said he knew the cops and Rufus knew the cops and as far as he Granville was concerned they were doing them a favour by turning up for the cops' meeting and since he hadn't had any breakfast why didn't they go straight in the Mansion House and see if the cops had any coffee and wads going?

Rufus said you got slaves going from Lagos to Kingston. He said you got seven hundred thousand a year leaving Lagos and only three hundred and fifty thousand reaching Kingston, so whose fault was that?

Granville said he was so famished he could bite that pigeon's head off and suck his blood out raw but he expected it was Mr Whiteman's fault. Rufus said no not entirely, it was also the fault of Mr Portagee, Mr Harrab and Mr Blackman hisself for selling God's black people to the white people in the first place.

But if they hadn't, said Rufus, then he and Granville would not have the freedom to stand in the middle of this beautiful city on this beautiful morning harguing and discussing so that was a kind a plus there. Not much of a plus, agreed, but small was better than none as the white guy said to the black guy.

Granville said it was a dipstick of a plus as far as he was concerned and any case he was hungry, like really hungry, so could they go in the Mansion House now please. *Now please.*

Rufus redrew the left hand side of the triangle and said that was Kingston to Bristol and Granville was too gravalicious.

Granville said, 'What the fuck is gravalicious?'

Rufus said, 'If greedy wait, hot will cool.'

Granville said it was all right for Rufus, he'd had a zonking great six-inch joint for breakfast, and Rufus said why not, it was better for you, was Jah's way to clear the mind and purge the bowel, and what you got from Kingston to Bristol was, counting them off on his elegant brown fingers, rum, sugar, chocolate, coffee and tobacco. And bananas. Which was a whole lot a plusses because all dem ting make Bristol rich, all dem big concerns like Wills and Harveys and Averys and Frys and Fyffes and such, and all dem ting was to do with pleasure, and so what you got from Kingston to Bristol was pleasure; pure profit and pleasure.

Then he redrew the right side of the triangle.

'What you get from Bristol to Lagos?'

Granville thought, frowned, shook his head. 'What?'

'Cruelty and greed,' said Rufus sombrely. 'What the black man always get from the white man.'

Cromer opened the door of the Ladies and shoved his arm through. 'Hello?' The first aid kit was in his hand and the camera hung by its strap from his wrist. 'Hello?'

'Aah.' A low moan, more like a man's voice than a woman's. *Whatever you do, John, don't go in the khazi.*

He pushed on both inner doors at the same time. She was in the cloakroom, lying on one of the chaise longues, her eyes closed, her hand to her face, the back of her head toward him. When she opened her eyes, they saw each other through the mirrors behind the vanity units. He moved to her, hoiking one of the small bow leg chairs with him and setting it down beside her. She looked stricken, her eyes seeking his for safety, reassurance. He could feel himself wanting to take her in his arms, mother her, love her, make her better.

Come on Cromer, get a fucking grip.

'I've called the paramedics. How is it?'

She took her hand away. The shiny redness had dulled, with the result that the three finger-stripes stood out livid against the pallor of her neck. Her mouth opened, but nothing but air came out, air and a grimace of pain shooting up behind her eyes. He could smell spearmint.

She tried again. 'My jaw.'

He recalled the basic drill on first aid and fist fights.

A, B, C – Airways, Bleeding, Consciousness.

Always look at the good eye first.

'Can I see?'

She turned her face towards him and closed her eyes. The right side of her face looked OK. He leaned close to one side. 'Can you open and close your mouth for me? Slowly – without hurting yourself.'

She nodded. This time she was watching him, looking for a reaction. He focused on the point just below the right ear where the upper and lower jaw-bones articulated. They moved freely.

'Thanks. Can I see the other side?'

She tilted her head, and moved her mouth again.

Under the skin by her left ear, he could clearly see the movement of what looked like cartilage – a lump about the same size as a lozenge of chewing gum. 'Can you give me your hand?'

He put his thumb in her palm and four fingers on the back of her hand so that she could still move her fingers.

'I want you to touch your face here, just below your ear.' He moved her hand to the side of her face. 'Can you feel anything?'

Her two middle fingers moved tentatively up and down over the swollen skin. 'Something moving, sort of – clicking.'

'Right. That's cartilage, OK?'

She was nodding and frowning at the same time.

'Now, the good news is that it's not dislocated exactly but the swelling has moved the cartilage so it's not quite where it's supposed to be and it's not acting as much of a cushion and that's why it hurts, OK?'

A look saying how come you know all this.

'We get a lot of Saturday night fights outside the boozer, and these guys, they're great big heroes one minute and the next minute they're lying in the gutter bawling mummy mummy mummy he's broken my jaw.'

Her mouth trying not to smile.

'Most of the time it's something like this, OK?'

'Right.'

'Right. You're doing well. Average bloke'd be in tears by now. Now listen. I want you to keep your fingers where they are, open your mouth as wide as you can without hurting yourself or making it worse, and then I want you to sort of not exactly push at it but massage it gently, in a sort of circular motion as if you were putting cream on, if that makes any sense.'

She had a wisp of hair straying over her ear. He had to stop himself pushing it off her face and kissing her. She moved her fingers round and round on the skin beneath her ear, her eyes fixed on his, and his on hers. He could feel and smell her closeness. Warm. Musky. Oh shit.

After a while she stopped massaging her face and moved her jaw this way and that. 'It's not clicking any more. Still hurts, but not so much.'

'Good.' He shifted back in the small bow-leg chair and tried to hide the erection bulging through his trousers like a fucking tree root just because he was sitting next to her.

As he moved his knees to sit sideways on to her, he saw that she was looking directly at it. When she smiled at him he felt his whole face and neck glow burning red.

'Look – I think I better ask you some questions.'

'I think you better had.' Her eyes were still dancing. 'Don't worry.' She put her cool hand in his hot one. 'Your secret's safe with me.'

'Sorry.'

You're still on probation don't fuck up now, John.

'Don't be.' She leaned towards him. 'I owe you.'

Drawing back, dropping her hand, fumbling for his notebook and Flexigrip Papermate, putting it on his knee to stop himself shaking. Looking up at her. 'If you start having pain, just hold your hand up and we'll stop, OK?'

'Fine.'

'I just want to get the basics before the paramedics turn up. Let them do the pictures, too – unless you want to?'

'No thanks.'

Putting the camera on the carpet, wiping the sweat off his hand. OK. Name?'

'Opal. Opal Macalpine.'

Opal. He never heard of anybody called Opal before. 'Is that Mc or Mac?'

'Mac small a.'

'Thanks. Address?'

'Where I am now, you mean?'

A lot of young women said that. It usually meant they were living with a boyfriend but had another place where their parents thought they were. He hoped not.

'Your current address, yes. Where you'll go back to.'

'Fourteen Palmer Street, St Pauls.'

Not the best address in the world: not even the best address in St Pauls.

'Anybody you want us to contact?'

'Like who?'

'Partner?'

'No.' No hesitation there. He started to feel better.

'Relative?'

'No.'

'Solicitor, doctor?'

'No.'

'OK. Just say if you change your mind.'

'Right.'

'How're you feeling?'

'Bit shaky, better than I was.'

'We can stop any time you like, you know.'

'Yeah.'

'On we go then. Age?'

'Twenty-two.' Jesus Christ. Same age as Louise. He

57

would have sworn she was five or six years older.

'What's the matter?' She had picked up on it.

'Nothing.'

'Why – how old are you?'

'Twenty four.'

'Well then, there you are – John.'

'How the –'

'You said in the hall. And it's on your jacket.'

'Oh yeah. Right. Now this is the difficult bit. Can you describe your attacker?'

'Sure. I know him.'

They usually did on a domestic, but it was a thing he'd learned from Vic. You let the punter think he's in control and he'll tell you more than if you try to push him – or as Vic said, You just sit back and watch them digging their grave with their teeth.

'You know his name?'

'Julius Spicer.'

'Address?'

'Fourteen Palmer Street.'

'Where you live?'

'That's right.' Looking at him straight. 'But not with him.' Time to dig a bit deeper, but go easy, don't get official or she'll clam up.

Make them think you're their best friend, John: their only friend.

'How old would you say he was?'

He watched her thinking back. 'He's got to be late fifties.'

'His place or does he rent it?'

'It's his place. He rents me the upstairs.'

'He been there long?'

A shrug. 'Twenty years. Some time in the seventies anyway.'

'Before that?'

'I don't know. London. Barbados. He once said something about wishing he could go back but he couldn't.'

Julius Spicer. Maybe there was a record. More likely he'd changed his name. Check it out.

'Look, you don't have to answer this if you don't want to, but when he hit you, had he spoken to you first?'

'Oh yes.'

'Did he seem friendly or unfriendly?' It was the difference between assault, assault and battery, ABH and GBH: basically, it came down to intent; in this case the photos and what the paramedics had to say should be enough to send the guy down for GBH and wounding with intent – if, and it was a big if, the higher-ups and the DPP thought it was worth the hassle.

'He started off friendly enough, then – then we got into an argument.'

'You care to say what about?'

She was thinking about it, looking as if she was going to clam up. Hoping he wasn't crossing the line between leading and prompting, and if he was, keeping his fingers crossed he was going to get away with it if it did get to court, he said, 'I mean, was it about money, were you late with the rent –'

'Housing Benefit people pay him direct –'

'Noise then, visitors, something like that. Keeping him awake?'

'Him? He sleep all day, Julius.' A touch of West Indian there. Maybe it was just her thinking about him bringing it out. He knew some coppers did the same thing, trying to talk the talk in the hope of getting through. Vic said it was unproductive: black people thought you were taking the piss.

Best thing is, John, is to call them Sir or Mr Whoever. Because if they start calling you Baas you've lost it, because then it's them that's taking the piss.

'Something personal, then?' It was as far as he could go. He waited. She looked down at her hands, spreading the lilac nails wide on her lap. Then she took in a deep breath as if she was nerving herself to go off the top board.

'You got a understand.' The West Indian thing again. 'Julius was my mother's – he was her man, not mine, never mine. Never was anything like that. Anyway, when my mother died, he look after me. But because he do that, sometimes he ask me things to do I don't want to do.' Another pause, sizing Cromer up. 'Like delivering stuff, you follow?'

'What sort of – stuff?'

'I don't ask. Sometimes I do it. Not always. When I don't, he always get mardy-arse and don't speak for a week.' Lifting her head defiantly to show the bruising again, 'But he never hit me before.

'What was it?' Time to get harder now. 'I need to know what he wanted you to do, Opal.'

Use their name when you can, John. It all helps to soften them up. If they think you're their friend, they'll want to be yours.

'I don't want to get him into trouble, you know.'

'Opal, he already is in trouble.'

Then, John, you let out a little line. You give them a little slack, a little chink of hope before you set the hook in.

'But if you tell me, maybe we can sort it out without going to court. If we go round and see him, talk to him, explain what he's done and what he could get, but if he promises to be on his best behaviour from

60

now on, and this was just a sudden lapse, well, we're all going to be better off. You won't have to run his errands for him, he'll stay out of trouble, and we'll save ourselves a load of paperwork.' Leaning towards her. 'It's worth it, Opal.'

She was biting her lip. What a gorgeous fucking mouth she'd got.

'He wanted me to be nice to these guys,' she said.

'Nice?'

'Yeah.'

'He ever ask you to do anything like that before?'

'No, never.'

'He say why?'

'He said they were getting on his back, and he needed some time to make his moves.'

'While you were being "nice" to them?'

'Yeah.'

'He say how many?'

'No.'

'He say anything else about them?'

'He said they were all Turks but I shouldn't worry, they had plenty of money, and he'd give me five hundred up front.'

Turks. Holy shit. Time to wrap this up and tell Vic.

'He showed me,' she added.

'What?' The fuck was she talking about?

'The five hundred.'

'Oh right. Opal, this is important. He say how many of these Turkish guys he wanted you to – look after?'

'No. He didn't know.'

'Why did you come here, of all places?'

'He said this is where he'd be. If he could make it.'

'"If he could make it"?'

'That's right.' She touched her cheek. 'After I saw how bad he hit me I wanted to show him up, show him and everybody what he'd done.'

'And what time was all this?'

'Four a clock this morning.'

'Four o'clock he wakes you up to get you to go out and "be nice" to a bunch of Turks – for five hundred quid?'

She was looking at him steadily, much colder now.

'What did you say, Opal?'

'What you think I said?'

'You don't have to answer if you don't want to, Opal.'

She put her chin up. 'I told him to fuck off.'

'Good for you.' Cromer wanted to cheer, put his arms round her, hug her. 'One last thing. When he woke you up, did he knock, has he got a key, did he force his way in, or what?'

'Nothing like that. I was already awake and out a bed.'

'At four in the morning.'

'Yeah. Like I said he sleeps all day and does what he has to do, his work you want to call it that, at night.'

'So he was awake and he heard you moving about?'

'No. He said he heard the kiddy crying.' Watching his face carefully. 'When you got a kiddy, John, they're awake, you're awake.'

Smiling at him quite differently now.

6

'She's got a kiddy,' said Cromer.

Vic stretched his legs into the footwell and pushed the passenger seat right back. 'There's always something, John. Make for St Pauls.'

Cromer fired up the maroon Escort. 'Little girl. Esme.' He blipped the throttle a couple of times, grinned at Vic. 'She showed me a picture. Lovely little kiddy, about eighteen months.'

'Very nice,' said Vic. 'She mention the father at all?'

'No. Why?'

'Just wondered.'

Cromer shoved the Escort into gear. 'Not black, if that's what you mean.' The Escort leapt forward, front tyres squealing.

They drove in silence across Bridge Valley Road and up on to the Downs. It was turning into a warm April day. Vic opened his window, smelled the new-cut grass, lit a Marlboro and waited for the kid to stop looking so fucking wounded.

Finally Cromer said, 'What Sam say?'

'He was fucking furious, John.'

'Par for the course.'

'He said what these black toerags think they're on, crashing my fucking meeting. What they think it is, fucking open day?'

Cromer said, 'He's too fucking old.'

'Not much older than me, John.'

'Yeah but you're out on the ground aren't you?'

'So?'

'You got some idea how rough it is. Sam and Parnesy, they see more than two blacks together, they think it's fucking Rorke's Drift all over again. Same with women on the Force –'

'You been talking to Caroline Coombes by any chance?'

'No. It's fucking obvious, Vic. You can bring all these fucking guidelines in, equal opportunity, no discrimination, all that stuff – you can't make it stick unless you really fucking want to. And Sam and Parnesy and the rest don't. Too fucking old, too fucking managerial, too fucking white –'

'Reading the fucking *Guardian* again –'

'Common sense, Vic. You got a young population, you need a young Force. Young-thinking anyway. All there is to it.'

'You're an arrogant young fucker, you know that?'

'Not fucking quitting though, am I?'

Vic let that one slide and said, 'How's Louise then, John?'

'That fucking bitch –'

Vic said, 'See what I mean?'

Face closed, Cromer drove the Escort hard along Ladies Mile. Then as they pulled up at the junction, he turned to Vic and said, 'Sorry, mate.'

'That's all right John. All I ask is don't make a cunt of yourself over this.' He punched Cromer's solid shoulder. 'No more than you are already, anyway.'

As they waited for a gap in the heavy morning traffic, Cromer said, 'St Pauls where?'

'What Sam said was, John, You found the fucking

woman, you deal with Julius fucking Spicer. But don't go in heavy-handed.'

'Sam, protecting the guy that fucking hit her?'

'My guess is he's one of Sam's snouts – contacts, anyway.'

'Playing it fucking close to his chest, isn't he?'

'He's entitled, John. We're all entitled to protect a contact. Even you, John. Sam doesn't like the sound of these fucking Turks any more than we do.'

'Not this fucking heroin thing again –'

'Nobody likes losing seventy-three k of Class A. Not them and not Sam. So put your lights and your nee-naws on and drive like fuck to Palmer Street – and just remember what happened to that other cuntstruck fucker.'

'What other cuntstruck fucker?'

'Detective Chief Inspector Barney fucking Barnard. Hadn't been for him wanting to stick it where he shouldn't, he'd still be alive, Maelee Thomas would still be alive and none of this would've ever happened.'

Sirens yipping, lights flashing, the Escort shot right then pulled left by the Water Tower. Charging over Westbury roundabout and down into solid Victorian Redland they screamed over Cotham Hill and dropped again towards Gloucester Road: the dividing line between the mainly-whites from the mainly-blacks.

'You can switch off now, John, we don't want everybody to know we're coming.' In the sudden silence Vic said, 'Where's the kiddy now?'

'With the babysitter, 25 Palmer Street. Across the road.'

'The mother?'

'Paramedics are taking Opal to A & E, get her jaw X-rayed.'

Vic took out his mobile. 'I'll call Ellie, tell her to look out for her.' Vic keyed in the A and E number. 'Favourite is pick up the kiddy, then go see this Julius character. And John –'

'What?'

'Let's remember Sam wants us to be nice to him, all right?'

'He fucking hit her, Vic.'

'Yeah. Unless she's lying, John. Ever think of that?'

Palmer Street was in the middle of St Pauls, and St Pauls was in the middle of the city; a rough diamond or, as Sam Richardson put it, a 'bloody great black cloud', just to the north of the main shopping drag.

West of St Pauls, jutting out of the city like a concrete *Titanic*, was the Bristol Royal Infirmary where Ellie Wilcox was a Senior Staff Nurse waiting for the ambulance to arrive with Opal.

Half-way down Cotham Hill Vic said, 'Left here, John!'

'Fuck you mean, left?'

'Just go down fucking Elmsleigh, will you? You're not losing anything –'

'Fucking hell, Vic.' Sawing the wheel round. 'What for?'

'Where I used to live, isn't it? When I was married to that cow Pat – Trish as she now calls herself –'

Vic grunted as they passed the FOR SALE board at the bottom of Elmsleigh Road. 'Still on the market. Fucking great.'

Cromer said, 'I don't get it.'

'What's that, John?'

'I thought you and Ellie were shacking up.'

'We are.'

'Well you want this fucking place sold, don't you? For the mortgage.'

'Tell you've never been divorced.'

'Getting fucking close without being fucking married.'

'You've had one sniff, John, one sniff of a bit of fresh,' said Vic. 'We're all allowed a sniff.'

'You're just cutting off your nose, though. I mean, if you don't want the place to sell just to spite your fucking ex.'

'You know what the cow said? On the phone?'

'What?'

'She said, "At least, Victor, after all these years I've got myself some decent transport, say what you like about the man."'

'Fucking hell, Vic.'

'Fucking BMWs,' said Vic. 'Cunt wears a blazer.'

They came down fast off Nine Tree Hill and shot the lights across into Ashley Road on the edge of St Pauls.

'Bit of luck,' said Vic.

'Fucking skill, man.'

'Whatever,' said Vic. 'Just take it easy now we're here.'

Bordering and enclosing St Pauls like the bent uprights of an old-fashioned window-cleaner's ladder were Ashley Road to the north and Newfoundland Street to the south. Between them, like a mass of broken rungs, lay a score of more or less residential streets filled by a mix of pastel sixties council flats, big old places with cracked and dusty windows, and neat, jazzy-painted terraces of two-up-two-downs. Palmer Street was in the middle of the ladder, one of the terraces.

'What we want, John, is a car at each end and an OSG van behind us. Preferably full of uniformed gorillas.'

'Be nice.

'What we got is you and me. Cuntstruck and Gimpy.'

'Thanks,' said Cromer. 'What d'you reckon?'

'Whole street's not much over hundred yards. Can't be more than fifty houses all told.'

'Number 25's in the middle then.'

'Yeah,' said Vic. 'Drive slowly past and try to look like a white guy who's lost the plot.'

'Only white guys down here are cops and machine-gunners.'

'Machine-gunners?'

'What they call debt collectors.' Cromer rat-tat-tatted a knuckle on the dashboard. 'Way they knock on the door.'

They had gone about twenty yards when the first bottle hit the road in front of them.

'Heinz Tomato Sauce,' said Cromer. 'Two o'clock.'

'Take no notice, John.'

Seconds later a Cola bottle whanged and skidded off the Escort's rear window. At the end of the street a green and white trail-bike wheeled round and sped off. Cromer glanced in his mirror. 'He doesn't fancy it either.'

'Kids,' said Vic. 'Hiding behind these fucking old bangers they call transport.'

'Foot down – or do we have 'em?'

'Not with my leg. Just keep going, John.'

'Jesus Christ.'

'What?'

'That's no fucking old banger.'

Up ahead, half-hidden by a roofing firm's rusty old flatbed, a dark-blue S-reg Mercedes 300D stood at an angle to the road, driver at the wheel, kerb-side rear door wide open.

As Vic and Cromer drew level the door to number 25 was dragged back and two dark-haired sallow-faced men were bundling a skinny blonde with a baby towards the Mercedes. Both the girl and the kiddy were screaming.

'Fucking hell, Vic.'

Vic was already half-way out of the passenger door. 'Airbag the fuckers, John. Hard as you fucking can!'

Cromer jammed the Escort into first and, as Vic ran and stumbled towards number 25, accelerated the last couple of yards and caught the Mercedes amidships. A series of reports like firecrackers, and for a split second the inside of the Mercedes filled with airbags and clouds of condensation front and rear.

By the time Vic had rugby-tackled the girl and baby to the pavement, the two dark-haired guys had piled into the back doors of the Mercedes and were shouting, yelling and screaming at the shocked and blinded driver to get the fuck out.

Cromer meanwhile had his foot hard down and was using the Escort to nudge the Mercedes up over the kerb and jam it against the low front-garden wall. Tyres scrunched and squealed and blue smoke rose and stank; then the driver finally got his act together and the Mercedes shouldered the Escort aside like a pile of scrap, surged off down Palmer Street, swung hard right and that was it – gone.

All that remained was a smell of diesel and a cloud of dark exhaust drifting up into the privet.

Looking increasingly glinty-eyed, DCS Sam Richardson tapped his teaspoon against the water-jug in front of him until almost everybody fell silent. His gaze travelled down the mix of black and white faces to his right until he made eye-contact with Rufus James, still quietly haranguing Caroline Coombes.

'Thank you, Mr Jacques.'

'James, hactually,' countered Rufus.

'I do apologise, Mr James. Nobody here called Spicer is there? Julius Spicer?

Rufus put his long elegant brown hand in the air.

Sam acknowledged him with exaggerated patience. 'You're not Julius Spicer as well, are you Mr James?'

'Jus' to tell you this type a thing ain't Julius' scene.'

'You know him do you? Old friend of yours, is he?' Rufus shrugged. 'I see him time to time.'

'Well, next time you see him, tell him I'd like a word with him, will you? Now, if we can get on.' Sam shoved a hand into his trouser pocket and pulled out a ten-inch bar of parcel-taped soft granular material. He slapped the bar on the table and pointed at it. 'Part of what all this is about is that. Heroin.' He glared down the table. 'Which, as we all know, don't we Mister James, is a Class A prohibited and proscribed substance under the Dangerous Drugs Act 1920 and all subsequent revisions thereof.' Sam tapped the package. 'I haven't mentioned it before because it didn't seem germane to the issues involved. Now, sadly, as a result of information received, it does.'

Rufus put his air again. 'One question –'

'One moment *please*,' said Sam. 'Before we go any

further, I would like, if I may, Mr James, to fill you in –'

Parnesy next to Sam, spoke behind his hand. 'Nice one, Sam.'

Rufus left his arm in the air, two fingers bent like a bishop giving a blessing. 'One question –'

'To fill you all in on the background –'

'One question –'

'You do understand English, Mr James?'

'Sure –'

'Well just keep it shut for a minute, will you?'

Sam saw Caroline raise her hand and, smiling, put her index finger against her lips. It was the same gesture Sam had seen his wife use to bring a rowdy class of remedials to instant silence.

Rufus brought down his right arm.

Maybe that was the way to treat the buggers, humour 'em, treat 'em like bloody kids.

Sam gave Rufus a thin, lipless smile. 'Thank you, Mr James. Your turn will come I can assure you –'

'Tank you.'

Still smiling, Sam hefted the parcel-taped packet in his hand. He left it to their better judgement, he said, as to whether this heroin here was the genuine article or not, but just in case any of them should feel tempted, Mr James, it wasn't. Now then, as he was sure they all knew but just to reiterate and make absolutely certain, he said, the circumstances surrounding the death of Maelee Thomas were as follows.

Just before Christmas seventy-three k of finest Turkish H had gone missing. As far as they could establish, he said, a pair of miscreants, one black, one white, by the names Baxter and Lang respective, had driven down the M4 from the Smoke to deliver five k of cocaine to the local citizenry, 'as it might be yourselves'. Fifty or so dealers had mingled theirselves with ordinary punters having a legitimate knees-up and dance in the assembly hall of Westminster Road Community Centre, the old Infants and Junior as was.

So far, so normal.

Then the police raid went in.

'At that point,' Sam said, 'things in the neighbour-hood became rapidly and progressively shitfaced, if you'll pardon the expression, Mr James.'

Rufus leaned back in his chair and sucked his teeth. 'Things fell apart. The centre did not hold. Murder, arson, robbery and death stalked the streets of St Pauls.' He jutted his chin at them. 'A toerag dies, an addict, shot in the face in the toilet. One of the finest officers this Force has ever known, my personal friend and colleague Detective Chief Inspector Barnard, is shot in the back of the neck in the basement of the old Hillside asylum. Stark naked, ladies and gentlemen. In a cage, like a bloody animal – because of this!' Sam threw the parcel-taped package flat on the table. His voice, red-raw with outrage, fell quiet. 'And of course, poor Maelee Thomas was killed as surely by this substance as the bullet that struck her as she tried to escape from that smoke-filled school hall.'

Sam waited. No one spoke. Even Rufus was silent.

'That heroin,' said Sam, 'was picked up by Lang after Baxter was shot dead by police marksmen. The landlady of the King of Prussia, Avonmouth, recalls Lang, with a headwound, talking to some Turkish gentlemen. Later Lang drove off in a white van with Turkish gentlemen in cars front and back. Lang skedaddled at our roadblock on the New Severn Crossing. The Turks, some of whom were bona-fide merchant seamen, admitted they had spoken to Lang out of concern for his head wound, but knew nothing of any white van, and claimed their colleagues were merely giving them lifts to their families in Cardiff and London. My officers checked and corroborated their stories and we had no option but to let them go about their business. Next day, a burnt-out white van, later discovered to have been stolen, was found near the New Severn Crossing: Lang's charred remains were inside. He had a fatal four-inch puncture-wound in the back of his skull now known to have been caused by a twenty-ounce stainless-steel fireaxe. Traces of heroin consistent with leakage from a split parcel or parcels were found round and about. The rest of the heroin is still missing. Close to seventy-three kilos.' Sam leaned forward on both hands. 'The largest amount of heroin ever to appear in this fine city of ours, and enough to ruin scores of young lives and leave families scarred for ever.' Sam paused to scan every face in turn. Mark my words, ladies and gentlemen, my colleagues and I *will* seize this evil substance – and the foul black-hearted scum who deal in it.'

Simultaneously, DCI Parnes's mobile went off and Rufus stuck his arm up again. As Parnes withdrew to the bay window for better reception, Sam said, 'And that, Mr James, is the background to this procession of yours. I hope, ladies and gentlemen, that you can see why I remain opposed –'

'Can I harsk a question?'

'– to certain aspects of such a procession. We have already had one riot, and several deaths –'

'Can I harsk a question, please?'

Sam said wearily, 'Arsk away, Mr James.'

73

'As funeral director responsible for the arrangements of Maelee Thomas' burial an' memorial service, Mr Richardson –'

'Yes, Mr James?'

'When will the body of the deceased be released into my possession?'

'What?'

'What I said was –'

'I heard what you said, Mr James. What I don't understand is what you're talking about.'

'What I am talkin' about, Mr Richardson, is you can't have a funeral without a body – you understand me?'

'Yes, I understand that, but –'

'Every time I call the coroner's office they say I got a get a release from the Police, an' every time I call the police they say there is a question of evidence and send me back to the coroner's.'

'Mr James, are you telling me –'

'What I am tellin' you, Mr Richardson, is gettin' kind of late – twenty-four hours, do what I got to do –'

'Sam!' Parnes hurrying back from the bay window mobile in hand. Listening and talking at the same time. Sweat beading out on his neck. Staring at Sam. 'Five kids. In a squat. Down by the Feeder. OD'd on heroin. Taking a breath, swallowing. 'They're all dead, Sam.'

'Shit. When?'

'They think Friday night.'

'Fuck.'

'Mr Richardson –'

'One minute, Mr James, please –'

7

'John, you get a number?'

Cromer was on his knees jacking the crumpled right front of the Escort off the tyre. 'I got PYC or RYC –'

'250 S or E?'

'Something like that – S reg anyway –'

'Leave that now, John –

'What?'

'Get the woman and the kid inside – before they all start yakking.'

Cromer looked up. Neighbours' doors were opening on both sides of the street. 'Oh, right.' He watching Vic limping round to the passenger door. 'You OK?'

'Yeah.' Vic half-fell into the passenger seat and grabbed for the radio mic. 'John –'

'Yeah?'

'Put the jack in the boot before they nick it.'

'Right –'

'Woman's name's Perrott. Nova Perrott.'

'Got it.'

As Vic got on to National Vehicle Registrations he heard Cromer saying, 'Come along now come along – show's over.'

The front door slammed.

By the time Vic had finished with the NVR people, a yellowstripe patrol had shown up from Trinity Road.

The driver was a white PC name of Lever; his partner was a stocky young black woman Vic hadn't seen before. Both were in white short-sleeve order.

'Jesus,' said Vic, 'summer's come early.'

'Always does down here,' said Lever. 'Anything we can do, Vic?'

'You can try pulling the front out so we can drive the fucking thing.' The stocky black WPC looked at him askance.

Lever said, 'WPC Diane Bradley, Sergeant Hallam, Central CID.'

'Hi.'

'Hi,' said Vic. She had a firm no-nonsense handshake. 'See if you can get any descriptions off the neighbours – usually turns out they're all watching telly.'

'Maybe to you, Sergeant, but I was born here.' As she swung away, Vic saw Lever was grinning.

'Doesn't mess about, does she?'

'They say she's the best thing that's happened round here since sliced breadfruit,' said Lever. 'Makes the job almost do-able.'

There was a pram and a double pushchair in the narrow hall of number 25. Vic sidled himself past. He was already thinking about Nova Perrott. She was a bit of a hard nut – had to be, white and living round here – but she'd been a mate of Maelee's, so maybe that was the way to crack it.

No use going at her head on, she'd clam up.

The kitchen door was open. Cromer was unselfconsciously joggling baby Esme in the crook of his arm and wiggling his little finger for her to catch hold of, and when she'd caught hold of it, he'd nuzzle her in the neck and she would chuckle and let go until he wiggled his finger in front of her again. She was a bright nice-looking kid with dark soft shiny hair and the same creamy skin and lustrous eyes as her mother. In a playpen on the tiled floor two other toddlers, a big brown-skinned boy and a pale young girl with thin fair hair were looking up at Cromer goggle-eyed.

Nova said, 'She was screaming her head off till he took her offa me.'

'You should have been a mother, John.'

Cromer looked up. 'Anything on the Merc?'

'Plates off a '77 scrapper, yard in Eltham.'

Nova said, 'Here, I knows you, don' I?'

Vic looked at her pinched pretty face. Her yellow T-shirt, skimpy enough to show her nipples through her bra, had a red slogan printed on it:

FUCK ART
LET'S DANCE

'D'you know Inspector Coombes, Trinity Road?'

'Yeah, course I do.' Tilting her chin. Then, recognition dawning: 'Ey, you're that mush she fancies, incha?'

Vic grinning. 'Am I?'

'Way she was looking at your arse.'

'Who's a naughty mans?' said Cromer to Esme.

'They were all taking the piss, John.' Vic turned back to Nova. 'Trinity Road, wasn't it? The night of the riot, before it started – you were there with Maelee.'

'So?' Very quiet, very cautious now.

'You going to the funeral tomorrow?'

77

'How can I with this lot?' Looking at the kids, then looking at him. Looking at him hard, then tears welling up. Biting her lips shut, trying to hold on to herself but the tears coming out over the mascara anyway. 'Poor cow.'

Vic reached forward a hand. 'I'm sorry.'

Nova looked at his hand, then took hold of it and squeezed enough strength out of it to reach across to the Boots box on the table for a leaf of peach tissue to wipe her eyes. She looked at the smudged mascara on the tissue and threw it in the empty fireplace. 'Yeah, everybody's sorry ain't they? It's me looking after her kiddy though, innit? Her kiddy, my kiddy –' glancing at Esme '– everybody's kiddy . . . All my life is now – shoving yellow stuff in one end, wiping it off the other.'

'You were with her, weren't you?'

'What?'

'You were with Maelee when she died, weren't you, Nova?'

'So?'

'Did anybody ever ask you about it?'

'Only Miss Coombes.'

'Inspector Coombes?'

'Yeah. That was before though.'

'Before what?'

''Fore I found out where she was. When I did I went there.'

'To the General?'

'Yeah.'

'What happened, Nova?' She shook her head and reached for another peach tissue. Vic could feel Cromer looking at him, eyes burning, willing him to stop. He leaned forward, took hold of her hand again.

'Nova, has anybody – did anybody – ever ask you to make a statement?'

She looked up, her expression hardening. 'Did they fuck.'

'So what did happen?'

'Fuck all, as usual –'

You're losing her, Hallam.

'You tell us, maybe we can get something done. We're not all arseholes, are we, John?'

She glanced at Cromer holding the kid on his lap, his eyes brimming. 'She bled to death, din't she? In the General. In the corridor outside where they do's the operations.' Vic watched her summoning up the strength to look back. 'I was with her but there was stretchers everywhere, see, all down the corridor out into reception and everywhere. They didn't think she was too bad, like, because she was quiet. One of the junior doctors had a look at her, where she'd been shot in the stomach – about here –' pointing to her own midriff, running a finger along an imaginary appendix scar, '– but because she wasn't moaning and screaming her head off and everything and there wasn't hardly any blood, they said she could wait a bit.' She swallowed, took another tissue from the box, looked Vic straight in the eye. 'She'd been shot in the womb, what they call internal haemorrhage. When it filled up and burst she was dead.'

After a while Vic said, 'You think you could make us a cup of tea, John?'

Sam had taken Parnes into the billiard room, and left Caroline Coombes in charge. Her patch, let her deal with it, Rufus and the rest. Sam waited until Parnes had closed the door then swung on him.

'What the fuck's going on, Parnesy? This is you, isn't it?'

'Jesus Christ, Sam, all I did was take the call –'

'Not that. In there.' Gesturing towards the conference room.

Parnes looking blank. 'What you talking about?'

'That black cunt, in there –'

'What about him?'

'He says there's no fucking body.'

'Well he's a fucking liar –'

'He says he's been given the fucking runaround –'

'He's giving us the fucking runaround – what they do, Sam –'

'Parnesy, he's organising tomorrow's fucking funeral, and he's claiming we've set him up on a fucking yo-yo between us and the Coroner' s –'

'So?'

'Jesus Christ, Parnesy, give me fucking strength – is he or isn't he?'

'What?'

'Being fobbed off. Fucking yo-yo'd.'

'Course he fucking is.' Now it was Parnes's turn to act aggressive. 'What you wanted, wasn't it? No body, no funeral. No funeral, no procession. No procession, no riot. You were the one said you were opposed. You said so just before I got that fucking phone call.'

'So it *was* you?'

'Me what?'

'Set him up.'

'Doing my fucking job, for Chrissake –'

'All right. Let's assume, for the moment, up to now, delay-delay-delay has been the way to go –'

'Thank you.'

'Better for us to keep them on the hop –'

'Exactly –'

'Than t'other way round.'

'Right,' Parnes was nodding vigorously. 'So what's the problem?'

'The problem,' Sam said, 'is this black cunt. What's this "question of evidence" crap he says we've been fobbing him off with?'

Silence.

Parnes looking at Sam as if Sam had suddenly contracted Alzheimer's. 'Don't tell me you don't fucking know.'

'I don't fucking know.'

'It's not crap, Sam.'

'What's not crap?'

'This "question of evidence" thing.'

'What is it then?'

Parnes said, 'Oh shit.'

'Come on Parnesy, never mind "Oh shit".'

'Forensic said they were passing it up the chain yonks ago.'

'What?'

'I assumed we were sitting on it.'

'"We"? Who's "we"? Not fucking chickens, Parnesy –'

'Hang on a minute.' Parnes dabbed at his mobile, turned away, walked to the billiard room bay window, spoke, listened, came back. 'Forensic say it went straight to the CC's safe.'

'Not a fucking mind-reader either – what went straight to the CC's safe?'

'The slug that killed Maelee Thomas, Sam.'

'What?'

'Plus the Forensic report on its provenance.'

'Which said what?'

'It came from DCI Barnard's Smith & Wesson .38.'

'Fuck.'

'I thought you fucking knew, Sam –'

'Well I didn't fucking know, did I?' Sam fixed Parnes with his herring-gull stare. 'How did *you* fucking know, Parnesy?'

'I was there when they dug it out of her, Sam. I watched them do the tests.'

Sam continued to stare at Parnes. Then he turned on his heel and paced, quite slowly, all the way round the shrouded billiard table until he came back to Parnes.

All he said was, 'I think you should tell Mr James he can have the body as soon as he likes.'

'What about you, Sam?'

'I'm going down the Feeder to look at a few stiffs.'

8

While Cromer was out brewing up in the small back kitchen Vic said, 'Right, take me through this morning from the knock on the door.'

'Didn' have no chance, did I?' Nova folded her arms in memory of the assault. 'No sooner I slipped the chain, they was in, the pair of 'em.'

'They speak English at all?'

'One did. "You shaddap you face I fuckin' kill you."'

'Anything else?'

'No, he just fucking whacked me, didn' he?'

'Where?'

Nova lowered her head and put a hand to the bottom of her skull. 'Here.'

Vic looked through her pale blonde hair. The scalp was reddened, but no more. 'Then what?'

'I shut up, didn'I? Then the other one gets me, arm up behind me back, shoves me in here. I'd only just finished changing Esme, hadn'I? Pampers on the table and everything. The one as got me is copping himself a feel, one hand all round the top here and the other trying to shove a finger up me jacksie, dirty bugger. I can smell him on me now, that sweet stuff they puts on their hair, like coconut oil but sweeter – and then the other one's picking Esme up, and Erin and Jamie are screaming blue fits –'

'How did they know to go for Esme?'

'One of 'em said, "Girl?" Well, they could see it wasn't Erin, couldn't they, her bein' fair, an' they could see Jamie was a boy.'

'Erin's your daughter?'

'Yeah, and Jamie's Maelee's – and I'm going spare now, aren' I, so the other one punches me here,' pointing to the base of her rib cage, 'and fucking winds me, next thing I know they've got me, her, the bag with her things in, and we're going out the front door, jabber jabber jabber, when wallop you come along –'

'And Erin and – Jamie?'

'Never touched 'em, never took a blind bit of notice.' Looking at Vic. 'I haven't had a chance to get down the papershop.' Weighing him up. 'Haven't got a fag on you, have you?'

Vic pushed across a packet of ten Marlboro. 'Keep 'em.'

'Thanks.'

'How's the ribs?'

'Sore.' She lit up, breathed in, flinched. 'Ow –'

'Anything else, scratches or anything?'

She held out her arms. They were bony but there were no needle marks or bruises, just red friction burns round her wrists. 'I don't bruise that easy. Nothin' to bruise, I spose –'

'How d'you feel now?'

'Bit shaky,' drawing down on the cigarette. 'All right, really. More relieved than anything –'

'We're going down to A and E later, I'll get you looked at.'

'Can't leave three kiddies, can I?'

Vic let that one go and said, 'When Opal came round here with this one,' Vic extended his little finger

84

to Esme, as Cromer had, but she turned her face away, 'what time was it?'

'I think it was around fiveish but I couldn't swear, I was half asleep.'

'Funny time to go visiting with a kid.'

Nova shot him a look that said, *How would you know?* 'What she say?'

'Oh, she'd had a row with old Julius, he'd whacked her one and she needed somewhere to sit down and think. So I left her to it and went back to bed.'

'She say anything about Turks at all?'

'Only what Julius wanted her to do.' She took a deep drag on the Marlboro and blew the smoke out in a thin grey stream. 'Look Mr Hallam, I know what everybody thinks, they think any young single mother lives round here has got to be on the batter. Well, I ain't, and Opal ain't and neither was Maelee. I've had men up to here.' She cut a forefinger across her throat. 'If one of 'em came in here on fucking fire I wouldn't piss on him to put him out.'

Vic watched her stub the Marlboro into shreds. 'This guy, Julius. You think he'll be at home?'

'Unless he's done a runner. You'll have to knock hard, mind. He kips all day.'

Cromer came in with three teabagged mugs in one hand and a milk bottle in the other. He set the mugs down on the table and waved the milk bottle at Nova.

'Shall I be mother?'

Outside, Lever was standing next to the Escort. 'Well, it's driveable, just.'

'Thanks, Don.'

'New headlamp, side cluster, wing, bonnet, bumper. Nothing five or six hours of paperwork shouldn't fix.'

Vic said, 'Can you stay on the door, Don, 'til we've finished at number 14?'

'Sure.'

'Where's your mate?'

Lever nodded down the street. WPC Diane Bradley was coming out of a house a couple of doors away. A short olive-complexioned woman in her forties with frizzy black hair was telling her to take care. The WPC came up to Vic. 'I've just been talking to the Ioannides. They're Greek Cypriot. They said what they heard was definitely Turkish.'

Vic said, 'Yeah, well they would, wouldn't they?'

The WPC cocked an eyebrow at him. 'Yeah, these white people, so racist, know what I mean?'

Vic grinned. 'Thanks.'

'No problem.'

Vic hauled himself across the road to number 14.

Maybe Cromer was right. Maybe she was right. Maybe everybody else was right and he was wrong. Maybe.

Number 12 was empty and number 16 was separated by an entry. Number 14 had a concrete yard just big enough to park a bike, a shuttered front window, a Cardinal-red front step and a panelled mahogany front door with a lion's head black knocker. Set a foot apart, one above the other, were a Chubb lock and a Yale. 'You go round the back, John.' He gave Cromer chance to get down the entry then lifted the lion's head knocker. It was stiff with paint and hard to get a swing on.

Don't get many visitors, do you, Julius?

Cromer's shout echoed down the entry. 'Vic!'

Julius was lying naked on the cork-tiled kitchen floor in a thin pool of his own blood from a seven-inch slit in his side. He was lying on his right with his knees drawn up and his hands taped behind his back. There was more white tape round his ankles. His eyes were open and the whites had a milky bluish sheen to them.

Cromer was looking a bit drawn so Vic said, 'Better give him the kiss of life, John.'

'You what?' Then, 'Oh fuck off, Vic.'

'You haven't touched anything?'

'No fucking fear. Door was on the latch.'

'Not over-worried then, was he?'

'Who?'

'Whoever did it.'

'Vic – this *is* Julius Spicer, right?'

'Oh yeah, it's Julius. I've had him in a couple of times for questioning. Never anything on him, though. Too fly – 'til now.'

Vic pulled on a pair of latex gloves, moved to the sink, looked into the plughole, then opened the door underneath to look in the swing-lid wastebin. It was empty. He pushed the door shut with his toe.

Cromer, belatedly pulling on his own gloves, said, 'What d'you reckon?'

'Tidy job. We're not going to get much here.' Vic looked closely at the blistered lips and the long red slit in Julius' left side. Frowning, he moved to look at the taped-up feet, took out a plastic bag, slipped it on his hand and used it to wiggle the big toe. Leaving the bag over the foot, Vic stood up and checked his watch. 'Not that long ago. He's still warmish.' He took out his mobile. 'What time Opal tell you she left?'

'She said they had the row some time after four.'

'Nova said she was round her place fiveish.'

They stood there, looking at each other.

Cromer said, 'You don't think –'

'I don't think anything, John. Neither should you.'
Vic moved to the back door.

'Where you going?' Cromer sounding nervous.

Vic said patiently, 'Listen, John. What we've got here looks like murder, right?'

'Right.'

'It doesn't look like an accident and it doesn't look like manslaughter. It looks like cold-blooded deliberate fucking murder.'

'Yeah, but –'

'John, not just Opal, but everybody, Nova, neighbours, everybody on this fucking street is going to be interviewed to fucking death. Nothing you nor I can do about it, so don't fucking try.'

Cromer nodding, getting a grip again. 'Yeah. Right.'

'Any consolation, I'd say it looks professional. The tape, all the rest of it. On the other hand –'

'What?'

'She was in the vicinity, she said they had an argument –'

'I know –'

'Then you know what she's got coming, don't you?'

'Yes.'

'Good. Just don't fucking tell her.' Vic opened the back door and took a lungful of fresh air. 'Now, I'm going to get the camera and call the bodybag brigade. You have a look round upstairs, but don't move anything.'

'What am I looking for, anything special''

'He's a dealer, isn't he? Was anyway –'

'Oh, right.' Cromer was still looking bothered. 'Vic –'

'What is it now, John?'

'What d'you reckon that smell is?'
'That, my son, is blood, shit and burnt flesh.'

Cromer climbed the stairs, careful not to touch the handrail. Up here, the smell was still claggy but more like pork scratchings and less like shit. All three doors – bathroom, front and back bedrooms – were open.

Cromer stuck his head round the bathroom door. The narrow room had been trashed and the stained bath held a violent technicolor mix of shampoos, baby lotion and smashed medicine bottles. The front bedroom was the same: drawers yanked out and tipped, the mattress slashed, hardboard ripped out of the fireplace. He went into the back bedroom. A basket-weave cot was turned upside down next to a single bed. Opal's bed. That too had been slit and gutted.

One second he was juiced up, hot with anger – *I'll kill the cunt* – and the next he noticed he was automatically checking for come-stains. When he found nothing but a tight-curled black hair he felt his anxieties lightening, his mood easing.

Jesus Christ, Cromer, what a state to get into.

He picked up the hair and rolled it between latexed thumb and forefinger: it was what they told you in Forensic Basics. If the hair was round and smooth it was head hair; if it was thicker and you could feel it rolling, then it was triangular in section, and probably pubic.

Probably pubic.

Cromer's mind went off God knows where.

'You still up there, John?' Vic's feet were clumping awkwardly up the uncarpeted stairs. Cromer dropped the black hair on the bed and felt the blood rising up his neck into his cheeks.

Vic came in. 'This her room?'

'Yeah.'

Vic took a closer look at Cromer's reddening face. 'Not having a quick J. Arfur are we?'

'Leave it out, Vic –'

Vic glanced at the slashed mattress. 'They all like this?'

'Trashed to fuck, bathroom and all. Somebody must have heard –'

'Next door's empty, John.'

'Oh.'

'Anyway, he was wasting his time whoever he was. Guy's a long-time dealer he's not going to be holding in his own house, is he?'

'What Forensic say?'

'They've got a rush on.' Vic put the Olympus on wide angle and shot the room from the doorway. 'They've just found five bodies down the Feeder.'

'Five.'

'Yeah. All kids, all white, all OD'd on heroin according to Parnesy.'

'Holy shit.'

Vic nodded. 'Looks like the war's started without us.' He moved to the window, stared out. 'This is a shit deal, John.'

'You can say that again.'

'No, not just Julius. This whole fucking deal.' He took a shot of the room and the doorway from the window. 'Too much heroin.' He clicked the Olympus shut and handed it to Cromer. 'Sam wants me down there. Traffic are sending a red-stripe.'

'Why? I can take you –'

'No John, you got to stay here, take the snaps and wait for Forensic.'

90

'Right. I'll see you down there –'

'No, John.'

'You what?'

'I want you to pick up Nova and all three kids –'

'Nova? Why Nova?'

'Nova and all three kids, John. You pick them up and take 'em down to A and E. Ellie knows you're coming.'

'What about Lever and Bradley?'

'They got to tape this place off.'

'Yeah, but why do I get to be fucking nursemaid?'

'Because you're fucking good at it, my son.'

'Fucking hell, Vic –'

'Look at it this way – you get to stay with Opal and you don't take your fucking eyes off her. Got that? Shouldn't be difficult. Not for a man in your condition –'

'For Chrissake, Vic –'

'I mean it, John. She goes to the khazi, you go to the khazi. And you stand right outside the shithouse door with the kid in your arms if necessary. Got it now? You don't let either one out of your sight. These guys, Turks or whoever they are, they've tried it once, for some fucking reason – they could try it again.'

'You reckon?'

'Your chance to be a knight in shining armour. Don't fuck up.'

In the distance a traffic patrol siren grew louder. Vic moved through the bedroom door. 'I'll see you down A and E.'

Cromer heard him hopping down the stairs favouring his bad leg. A couple of seconds later the back door banged shut and the traffic patrol siren wound itself up again.

9

The Feeder Canal was a mile and a half downhill to the south-west. It had been constructed to feed water into the Floating Harbour and keep the level constant. Half-way down was a row of boarded-up houses, their frontages swarming with reflected blue and orange lights.

The usual sad people, mostly old men and women with one or two young mothers with pushchairs, were watching from behind the DO NOT CROSS tapes. As the traffic patrol drew alongside, Vic saw that four of the chipboarded windows were covered in white-washed lettering. Taken one after the other, the windows read:

FOXES HAVE HOLES
BIRDS OF THE AIR HAVE NESTS
BUT THE SON OF MAN
HATH NOWHERE TO LAY HIS HEAD

'Some of 'em have now,' said Sam's voice behind him.

'Hallo, Sam. What's the score?'

'Four down, one to go. They're still straightening him out. Fancy it?'

'Not a lot.'

Sometimes you got one in a twisted position and you had to pull him straight to fit the stretcher. And sometimes, as you pulled and pushed, the joints cracked, and air wheezed out through drawn-back bluish lips.

'Come on – perks of the job.' Sam put his head down and shouldered into the big back room.

Two blanketed windows let in pinholes and stripes of strong morning sun. The floorboards were bare and the fireplace was choked with half-burnt wallpaper and splintered skirting.

A green-overalled paramedic was laying out the skin-and-bones body of a dark-haired young man. He wore black jeans and a silk-backed chalkstripe Oxfam waistcoat. The sleeves of his collarless flannel shirt were rolled up above his knobbly elbows. There were needletracks in the crooks of both arms, small indelible-pencil blue points, with surrounding lividity bruising and smeared blood running down both forearms. The paramedic said when they found him the empty needle was still in his arm.

Sam said, 'What about the others?'

'All blokes,' said the paramedic. He pointed out the chalk body outlines. 'That one had the needle in his hand – one on the floor had a needle half full of blood underneath him – him by the window had managed to mess himself thank you very much – and matey by the door here looked as if he was scrabbling to get out.' The paramedic drew a green sheet over the thin young man's face and gave them a mild bespectacled smile. 'Can't say I blame him really.'

Calder, the police pathologist, was on his hands and knees, brushing traces of icing-sugar-white heroin into a transparent plastic evidence bag.

'Morning Mr Calder.'

'Morning, Sam, Vic.' Calder, a solidly built man in

93

his late forties with clean pink skin and large glassy eyes, stood up awkwardly, knees cracking, and shook the evidence bag in their faces. 'Four or five grams of pure China white. Say five hundred quids' worth.' Shaking it harder in front of Sam's face. 'And that's what's left over, Sam. That's what's they left behind.' He dug in one of the dark blue POLICE holdalls that made up the murder bag and held up a bagged audio cassette. 'This was on nonstop playback.'

Vic peered forward to read the hand-lettered black and green Gothic label: ' "Kurt Cobain Lives". '

'Who's he when he's out?' said Sam.

Vic said, 'Singer, supposed to have invented grunge.'

'The fuck's grunge?'

'Well, it's like heavy metal –'

Savagely, annoyed at not knowing something, Sam grunted 'That's all shite, that is.' Then, bending forward to address the green-sheeted body of the young thin-faced man, 'Isn't it, my son?'

'Cobain OD'd and shot himself,' Vic added.

'Silly cunt,' said Sam. 'What was he, black?'

'White.'

'Fucking mad then,' said Sam. 'What about this lot, Mr Calder?'

'I'd say we're looking at a communal shoot-up,' said Calder.

'What I thought,' said Sam.

'Needles in, blast-off lads, five seconds later the rushes start. And they're big, they're massive. And then they're too big and all their motor functions start to shut down. Twenty seconds later they're all on the way out. Looking at each other, unable to move. Knowing there's no coming back.' Calder nodded at the outline drawn scrabbling against the door edge. 'Twenty very long seconds after that they're all dead. Death by vomit, asphyxiation, congestion of the lungs, take your pick.' When Calder smiled, Vic noticed, his eyes grew even larger and glassier, as if impressed by his own self-command.

Sam paced his way slowly to the nearest window and looked out. Weeds, washing machine shells, a Sainsbury's trolley and a pink mattress with its dark grey guts trailing out. He turned back to face Calder.

Now, Vic noticed, both of them were smiling, like adepts congratulating themselves. The presence of death affected Vic differently: a cold, damp, sinking feeling, almost a smell, like looking into a street sewer as the lid was taken off. There was nothing to do but wait for the wave of blackness to pass, and wait for your own warmth to rekindle itself.

Sam was saying, 'Can you clear up one thing for me, Mr Calder?'

Calder folded his white-coated arms. 'Try me.'

'We're not talking suicide pact here, are we?' Moving up close to Calder, as though to compare smiles. 'I mean we are just talking accidental overdose leading to accidental death, aren't we?'

Calder shrugged his thick shoulders up to his ears, said nothing.

'Because if we're talking accident, fair enough. But if we're talking pact, it's hundreds of police hours and arseholes off the telly all over the place. If you get my drift.'

'No deal, Sam, there's too many of 'em.'

'Just a thought, Mr Calder.'

'One yes, two yes, but five – it'll be a feeding frenzy,

Sam, nothing you or I can do about it.' Looking fairly well pleased at the prospect.

'All I'm saying, Mr Calder, is if you don't mention pacts, cults, any of this Kurt whatsit shit, I won't. We won't.'

Calder shook his head, bent down, zipped up the two other POLICE holdalls.

'All I'm saying, Mr Calder, is we don't want any more, do we? We don't want any fucking copycats.' Sam waited patiently for Calder to stand up. 'See what I mean?'

'You're not going to give up, are you, Sam? You're not going to get off my back, are you?'

Sam grinned. 'I hadn't thought of it, no.'

Calder flicked open an old-fashioned square black notebook and leafed through its squared graph paper pages. 'All I can tell you, Sam, is that tests on heroin recovered at SOC, comprising three samples, registered 89, 94 and 91 per cent purity.'

'Meaning what?'

'I've never come across anything much over 70 before. Most ten-quid wraps come in anything from one to 40. This is pharmaceutically pure, compared.'

'Which gets us where, exactly?'

'Never mind pacts, Sam, every one of these lads signed his death warrant the second he shot up.'

Cromer left Nova and the three kids at A and E reception with instructions to ask for Chief Staff Wilcox, and walked out from under the canopy to call Vic.

A kid in camo pants astride a green and white trail-bike was looking in through the Escort's hatchback. When he saw Cromer he pulled his reflective vizor down and sped off, one para boot trailing, up over the kerb and through the anti-ramraider bollards. Cromer moved to check the hatchback. It was shut, but inside, on the rear seat, was a child's dummy on a pink plastic teething ring.

Jesus – it had to be the same kid – had to be.

He took out his mobile and sat down on one of the bollards. There was a sprinkling of cigarette ends round its base.

'Vic?'

'Hang about.' Cromer heard Vic's feet clumping awkwardly across bare boards and then a door opening and closing. 'OK John, I'm out the back, in the fresh air again.'

'What's it like?'

'Could be worse, last body's leaving now, Sam's getting all unnecessary with Calder – like that. You?'

'That kid on the green and white trail-bike, end of Palmer Street.'

'The one you said didn't fancy it?

'Yeah, when the bottles started flying.'

'What about him?'

'Him or his fucking double just turned up here. Outside A and E. Looking in the back of the Escort.'

'What for?'

'Nothing in there but a kid's dummy. I start towards him, he's off like a long dog.'

'Get a number?'

'No. Back end was all splattered in shit.'

'Sort of shit?'

'Thick grey stuff, like builder's compo.'

Silence.

'Where are they, John?'

'Nova and the kids are in A and E.'

'Opal?'

'Still in X-ray. There's a WPC with her.'

More silence.

'John, you should be there.' Then harder, 'You should be in that fucking room with her, John, I fucking told you –'

'Fuck sake, Vic, they've got her stripped off, wouldn't let me in there.'

'Fucking right, too. When they do, John –'

'What?'

'Tell her about Uncle Julius.'

'Me?'

'You saw him first, son.'

'Yeah, but –'

'It'll sound better coming from you, John. She likes you.'

'Oh yeah –'

'What?'

'Not exactly the greatest chat-up line in the world, is it?'

'What isn't?'

' "Oh hello Opal, your uncle's dead." '

'Stepfather, John. Get it right.' Another pause. 'I want to see if I can get Calder to bump Julius up the list, then I'll be with you. Tell Ellie –'

'Vic –'

The line went dead.

10

Lance and Senda sat in the Ford Explorer watching the smart-ass Saudi-looking kid driver tooling round Severn View Services car park. Going round twice until he found a slot close to the doors and facing the exit lane. The kid left the big 4 by 4 parked nose-out on the sloping ramp and switched off. 'If you'll excuse me, gentlemen, I'll inform Mr Sabbahatin of your arrival.'

Lance said, 'Hey, kid.'

'Yes, Mr Bull?'

'You always park like that?'

'Like what, sir?'

'Like you was expectin' some duckin' and divin'.'

The kid lifted his mobile from its hands-free stand. 'Just basic precautions, Mr Bull, sir.' No smile, nothing. He turned to Senda. 'Mr Senda, sir, if you could place your chador, and your other belongings in the storage area beneath the rear parcel shelf – I shall be staying with the vehicle –'

Senda turned his head and looked the kid up and down, taking in the narrow red bow tie, the blazer, grey trousers and lacquered ox-blood loafers. 'You a brother?'

'In what way, sir?'

'The Brotherhood, the Nation.'

The kid opened the driver's door. 'If you mean the Nation of Islam, sir, the answer is no –'

Senda grabbed the kid's left wrist. 'Then why a fuck you dress like one?'

The kid looked down at his wrist, then at Senda's dusty expressionless eyes. 'We find a smart appearance makes our job easier.'

'Easier than what?'

'Vis-à-vis the police – and so forth – Mr Senda, excuse me, you are hurting my wrist.'

'Yeah,' said Senda. 'OK.' He let go. 'So long as the Brotherhood don' come checkin' you, you hear?'

'Yes sir –'

'Else, you in serious disrespec'. You diss, you get dissed, you hear me nah?'

'Yes sir.'

Lance said, 'You a Turk, kid?'

'No sir.'

'You sure now?'

'Yes sir.'

'How about your folks?'

'From Cyprus, Mr Bull.'

Senda said, 'North or south?'

'North, Mr Sender, sir.'

Senda sucked his teeth, looked at Lance, said nothing.

Lance said, 'You talk to this Shabba guy, you talk English, OK? Way we can all hear, OK?'

'Yes, Mr Bull.'

'Is cool.'

'I have to get out of the vehicle, sir – a question of range within the building.'

'Sure, and we can stretch a leg too, what you say Sen?'

'Irie.'

*

100

Severn View Services stood on a low rise overlooking the Severn Road Bridge. From the first-floor cafeteria the south side looked down on black and yellow acres of car park and toll booths; on the north side, a row of anti-glare picture windows opened up on a two-mile width of mud-coloured Severn. It was coming up high tide and the river was running a splashy swirl round the bridge-piers. Out in the middle and up towards Sharpness overfalls and eddies bloomed and spread round the tug-led barges threading the grey whaleback mudflats: even in the bright April sun it looked a fast and treacherous place to get caught.

Sabbahatin, tall, heavy-set, late forties, sharp Italian suit and sunglasses, was watching the river-traffic. Behind him, on another chrome-edged table, cowed and sullen, were the two guys from the Mercedes.

Sabbahatin lifted his mobile. ''Allo?'

'Good morning, sir. I have the two gentlemen with me now, Mr Sabbahatin.'

Sabbahatin stood up and took off his sunglasses. His eyes were black as olives, surrounded by patches of dark liver-coloured skin, and his face, once firm-fleshed, had the damp jowly look of someone on long-term cortisone. 'Nereyeh?'

'The car park – by the doors, sir.'

'Wait.' Sabbahatin ignored the two guys and shouldered his way through the tables. He had a big, stiff-looking upper body but seemed light enough on his feet. 'Why you speak fucking English?'

'As I said, sir, I have the two gentlemen with me now.'

Sabbahatin reached the first-floor concourse overlooking the car park. 'OK, I see you.'

The two blacks were standing each side of the kid,

the big guy scanning the windows, the short, hard-faced guy looking down the exit road.

'Tell 'em tables by the river – tamam.'

'Thank you, sir. Guleh guleh.'

Lance swung round fast. 'What's this hully-gully shit?'

The kid closed down his mobile and slipped it in his shirt pocket. 'Nothing, Mr Bull, it means goodbye, that's all.'

Lance looked at Senda and Senda nodded. 'Like take care, be happy. They say shit like that all a time.'

At the tables overlooking the Severn, the glazing cut all sound; the bronze tinting exaggerated the browns and greens, made white skin ruddy and brown skin metallic.

Sabbahatin was drinking black coffee and iced water. He indicated a couple of chairs at his table and scraped his own chair round so that the morning sun was behind him. When Lance and Senda were seated and the two sullen-looking guys gone for more coffee and Fantas, Sabbahatin took off his sunglasses, stared at Senda. 'Tell me about this other black piece a shit.'

'Your smart-ass kid already tol' you.'

Sabbahatin nodded. 'Now I want your black-ass version.'

The mortuary attendants were wheeling the remains of Julius away as Vic walked in. Calder laid down his voice-operated Sony and snapped his examination gloves off. 'You'll get a copy of the tape as soon as I can get somebody to type it up.'

Vic said, 'I don't think I can wait that long, Mr Calder.

'Way it is, Vic – five other customers out there –'

'What I was hoping, Mr Calder, is that you could tell me what you think they did to him. That's all I need to know at this stage.'

'No names, no pack drill?'

'Suits me,' said Vic.

Calder looked over his spectacles. 'Any problems, of course, I deny you were ever here and it's your backside in the bacon-slicer.'

'It usually is,' said Vic.

'Right. In words of one syllable, Vic, they shoved one cattle prod up his arse and another down his throat and tried to get them to short out through his guts. Luckily it doesn't quite work like that or he'd have been barbecued from the inside out. With me so far?'

Vic nodded. 'What it smelled like, when we found him.'

'Right. Now on, I'm translating – yes?'

'Fine.'

Calder flipped open his black notebook, licked his finger through the pages. 'Serious to severe burning, lips throat oesophagus larynx.' Calder flipped over the page. 'Ditto, anus rectum lower bowel. Perforation of bowel wall. Ditto bladder. Ditto scrotum plus severe testicular bruising and swelling. Calder looked up. 'Big as aubergines by the time he got here, Vic. Big as fucking aubergines. Same colour, too.'

'Poor bugger.'

'Two lots of twenty thousand volts through the marley bag,' said Calder. 'Bound to make your eyes water.'

In the next room a mortuary drawer slid, and slammed shut.

Vic said, 'Any ideas on cause and time of death?'

'Cause is heart but I need to talk to my torture mate before I say anything else.'

'Time?'

'Going on the usual recipe six-thirty. Ish.'

'Still warm when we found him.'

'Give it half an hour either way.' Calder flipped his notebook shut. 'Say between six and seven. Maybe earlier if the kitchen was warm.'

'Right, thanks.'

'Vic.'

'What?'

'He'd been worked over for a good half hour before this heart business. Someone who knew what they were doing.'

Vic found himself looking at the dissection table where Julius had lain, Y-cut from nipples to groin and grey as a fish. The water was still rusty pink in the runnels. 'Let me know what your torture mate says.'

'Will do.'

Vic walked up the damp exit ramp into the sunlight and breathed a deep lungful of formaldehyde-free air. Six corpses and the day still fresh.

It had started, all right.

Sabbahatin heard Senda out in silence, then he nodded. 'Is what the kid say. But how I know you still ain't shitting me?'

Senda sucked his teeth, said nothing, stared out of the window.

Lance said, 'We don' work like that.'

'I ain't talking you, I'm talking him.'

Lance tried again, 'Listen, Mister Shabba –'

Senda cut in, 'OK man, is cool. I know these people, they don' trust any fucker, right?

Sabbahatin, unsmiling: 'Right.'

Senda said, 'So what you problem, friend?'

Sabbahatin considered he had several: first the old black piece a shit was dead; second his two goons had smashed up the Merc and missed the woman's kid; third was the fucking police looking for the fucking Merc, and fourth here was this other black piece a shit calling him friend, for fuck sake. Finally, he said, 'You trying to get this guy to talk, right?'

'Right.'

'So why you stick that fucking thing down his throat?'

All Senda did was look at him and nod.

'You hear?' The 'h' sound very harsh – like he was hawking up, getting ready to gob on Senda.

Lance said, 'Stay cool, Sen.'

Senda, still nodding, said to Sabbahatin, 'I hear you.'

Sabbahatin spread his hands. Gold rings on both little fingers, a long nail, polished and tapering, on the third finger of his left hand. 'So tell me.'

'Was over by then.'

'That supposed to fucking mean?'

'The guy was finished,' Senda. said. 'He got nothin' else to say. He got nothin' else to say because he don' know nothin' else to say.' Leaning forward. 'He don' know from shit where this so-called H 'spose to be. You hear me? He don' fuckin' know –'

Sabbahatin said, 'So you say –'

Senda leaning even closer, right in the man's face. 'You and you kid driver think this is a first time I ever done this?'

Sabbahatin's mobile rang.

Senda ignored it. Tapping the base of his throat, he

105

said, 'You do the guy's gizzard so he don' mek no noise when you come to grip his 'eart – you with me, you hear me nah?'

Sabbahatin turned away from Senda, turned right round to show him his back, pulled his mobile. ''Allo.'

The kid driver said that Richie had arrived.

Sabbahatin said OK, send him up, he would talk to him. He closed down the mobile, stood up, took a folded tenner from a thick gold money clip, dropped it on the table, told Lance and Senda to go get some fucking breakfast, picked up his espresso and left.

Richie chained the green and white trail-bike to a hoop near the Ford Explorer. The driver kid watched him striding up through the car park carrying his helmet over his left arm like a shield. He was compact and muscular, cropped fair hair, small head, neat features, frank blue eyes. He was wearing camo pants, fourteen-hole para boots, a black leather biker's jacket.

Sabbahatin looked down on Richie from the first floor concourse. He thought Richie had a good confident swing to his shoulders and a fighter's balls-of-the-feet bounce to his walk – smiling for once as he remembered the old rhyme:

> There is a blue-eyed boy
> across the river
> With an arse just like a peach
> But alas I cannot swim –

Maybe this one would turn out better. At least he wasn't fucking black. Yeah. Maybe this was third time lucky.

Maybe –

Inshallah –

Sabbahatin sat down at the nearest table facing the automatic doors to the concourse. The two guys from the Merc put their Fantas down on the table behind him.

Watching his back – at least they'd got that fucking right.

Sabbahatin pulled the stainless steel sugar bowl towards him and stirred four lumps into his espresso to thicken it, sipped, then snatched a gulp of iced water.

Fucking lying English-shit coffee.

The concourse doors hissed apart. Richie came in, waited for Sabbahatin to give him the nod, and then sat down opposite him. He made to put his helmet on the table, thought better of it and put it on the floor under his seat, smiling up at Sabbahatin as he did so. 'Thanks.'

A soft voice and eyes like a girl.

Sabbahatin unbuttoned his suit jacket to lean forward over the table. White cuffs were fastened with square onyx links and dark wrist hairs curled over the bracelet of his black and gold Rado. He watched Richie taking it all in as he was supposed to, then nodded over his shoulder at the two guys on the table behind.

'You see all that Merc shit?'

'Yeah.' Richie grinned.

'Four grand damage and a cost of two hundred fifty a day to keep the thing out a sight in a fucking lock-up. All fucked. Not funny.'

'Sorry.'

Sabbahatin shrugged it off. 'What else you see?'

Richie bent down to his helmet. Sabbahatin looked at the two-inch twist of blond hair curling from the cropped nape of Richie's neck, shook a Benson & Hedges out of the pack in front of him. The kid came up holding a brown envelope with an engine-oil thumbprint in the corner and some figures underneath.

'Nine twenny-five the two cops make Julius' place. Ten minutes, cop in the crap suit leaves in a red-stripe. Ambulance, police van arrive. Three guys, white coveralls and wellies, go in. The young cop comes out, talks to the uniformed outside number 25, puts the woman, three kids in the Escort, exits Palmer Street nine five five –'

Sabbahatin reached for the envelope, tore it into small pieces, dropped it in the ashtray and wiped his fingers on his handkerchief. 'You follow them?'

'Sure.'

'Where?'

'A and E.'

'A and E?'

'Emergency. Casualty.'

'Which is where?'

'In the BRI. Near the Centre.'

'Traffic?'

'Fucking stacks. Fucking lights all over the fucking place.'

'Shit.' Then, looking hard at Richie. 'You seen?'

'Nah.'

Richie was smiling at him. Sabbahatin put the end of his cigarette just above the back of Richie's hand. 'Nice-looking kid like you, you fucking smile, you shouldn't fucking lie.' Lowering the cigarette until Richie winced. 'Don't fucking lie to me. Ever. Now – he see you?'

'I had my fucking helmet on, man –'

Sabbahatin let the cigarette burn him.

11

Ellie Wilcox was twenty-seven years old and had been a Senior Staff Nurse for three years. She wore a thin pale blue uniform with a broad black elasticated belt which showed off her good strong bust and magnificent backside. Clothed, Ellie looked reasonably attractive: blue eyes, fresh complexion, nice mouth, but in hospital flatties maybe a little on the heavy side. Naked and straight out of the bath, as Vic never tired of seeing her, the generous solidity of her flesh with its fluffy bush and warm pink belly and loins made Vic think first of art and then of mad last-gasp fucking. They had been together four months and even when they were both knackered they couldn't keep their hands off one another. Ellie knew it was a fever and would pass, but Vic couldn't believe his luck and was sure it made his leg better.

Sometimes, when Ellie was alone in the bare police maisonette Vic had pulled on a three-month temporary basis, she would take out the ring Vic had given her and show it, fingers spread wide, to the sunlight.

It was his mother's mother's – a thick, worn roll of pale Victorian gold with a single diamond bedded in it. She would turn it through the spectrum, squinching up her eyes to catch the kingfisher-flashes, then twist it round on her finger to be held up as a plain gold band. It was an eternity ring really, but so what, when she was married then she'd have both, wouldn't she?

109

Marriage, then two kids, no more, and back to nursing before she was forty. Ellie knew she was nothing if not sensible, and liked to have things worked out.

But first Vic had to sell his flat and sort his future out. Properly. Never mind fishing boats.

Then her mother. Going deafer every day. Stuck in a fourth-floor council flat in Shirley, up near Birmingham. They wouldn't let her live there for ever, so that was something else she'd have to deal with.

Meanwhile she'd got three kiddies and two single mothers to sort out.

Thank you, Vic, thank you very much.

She marched straight out of her office into Cromer.

A big, strong, nice-looking lad, with an interesting bulge in his trousers, but seriously under the cosh fiancée-wise, according to Vic.

And looking pretty bloody hangdog at the moment.

'Hallo, John.'

'Ellie.'

'What's up, our kid?'

'Just had a bollocking, haven't I?'

'Who from?'

'Your friend. Sends his love, by the way.'

'Nice of him.'

'He'll be here in a few minutes.'

'He'd better be.' Ellie set off down the corridor. 'I want a word with him – this isn't a mother and baby ward, you know.'

'No.'

'What'd he have a go at you about?'

'Opal. Not sticking close enough.'

'Any closer you'd be had up.' Turning to him, cocking her head. 'You like her, don't you, John?'

'What's that supposed to mean?'

'Oh come on, John, your eyeballs are on stalks and your tongue's hanging out every time you look at her.'

'Well thanks –'

'If Vic can see it and I can see it, she can see it.' Ellie turned away and set off, brisk as ever. 'One look from Worried Brown Eyes and you're hooked, my lad.'

'Jesus Christ, supposed to be looking after her, aren't I?'

Ellie's quizzical blue-eyed stare: 'Is that what you're going to tell Louise?'

'What?' For a moment Cromer's expression read Who's Louise, and in that instant Ellie knew he was in real trouble, and if he wasn't, he was going to be.

Opal and Esme were with Nova in the children's area, a waiting room with a blue plastic slide and a playpen with a few coloured bricks. Cromer looked through the wire-mesh window panel. Esme was on Opal's lap watching Erin and Jamie in the playpen squabbling over the bricks. First Erin, Nova's kid, hit Jamie, then quickly started howling herself. Then Jamie, who was Maelee's kid and much bigger, frowned, looked puzzled, pushed all of the bricks but one over to Erin and looked up at Nova for approval. Nova had the makings out and had her back to the kids, surreptitiously rolling a joint. Erin now started howling because Jamie had got the only brick she really wanted. Jamie gave it to her, and having checked to see that Nova wasn't looking, took two other bricks instead. Erin, squealing with outrage, threw a brick at Jamie's face. When it missed she fell back on her head and started a full-out screaming, shrieking, heel-drumming fit. First, Esme laughed, but then as Erin reached nerve-ripping pitch, hid her face in her mother's neck and started howling herself.

You could see it all, Cromer thought, even in the playpen. Cunning, violence, theft, injustice, rage and retribution.

His gaze fell on Opal's beautiful calm face and Nova's bent, indifferent back. Maybe that was it. Maybe all this fucking howling and shrieking was all down to lack of love – or care – or attention – or something.

Yeah, said Vic's voice, and not just now, but for ever. So get a fucking grip, Cromer.

He pulled away from the window panel. 'I can't tell her in there, Ellie – not in front of that lot.'

'Tell her what?'

Cromer looked even more hangdog. 'I can't tell her her stepfather's been buggered to death with a red hot poker in front of all them kiddies, can I?'

Ellie tried to keep a straight face, lost it and leaned against Cromer snorting with laughter until she was red from the throat up.

Vic got the Traffic guys to drop him off on St Michael's Hill behind the Bristol Maternity Hospital. He walked up towards Kingsdown so he could get a clear view of the mass of interconnected buildings that made a brick-and-concrete ziggurat all the way down the one-in-five slope to Maudlin Street.

All in all, if you included BMH and the old BRI, the Bristol Royal Infirmary complex covered an area a quarter of a mile square: a sprawl of wards, labs, dorms and service buildings set at odd angles and squatted on by huge slug-like air-conditioning ducts. A constant low, humming noise; the clank of pots and pans; the sound of women laughing.

He checked in and told Security what he wanted.

They had him sign for a bunch of blue and yellow tagged keys and the Duty Officer let him out on to the narrow brick walkway between the buildings. 'Just keep going down and you'll get there in the end as the actress said to the bishop.'

What Vic had in mind was a basic recce and some time to think. Maternity was out as a safe unit: all you had to do was walk into the main reception piazza, buy some flowers and magazines, up the lift to any level you liked, and bang –

Pity, because a top-floor end-of-corridor four-bedder would have been perfect: easy to guard, easy to isolate, plenty of warning.

But no way you could risk it, not with mothers and kids all over the place.

The brick path zigzagged past kitchens, laundries, incinerators, stores. Every few yards a locked door with a stencilled yellow number. By the time Vic opened the third, on to Terrell Street, half-way down St Michael's Hill, he found himself wondering how the fuck the nurses ever sneaked in late at night. Maybe they didn't bother any more.

Terrell Street separated the two hospitals. Vic let himself in to the back of the BRI – a blue key this time – and at once the buildings became darker, older, full of shadows. Hart's tongue fern grew in the cement cracks and the damp air smelt of glycoliser and disinfectant; there were no cooking smells, no voices, just the constant hum of the air-conditioning.

Cameras, steel grilles, security lights, dusty Vent-Axias, greasy barred windows. Even a mad-fucker rapist would have to think twice.

Then he'd walk straight through the front doors and say he was visiting like everybody else.

Vic picked his way through scaffolding, insulation blocks, green wheelie bins and blank brick walls. Outside one steel-gated service lift was a scatter of cigarette ends. Some reason, they were nearly all filters.

He broke open a fresh pack of Marlboro, lit one, leaned back to give his leg a rest, and let his mind prowl round the job as a whole. His experience was that if you focused on one thing, went at it head down like Sam Richardson, you'd end up bashing away at one blank brick wall after another –

Like this bloody place.

Bashing away suited Sam; bullying and blagging and threatening to lose control and beat the shit out of you was what Sam was good at, what he did.

What he liked.

Vic preferred to circle, like a jackal, looking for a weakness, a way in. Then you listened, you sympathised, gave the bloke a fag, waited for the poor mush to dig his grave with his teeth, and that was that. Case solved and mine's a pint.

This was different. Everybody was dead for a start.

Remembering Julius on the trolley. Being wheeled out and banged up in a mortuary drawer, poor fucker.

He was where it started but what the hell was he all about?

What sort of dealer has bolts all over the front door and lets his killer straight in through the back?

Somebody Julius knew.

And Julius certainly knew the Turks. And he was expecting them – he offered Opal five hundred quid.

Or so she said. And what was she all about?

Why did the Turks go for her kid and not Nova's or Maelee's?

Because they thought Opal knew something, same way they thought Julius knew something.

Something about heroin – seventy-three k of it.

Had to be.

Vic ground his cigarette underfoot, pulled the greased steel gate open, got in the service lift and pushed 'G'. As he went up he thought about the five kids in the gaff off the Feeder.

Foxes have holes –

But why pass out heroin uncut when you can make ten times as much cutting it? What sort of dealer was that?

Maybe it wasn't Julius. Maybe it was coincidence. Maybe.

He slammed the concertina gate shut and set off down the dimly lit service corridor. Same old thing and par for the course.

The more questions, the more questions.

12

Ellie was waiting for him in the entrance to A and E. 'What time d'you call this?'

'Half ten – ish.'

'Nothing to grin about, Victor.' She tapped the nurse's fobwatch pinned above her left breast. 'Half an hour ago you told John you'd be here in a few minutes.'

'Where is he?'

'In the kids' room with the rest of 'em.'

'Is it locked?'

'Yes it is – and it's bloody inconvenient.'

She glanced over her shoulder into the main waiting area. Three white youths from a late-night fracas, a couple of builders, one holding a wound pad to his head; Scotch Mary, an alcoholic in her forties with a rag round her right hand and blood down her shins; a grey-haired old dosser who was effing and blinding and balling his gnarled old fists at the impassive black male nurse, ducking and weaving and trying to get past him to have another go at her. Watching them were a pair of pensioners in matching beige jackets with tartan collars. They were holding hands and picking crumbs of glass off each other, the woman shaky, the man fussing, both still in shock from what looked like a windscreen smash.

'Sorry,' said Vic, 'it couldn't be helped.'

'Not a crèche for unwed bloody mothers, Vic.'

'I can see that.'

'Where've you been?'

There was no point in telling her he'd been checking hospital security in case of another attack. 'I was down the mortuary with Calder. I told John to tell you.'

'He did.'

'Has he told what's her name, Opal?'

'Told her what?'

'About Julius.'

Ellie nodded. 'I was with him.'

'And?'

'He did very well.'

'How did she take it?'

'She went very quiet.'

'What else?'

'Then she handed him her little girl.'

'Not Nova?'

'Who?'

'Her mate – she didn't hand the kid to her mate?'

'Her mate was too busy separating the other two.'

'Then what?'

'Then we've got one mother and two kids screaming, John's holding Opal's kid and *she's* walking over to the window and staring out. Then she blows her nose, turns round, comes back and says, "Oh well".'

'"Oh well"?'

'What else would you expect someone like that to say?'

'Jesus Christ, Ellie –'

'Don't you Jesus Christ me –'

'The guy was her fucking stepfather for Chrissake, looked after her for God knows how long –'

Ellie shook her head. 'No love lost there. Not that I

could see. No tears, nothing. But then black girls don't cry, do they, Vic? So they say.'

'Come on, Ellie. She's not fucking black —'

She cocked her head, gave Vic an appraising, questioning look. 'You had a look at her kiddy, have you?'

'Kid's not black either —'

'Dark then. They can go darker you know —'

'Fuck's that got to do with it?'

Jesus Christ, fucking Brummies.

'All right. I don't expect a man to understand this —'

'Yeah yeah yeah —'

'There's such a thing as being too good-looking for your own good, Victor.'

'Is there really?'

'Yes, there is.'

'How?'

'You start expecting others to look out for you instead of looking out for yourself and before you know you're working down the City Road massage shops —'

'She's got right up your nose, hasn't she?'

'We see enough of 'em in here on the needle.'

'She's in trouble —'

'They usually are. She's a complete liability.'

'Ellie — they tried to snatch her kid.'

A look as if she couldn't believe what she was hearing, then rifling straight back at him: 'Who was looking after it — her?'

'Listen, Ellie —'

'No, you listen, Vic. You know what she said when she took the kiddy back off John?'

'What?'

'Looking up at him all goo-goo and asking him did he think they'd be able to go on living in the same flat.'

'Not the mess it's in now.'

'Not the point, is it?'

'I don't bloody know, do I?'

'Oh come on, Vic, don't be so bloody thick. You know he's stuck on her?'

Vic shrugged.

'She's too much for him.'

So there. Like it or lump it, I'm telling you straight. It was one of the things Vic thought he liked about Ellie. Now he wasn't so sure.

She was counting on her fingers. '*And* she's got the kiddy –'

'Yeah.'

'*And* he's supposed to be getting married.'

'His life.'

'I thought you were supposed to be his mate.'

'You know what they say, Ellie.'

'No. Tell me.'

'Standing prick has no conscience.'

'You buggers, you're all the same.' She looked him up and down, considering him. 'You want some toast?'

As they passed through the waiting room the grey-haired old dosser was telling the couple in the rain-jackets that he knew Scotch Mary was a fucking old whoor who shit herself shagging on the gravestones, but he didn't care, he fucking loved her, he loved her, the fucking old cow.

The couple looked transfixed. Vic let the door hiss shut on them.

'What was that all about?'

'Mary and him had a fight over a flagon of scrump and one of them dropped it.'

'Oh right.'

Life was fucking tragic when it wasn't a fucking farce.

There was a big old four-slice Dualit in the sluice room. It had been donated years back by the Friends and even now on busy weekends it made just about all the food the night staff got.

Vic watched her slot in four slices of thick white, switch on and reach the tub of reduced-fat Olivio out of the fridge all in the same brusque movement. Maybe that was how nurses were: what they lacked in finesse they made up in efficiency.

Ellie was saying, 'This is something else I bet you don't remember.'

'What is?'

'This. First time I made you toast.'

'Oh yes I bloody do.'

'When then?'

'First time I'd had tea and toast on a winter's afternoon since I was a nipper.'

'Certainly scoffed it back like one.' Looking at him, challenging him. 'And it wasn't bloody tea either.'

What was it with women? Did they think they owned the fucking past just so they could trip some dick-headed bloke up for not remembering? Or was it more than that? Some perpetual do-you-still-love-me-exam which if you forgot some bloody daft thing you were failed and fucked and never to be trusted again.

Vic said, 'No, you're right. It was French-style Leek and Potato Cup-a-Soup –'

'And what with?'

'Fucking croutons, of course – what else?'

Smiling now. 'You bugger –'

'Manky little bits of dried bread tasted like cardboard, and after you'd crunched them up you licked your lips with your pink little tongue, and –'

'And what?'

'And I thought, I wouldn't mind giving her one –'

'Oh, did you now?'

'To be honest, yes.'

'You didn't give that impression.'

'No.' Vic paused, wondering whether to go on. Wondering how well he knew her – how well anybody knew anybody –

'Why?'

'You'd just been raped hadn't you?'

'Oh, Vic –' She was biting her lip.

As he took her hand to say I love you, the toast sprang out of the Dualit.

She said, 'Seems like bloody years ago.'

'Yeah.' Then, knowing it still got to her sometimes, he said, 'I love you, Ellie.'

She looked at him, went a bit misty, then bucked herself up and started spreading the Olivio. 'Cupboard love, all that is.'

He grabbed a handful of her solid backside through the cool blue cotton. 'Not quite.'

Then Cromer walked in and said he thought he could smell scran, and did they have any rusks, stop the kids crying.

Ellie said, 'Got you running her errands now, has she? Be changing dirty nappies next.'

Vic said, 'Have you got a room where I can talk to her, on her own?'

Ellie put the four slices between two paper plates, dumped them down on the white enamel tabletop. 'There. Be my fucking guest.'

And slammed out.

Cromer said, 'What was that all about?'

'Your fucking girlfriend.'

'Oh right. I thought Ellie was being a bit cool.'

'Female solidarity,' said Vic.

Cromer looking baffled. 'Who with?'

'Louise, who d'you think?'

Going very quiet. 'Oh.'

To let him off the hook Vic said, 'You get a result on the X-ray?'

'Nothing broken, just bruising.'

Vic took off the top paper plate and bit into a slice of toast. 'Bugger.'

'What?' Cromer eyeing the toast going into Vic's mouth, his own mouth making small chewing movements.

'Nothing broken means they won't keep her in – oh, for Chrissake have a slice.'

'Ta.'

'Go and get her will you?'

'Vic.'

'Yeah.'

'Can I take the toast?'

'Fuck sake, John.'

'No, not for me, for the kiddies –'

'Yeah, go on. Fuck it. Why not?'

With Cromer gone, Vic sat on his own in the sluice room. Cream walls, beige floors, white cupboards, white sinks, white bins labelled SHARPS ONLY.

Six bodies. Two women. Three kids.

A load of heroin and a load of toerags looking for it.

Plus a lovestruck Cromer and a pissed-off Ellie.

A flash of being back on Timperley station in the

rain: no mac, no satchel, steel rails shining like swords and the train hissing and slithering away from him.

Fuck it. Things always got worse before they got better.

Lance had a tray laden with egg, bacon, sausage, tomato and chips and a strawberry milkshake. Senda had rice, chicken and beans, two bananas and an Orangina. They were coming back from the All Day Breakfast section when Lance said, 'Shit man, you see that?'

'Yeah, fucker burn that Richie guy.'

'Was me, man, I fuckin' mash 'im an' lash 'im —'

'Stick a pin —'

'Leave 'im fer dus', man.'

'Hey, Lance, stick a pin —'

'What?'

'We got a talk to this Richie guy. Talk nice, you hear me nah?'

Lance nodding, catching on. 'Yeah, I hear you.'

'Turk want a burn him, shit, he doin' us a favour.'

'Yeah,' said Lance. 'Sure. Way I'm thinkin'.'

'Listen,' said Senda, 'Man carry feelin's agin me —'

'Yeah, you stuck up to 'im.'

'So you play kiss-me-rass, seen?'

'Seen.'

'Is what old folks say,' said Senda.

'What?' said Lance, grinning already.

'When dog 'ave money, 'im buy meat. When flea 'ave money, 'im buy dog.'

Lance smacked his thigh in delight. 'Man I love that shit.'

'Yeah.' Senda showed his long yellow horse teeth. 'Sit where we can see.'

'You got it, Sen.'

123

Richie watched the two black guys put down their trays down on the next table but one. Then the big guy came grinning and ambling up to their table. He put the change – a pound coin, some silver and copper – down by Sabbahatin's elbow. 'Thanks, boss.'

Without looking, Sabbahatin slid his elbow out until the coins fell, clinked and rolled around on the speckled grey Duralay. The big guy kneeled down, picked up the coins and put them in front of Sabbahatin in the middle of the table and murmured, 'Sorry, boss.'

Sabbahatin did not look at the big guy and the big guy did not look at Sabbahatin. Instead, the big guy dusted his palms, glanced at the red watery blister on Richie's right hand, shook his head once and moved to sit down at the next table but one. The way the two black guys sat meant the big guy had his eye on the Turks at the table behind and the other guy could see what was going down between Richie and Sabbahatin.

Sabbahatin picked up a paper napkin, unfolded it and delicately pushed the coins to one side with it. Richie thought, you don't even want to touch your own fucking money, you must really hate those guys.

Sabbahatin said, 'You ever see those two clowns before?'

'One. I seen one before. The hard-faced guy.'

'Where you see him?'

'Palmer Street, outside the house.'

'Julius' place?'

'Yeah. He was wearing, you know, one of them women's black things, one of them binliners –'

'Chador.'

'Yeah, but you know, he walked like a man. You can tell.'

'He see you?'

They were both looking at the back of Richie's right hand.

Richie said, 'I don't think so.'

'Why you don't think so?'

'I was cuppied down by the bike –'

'You was what?'

'You know, crouched down. I got this new petrol tap, sticks 'til it gets warm –'

'What time?'

'Seven, just on seven.'

Sabbahatin nodded, went on staring at Richie's face, examining it, moving his head slightly from side to side to catch different angles, noting the small white scar across one fair-haired eyebrow, the flattening around the bridge of the nose, the slight, attractive puffiness of the lips ... Richie put his head down, avoiding Sabbahatin's gaze, then slyly looked up and smiled as if both pleased and embarrassed by Sabbahatin's scrutiny.

'What you looking at?'

Soft voice and eyes like a girl.

'You.'

At the next table but one Lance muttered, 'Kid's leadin' with his chin.'

Senda said, 'No he ain't. He workin' him.'

'What?'

'Pullin' him.'

Sabbahatin lit a Camel Light and held it out prissily between thumb and forefinger. 'You smoke?'

'No thanks.' Shrugging an apology with a feeble grin.

Sabbahatin took smoke in, blew it out, then leaned

125

forward, his voice grating. 'What you in this for?'

'I told you – money.'

'No you not. Answer the fucking question. What you in this for?'

Sweat prickling his scalp. 'Fucking hell, man, I'm doing you a fucking favour and you're giving me all this fucking grief –'

Seconds ago, Richie thought he'd got the bastard. Now he was sweaty, unsteady, his guts going loose and watery the way they had just after the bastard had burned his hand – before the anger kicked in and stiffened him up again. It was like having to take the first big punch in a fight: until you weathered that first shock, your legs were still wobbly. It was nerves mostly: fear of being on show, being hurt, being humiliated, all of those things that came from you putting yourself alone up there, before you started windmilling away and forgot everything except the rush and the deliberate infliction of pain.

'You heard me. I said what you in this for?'

'I told you – a share –'

'You told me nothing.' Sabbahatin's eyes, voice, whole upper body bearing down on him. 'What you in this for?'

'I told you –'

Sabbahatin grabbing his wrist, the skin of his hand surprisingly rough and warm. 'You ain't tell me shit –'

'I got to get out of this place and I need the fucking money.' Richie wrenched his arm free.

'Why? For who you need money?'

Panicky, saying the first thing that came into his head. 'These guys, I owe these guys –'

Don't fucking lie to me – ever.

Sabbahatin leaned back, took out a big off-white

silk handkerchief, coughed and spat into it, then wiped his eyes and stuffed the handkerchief back in his trouser pocket. 'Take your coat off.'

'What?'

'Show me. Show me why you owe these guys.'

Oh fuck –

Richie slid reluctantly out of his heavy leather jacket to leave it hanging on the back of the chair. He was wearing a white sleeveless T-shirt; as he tensed his forearms on the table his biceps stood out hard and round as apples.

On the next table but one, Senda said, 'What you reckon?'

Lance said, 'Harms ain't nothin', you do weights you get harms.'

'Yeah, but look at a set of him.'

Thick fillets of neck muscle triangled out from the back of the kid's head to the bulge of his shoulders.

'Yeah,' said Lance, 'he got a middleweight's neck on 'im.'

'Ain't he the pretty boy.' Senda showed his yellow horse-teeth. 'Now look at him leg, goin' like a treadle-machine.'

Out of Sabbahatin's line of sight, Richie had his weight on the sole of his right para boot and the whole of his leg was vibrating rapidly up and down.

'He up to somethin',' said Senda. 'But he don' know whether to flip, flop or fly.'

Sabbahatin said, 'Put your hands down and your arms out.'

Watching Sabbahatin's cigarette hand closely, Richie laid the backs of his hands on the table and pushed his forearms out. He felt a rough thumb run itself over the skin in the crook of his elbow, and then a fold of flesh was pinched hard between thumb and forefinger.

'What you sweat for?' said Sabbahatin.

'You burn me again I'll fucking kill you.'

'Yeah. Maybe.'

As Sabbahatin let go he ran his fingers down the insides of Richie's forearms and right across his palms to the ends of his fingers. 'You like that?'

'Fuck off.'

'OK. You don't have no needle tracks, you don't have no crack-itch, I touch you, you don't scratch like you got fleas all over –'

'So?'

'So what's this "I owe money" shit? What you in this for? Come on, you suppose to be in the fight game, ain't you? What you want in on this shit for?'

Richie said, 'Fuck the fight game. Fucked off with the fight game.'

'Why you fucked off?'

'All fucking promises, man. They want you to sign, they're all over you. Then they stick you in some fucking gym South London somewhere and you're fucking meat. You're fucking meat for their boys, their fucking favourites. It's a fucking arsehole market, you know? You get pissed off, you know? You stop getting better and you start getting hit –'

Sabbahatin nodded. 'You too fucking vain, too fucking pretty, you know that?'

Richie said, 'I don't want my fucking brains turned to mush and my arse reamed out time I'm thirty.'

'That ain't why. That's all shit. I'm asking you why? I tell you, no fucking lies, you fucking lie. Why?'

Time to give up – pretend to, anyway.

Looking desperate. 'I don't fucking know you, do I? Friday night I'm talking to this guy in this shithole called the Famagusta, this late-night drinking joint, next thing I know you're here they're here – nodding towards Lance and Senda. 'I'm told I'm working for fuck-knows-who for fuck-knows-what as fucking lookout, Julius has copped it and now all this shit is coming down on me and I don't even fucking know you. Do I?'

'No you don't.' Sabbahatin took a last drag on the Camel and stabbed it out in his saucer. 'So what do you know?'

Richie swallowed. 'Suppose I know where some of this stuff is.

'What fucking stuff?'

'This H you're looking for. That fucking stuff.'

'How you know?'

'I followed his fucking mule didn't I?'

'What fucking mule?'

'Old Julie's fucking mule.'

'You full a shit, kid.'

'Well fuck you.' Starting to stand up.

Sabbahatin waving him down. 'Who you mean, old Julie?'

'Fucking Julius, man. He's too fucking fly. He's too fucking fly to carry grass – let alone shit –'

'So you followed some fucking mule. What mule?'

'Her. I followed her.'

'Her.'

'Yeah.'

'Meaning what?'

'The mother. The kid's mother. I followed the kid's mother.' Waiting for Sabbahatin to catch up. 'The kid

129

your Merc guys fucked up on.'

'Where?'

'I'm outside Julius' place —'

'Why you outside?'

'Because I know Julius. I know what he fucking does, and how he fucking does it — and I want in, man.'

'You want in?'

'Yeah — basically —'

'And he don't want you in?'

'Some reason he hates my fucking guts, man,'

Sabbahatin nodded. 'So you follow the woman.'

'Right.'

'Where? Where you follow her?'

Richie grinned. 'That's for me to know, and you to find out.'

'Don't fuck with me, kid. OK? OK, now I tell you what you got. You got one end of one shitty little deal and that all you got, so let me tell you one thing, you think you laugh, you laugh other side you face, you keep fucking bug me, OK? Clear?'

'Sure. OK. I didn't mean it like that, Mr Sabbahatin.' Sabbahatin watching, waiting.

'I followed her to this squat.'

'Squat?'

'Yeah. Now can I tell you one thing?'

'I had enough of this shit —'

'I'm not trying to bug you, Mr Sabbahatin, I just want to tell you one thing.'

'What?'

'You should've brought me in at the start —'

'Fuck off —'

'You should've brought me in at the start and let me talk to Julius —'

'Talking shit –'

'And then Julius wouldn't be fucking dead and you'd be on your way with seventy-three k.'

Silence. Then, 'How?'

'Because I know these people – I know what Julius was scared fucking shitless of for a kick-off.'

'What?'

'Nick, Mr Sabbahatin. Going inside.'

Sabbahatin said nothing.

'You could beat seven shades of shit out of him and he'd laugh in your fucking face. You mention getting him sent down and he'd start crapping himself.'

Still nothing.

'I knew that. Why the old cunt hated me. Nobody likes their fucking weakness known, do they, Mr Sabbahatin?'

That got a flicker.

'I know the kids in the squat. And I know her too, the kid's mother. And I know she'll talk to me.'

Sabbahatin fingered his ear with his long nail, looked at it, then wiped the nail clean with the edge of a paper napkin. 'Okay. You fucking know, you fucking get it.'

'Yeah, I know. I did that, you'd fucking kill me.'

'Right. So, last time, what you in this for?'

Time to go for it.

Richie glanced down at his hands. 'I don't think I'm big enough on my own. I need looking after.'

He saw Sabbahatin swallow. 'Return for what?'

Looking directly at him, holding the look. 'What d'you want?'

Sabbahatin's flat expression did not change. 'You.'

'Deal.'

Richie pushed his hands across until their finger-ends met.

On the next table but one Senda hissed air in through his teeth. 'Fuckin' Turks, man. What I tell you?'

13

Soon as Opal walked in Vic could see why Cromer was stuck on her and Ellie pissed off. She was tall and busty, and seemed simultaneously flawless and vulnerable: even the three dull-red finger-welts on the left side of her neck made you want to look after her, protect her, make her better, make her smile.

She had her black ringlets pulled back off her face and tied with a piece of multicoloured velvet; her creamy gold skin, light hazel eyes, well-modelled lips, were all done, cared for and made up just so. Her black grosgrain top and long shiny black skirt looked uncreased, straight out of the box; she even smelled fresh and pleasant – something flowery-fruity, like walking into the Body Shop, top of Park Street.

'Hi.' A breathy, girlish sort of voice, sounding completely at odds with the rest of her. 'John said you wanted to see me.'

John.

Now Vic knew for certain what it was with Cromer: just to have a young woman like this looking at you, talking to you, made you feel warm, made you feel lucky. It was like she was there and suddenly the sun had come out.

He also knew that for all sorts of reasons, some beyond his control, some maybe to do with Ellie, he was going to end up giving her a bad time. It wasn't, he told himself, that he wanted to; what he wanted was to look after her, make her grateful, to shine in her eyes, make her laugh and, yeah, to be honest, the rat in him wanted to pull her.

Luckily, given the circs, that was a complete non-starter.

But that was the sort of effect she had: the more beautiful you are, Vic found himself thinking, the more you seem to float free of the shit the rest of us sludge about in, the bigger and bloodier the lumps you're going to get taken out of you.

And therefore the more fucking lies you're going to tell.

He offered his hand and kept it formal: 'Detective Sergeant Hallam, Central CID.' Her hand was warm and lotion-soft, with immaculate lilac fingernails. Vic wondered how you took care of a kid all day and still managed to keep your fingernails. Maybe Ellie was right – maybe this victim-shit was all a front.

'Take a seat.'

'Thanks.'

'Opal or Ms Macalpine?'

'Opal is fine.' She smoothed her bottom into the tubular steel chair.

Jesus, what a great-looking arse.

'I'm sorry about Julius.'

'Yeah.' She sounded guarded, noncommittal. Vic was sure she was a couple of jumps ahead where Julius was concerned. That was OK by him. No sense upsetting the applecart first off, better to get some kind of rapport flowing – no matter how dodgy.

He said, 'I knew him, slightly.'

'Really?'

'Yeah, I talked to him a couple of times. Nothing serious.'

'Oh, right.'

'Never struck me as the sort goes round whacking people.'

She smiled. 'Who does?'

Smiling back. 'Oh, we get 'em.'

'I guess.'

'He just came over as being too laid-back – too cautious.'

'Yeah, he was that all right.' An amused grin, as if Vic was an old friend. Vic smiling back again, letting her think he was being sucked in.

'Your mother ever say anything?'

'To me? No, never.' As she recrossed her legs Vic heard the soft ssss of one stocking against another. 'I don't recall – I don't think he ever hit her, certainly not to my knowledge.'

'They got on pretty well, then?'

'Yeah, he wasn' there all the time, y'know.' Just a touch of Caribbean lilt there.

'I see.'

'I mean, she had her place, he had his.'

'Right.'

'Ten, twelve years ago, you had to be more careful, on account of the Soash.'

'The DSS?'

'Yeah. Them days, they see a black man coming in, going out, well – that's cohabiting. They can mess you up big over that.'

Vic nodded, not wanting to spoil the flow.

'I used to hear them downstairs, you know, talking late at night, laughing, sometimes.' Another smile, this time showing her even white teeth. 'Maybe that's why they kep' together, because he wasn't there under her feet all a time.'

'Could be.'

135

'She used to say you live with a man you end up with a moan.'

'Where was she from, your mother?'

'Neebiss.'

'Neebiss?'

'Yeah, you know, Neebiss, in the Caribyan.' Saying it the way all Caribbeans said it, Ka-Rib-Yaan. 'Kitts and Neebiss.'

'Oh, right.'

Another one up to Ellie.

Now she was looking at him, challenging him. 'If you want to know about Macalpine, it's northern Irish —'

'Oh, right.'

'She was a Catholic, he was what she called a Prod.'

'Your father?'

'Yeah.'

'How did that work out?'

'Didn't. The two of 'em fought like cat and dog.' Another searching, challenging look. 'Worse than black and white.'

'What happened?'

'He used to get drunk and hit her and she used to drive him on and drive him on . . . He was a brickie, a travelling brickie. One day he just went on travelling.' Trying to sound as if she couldn't care less.

'A bit like me and my ex. No fun being dumped on.'

Sometimes the dodge worked: sometimes the thought of a common misfortune could help prise people open. This time it didn't. All she said was, 'Really?'

'Any idea where he is now?'

'No, and I don't want to know — last thing I want to know.'

Time to put more pressure on.

'When your mother died –'

'Oh Jesus –'

'And you went to live with Julius –'

Reining herself in now, watching him. 'Yeah, what?'

'You were how old?'

'Twelve.'

'Twelve?'

'Twelve.'

'And how old when you started running errands?'

'From then.'

'Did you know –?'

'No.'

'You ever collect money, or anything?'

'Not then, no.'

'When?'

She had that defiant look they all got when the questions started cutting closer. 'A couple of years, maybe longer –'

'When you were – what? Fourteen? Bit more streetwise?'

Looking away, saying nothing.

'What did you pick up for him? Money?'

'Mostly.'

'Other stuff?'

'Sometimes.'

'When did you know, Opal?'

'Know what?'

'Julius was a dealer.'

She went quiet, and then she said, 'I was told.'

'By him? By Julius?'

'No, kids, other kids.' Looking back. 'People wanting somethin', you know. Asking *me* for it.'

137

'And?'

'Was a big row. Big shouting match. A real bust-up.'

'You and Julius?'

'Yeah.'

'You remember when?'

'Yeah. Yeah, I do. When I was sixteen.' Tipping her head back. 'They can put you inside when you sixteen, you know.'

'That why you had the row?'

Smoothing her skirt down with both hands, brushing something invisible off her lap. 'I was fed up.'

'With him?'

'People call you Junkie Kid, Hokey-Cokey, stuff like that.'

'So you stopped?'

'Yeah.'

'Right.' Vic stood up, moved to the toaster and slipped a couple of slices in as if he'd finished and it was all over. Then he said, 'Why did you start again, Opal?'

She mumbled something. He turned round to face her. 'Sorry?'

'I said when d'you fucking think?' Her face was blank with total animosity towards him. 'When I had Esme.'

Not far to go now.

'Want to tell me about the father?'

'No.'

'Any reason?'

'None of your business.'

'Fair enough. When was the last time – I mean the last time you did a delivery for Julius?'

'Friday.'

Friday. Something starting to click.

'This was before he asked you – before he mentioned the Turks, all that business?'

'Yeah. Before all that business.'

Now it hit him, fast and blinding as a migraine. 'Was this – was this anywhere near the Feeder?'

Frowning, looking genuinely puzzled. 'Feeder? What Feeder?'

'Canal behind the Floating Harbour. Down by the docks.'

'No. Never heard of it.'

'Where then?'

'A pub called the Three Tuns, somewhere down Hotwells.'

'Right. What was it?'

'You learn one thing, it's you don't look.'

Vic said, 'OK. One last thing, Opal.'

'What?'

Vic sat down and put his elbows on the table. Facing her directly, he said, 'When you went to live with Julius, after your mother died – did he ever come on to you?'

'What?' Like a whip-crack. 'What?'

Vic ignored the fury he could see rising in her. 'Did he ever touch you, kiss you on the mouth, molest you, assault you, try to get into your bed or get you into his bed?'

Starting to scream at him, standing up, scraping her chair back. 'I've had enough of this! I don't know why you want to know all this and I don't fucking care – all I know is I can't fucking handle it! Now do you understand? I can't! I can't. I can't fucking handle it! Oh God, oh God – only one assaulting me is you! You hear me you fucking pig? So leave me, just leave me!

Leave me a-fucking-lone!' Breaking down, sobbing on the windowsill. 'Oh Jesus, Jesus, Jesus Christ –'

Cromer stuck his head through the door, his face red, his eyes round as gooseberries.

'It's all right, John, we've nearly finished. Opal –'

'Leave me alone!'

'Come in if you're coming, John, and shut the door.' He motioned Cromer over to Opal. She reluctantly let herself be turned into his arms and tried to bring her gasping sobs under control. Cromer's blue eyes glaring I'll-fucking-kill-you at Vic.

Vic said, 'Opal, I'm going to ask you again, then I'll tell you why. Hear me?'

Cromer said, 'For fuck sake, man –'

'John. Shut the fuck up.' Vic waited, then moved closer. 'Opal, can you hear me? Did he or didn't he?'

Her voice a whisper. 'Once. He did once.'

'What did you do, Opal?' Again, 'Opal, what did you do?'

She looked wrecked, her eye make-up and mascara run together in dark smudged pools. 'I was froze.'

'Then what?'

'I – I told him mother was watching him and telling me if he went on I would have to kill him.' Looking hard at Vic. 'One day I would have to kill him.'

'And?'

'He left me alone after that.'

'He apologise?'

'Sometimes, sometimes he would think – you could see it in his eye – but no, never. Not really.'

'Why?'

She took a handful of white tissue from the unmarked box on the windowsill and wiped her eyes. The action seemed to bring her at least part of the way back to normal. She said, 'Show me the man who can.' Throwing the tissue in one of the blue-lidded pedal bins. 'Only time they apologise is when they want something else.'

'Sounds about right,' said Vic. 'Did you kill him?'

'What?'

'Did you kill Julius or have anything to do with his death?'

A long silence. Cromer looking at him in total disbelief.

'No.' Looking very calm now.

'No. I didn't think you did.' Outside, a sparrow landed on the windowsill. 'Sorry about that. Reason I asked, Opal, is I need to be sure of you and all your circumstances before taking you and Esme into protective custody. You understand?'

'What?' Looking unsure again. 'What about Nova and –?'

'More the merrier.' Two slices sprang up. 'Toast?'

'What? Oh, thanks.'

'John, get on to Caroline Coombes, tell her we're on our way.'

As Cromer moved past the window, darkening it, the sparrow cocked its head at its reflection, pecked it, and whirred off.

141

14

Sabbahatin's mobile went. He began to stare at Richie as if he was being told the kid had Aids. He closed the mobile down, said something to the Turks on the table behind, stood up and spoke to Richie. 'You fucking know about this, you fucked.' Then he shouldered his way out through the sliding doors, across the concourse and down the stairs.

Richie swivelled back to the two Turks. 'What's happened?'

One shrugged. The other one said, 'You stay here.'

'What the fuck –'

A deep bass voice said, 'Hey kid, stick a pin.'

As Richie turned towards Lance, he saw Senda slipping out through the sliding doors. A rush of possibilities cascaded through Richie's mind: the job was blown, he'd been set up, the whole thing was a wet-job, and he was fucking star –

Senda strolled back in, hands in the pockets of his dark blue fleece. 'Talkin' to the kid driver,' he said to Lance. 'Then he get in and they both sit there. Neither one sayin' anythin', just lookin' out, like they was listenin' to the radio.'

Lance nodded. 'Hey, kid.'

'What?'

'Take a seat.' Lance pulled out a chair with its back to the Turks. Richie picked up his jacket, sidled across and angled the chair so he could clock any sudden movement from behind. As he sat down Lance said, 'You a bit fuckin' jumpy, ain't you?'

'Everybody's fucking jumpy.'

'Yeah, but you extra-special fuckin' jumpy.'

Senda said something about 'tunti' Richie didn't catch.

'Heh heh heh.'

'What'd he say?'

'Senda say I be fuckin' jumpy, that Turk was after my ring.'

'Yeah, well, shit happens, y'know.'

'You tellin' me.'

Senda said, 'Job got muthafucka writ all over it an' all the way tru.'

Richie shrugged. 'You stiffed the guy, not me.'

After a few seconds, Lance said, 'That what this Shabba guy tell you?'

Richie shook his head. 'I was there, man.' Grinning now. 'I saw him coming out in his fucking binliner.'

Senda said, 'You see too fuckin' much, boy –'

'Yeah. Maybe.'

Lance said, 'What else you tell him?'

Another shrug. 'All I said was, more'n one way to skin a cat.'

'Meanin' what?'

Senda muttered something about jooking the rass as of now and getting way the fuck out.

Richie said, 'I told him I knew Julius. Been on his case for fucking ages, hadn' I?'

'What for?'

Senda said, 'We wastin' we fuckin' time, man –'

'Hang steady, Sen.' Lance was eyeballing the kid like it was a weigh-in where you had to browbeat the other guy. Trouble was the kid was grinning back at him. 'What for?'

'I wanted in, didn'I?'

'In on what?'

'Julius' fucking scene, man.' Richie leaned forward across the table. 'Look, you was in the fight game –'

'Years back, yeah.'

'Yeah, but you was fucking known, man. Me, I had two fights, two fucking zeros, I was fucking BD and O. Broke down and out. I was fucking Chummy, man. You know who fucking Chummy is, don't you?'

'Yeah,' said Lance.

'You walk in the fucking gym, suddenly nobody knows your fucking name and it's "Hey Chummy, here's a tenner, give my bloke a spar, will ya?"'

'Yeah.'

'Ten years down the road, you've had your lights punched out and it's still Hey Chummy, but now you're swabbing gob and resin and lumps a gum off the gym floor for a fucking living. Well, fuck Hey Chummy.'

'Yeah, you right.'

'Anyway. Old Julie's got a nice little scene going so I says I'm having some a that, fuck the fight game, let's have some a that – but he won't fucking play, will he?'

'Why? Because you white?'

Richie shook his head. 'Because he hates my fucking guts.'

Senda said, 'Is all shit, man –'

'Is it?' said Richie. 'Is it? Listen, I had stuff on Julius would a sent him down the steps rest of his fucking life.'

Senda said, 'So why ain't you do it? Solve you problem.'

Richie gave him a sour half-grin that made the

144

right side of his mouth twist down like he'd had a stroke. 'I did that, no fucking punter's gonna trust me, are they? This game, it's all fucking trust, man.' He leaned back, lacing his hands behind his head. 'Then you two fuckers come down –'

'An' what?'

'And I'm bolloxed all ways up, aren' I?'

'Heh heh heh.'

Richie brought his two fists down on the table hard enough to make the knives and forks jump and rattle on their plates. 'Not fucking funny – not fucking *funny*!'

Senda said, 'Ain' it?'

Richie sighed and shook his head. 'Know the only thing scared the shit out of old Julius?'

Lance said, 'What?'

'Bein' banged up.' Looking from one to the other. 'He could take his lumps all right – you must've seen that – but you start talking about inside, bein' banged up in a six by twelve with ought else but a bucket a shit to talk to, and he'd go fucking spare. See what I'm saying?'

'Yeah,' said Lance. 'Seen.'

'What?' said Senda.

'If I'd told you and you leaned on him, just leaned on him, laid the Verne on him –'

'Who a fuck Laverne?'

'The *Verne*, man, HMP fucking prison ship, all the dealers end up – you'd laid the Verne on him, we'd all be on our merry little way, I'd be in for my share of seventy-three k – plus I'd have a nice pair a shoes to step into.'

Senda said, 'You got this all worked out, ain't you, boy?'

'You got to have a business plan.'

'Fuckin' sick –'

'You fucking slotted him, man, not me.'

Senda picked up his table knife and put his thumb half-way down its serrated blade. 'You like to say that one more time?'

Another lopsided smile but now the corner of Richie's mouth was quivering.

'Hang steady, Sen.'

'One more time I put that fuckin' smile tree inch lower an' it go from ear to ear. You hear me nah?'

Richie put both palms up. 'Yeah. No offence, man – just making a point.'

Lance said, 'Why he hate your guts, son?'

'Knew I was watching him, didn't he? Watching and waiting.'

Senda said, 'Why you not go to the Beas' youself?'

'What?'

'He mean the cops,' said Lance, 'the Beast a Babylon.'

'Oh right.' Richie leaned back, smiling. 'Like it –'

Senda said, 'So why you not go?'

'What you got to remember is this ain't the Smoke. This is Bristol – city of grass.' A shrug. 'What they call it –'

'City a grass?'

'Yeah. Always has been,' said Richie. 'I tell the cops, they lift old Julius, what happens? They tell their fucking snouts I put the mockers on Julius – I'm out a business before I fucking start –'

Senda said, 'That what you tol' the Turk?'

'Yeah. Good as.'

'What he tell you?'

'When?'

Senda said, 'Jus' now, when he got the call on a

mobile.'

'He said "You know about this you fucked."'

'This?'

'Yeah.'

'Meanin' what?'

'Fuck knows.'

All Senda said to Lance was, 'This whole job full a shit.' Frowning, he stood up, hunched his shoulders to detach himself and walked over to the bronze-tinted windows.

Outside the glass long muscles of shit-brown water twisted and shifted in the Severn.

Lance said, 'How old are you son?'

'Look,' said Richie, 'I don't even know that guy's name.'

'Senda.'

'Senda?'

'Right.'

'When'd he get off the boat?'

Lance's long Easter Island face went expressionless and stayed expressionless until Richie grinned and put up his hands. 'OK, sorry.'

'Yeah. You could be,' said Lance. 'How old you say you was?'

'Twenny-six.

'Where you fight?'

'Belfast. Dublin.' Looking down at his knuckles. 'I was depping, both times.' A frank blue stare, chin up and truculent. 'Last-minute fucking sub, they throw you in there, say it's all fucking experience, shit on you when you go down.'

'Yeah.' Lance leaned forward and pushed a finger into Richie's midriff. 'You goin' soft in the belly, you know that?'

'Out the game, aren' I?'

'Yeah, right.' Lance considered for a while. 'So how you see this fuckin' deal?'

'Not as fucking lookout, I can tell you.'

'Yeah, I figured.'

'Nor as fucking bumboy either.'

'You pulled him, kid. Me an' Senda watch you pull him.'

'Gotta have some fucking leverage, haven't you?'

'Ain't my scene.'

'Me neither.'

'Could a fooled me, boy.'

'Good.' The lopsided grin again. 'What's your dap-off anyway?'

'Pardon me?'

'What's your angle? Come on, Lance – one thing you learn in the fight game, everybody's got a fucking angle –'

'Me and Sen, we workin' a contrac' for the North London Brothers. End a story.'

'Not the Turk?'

'Like I said, we workin' a contrac' for the North London Brothers. With the Turk the Brothers got what they call a communication a hinterests.'

'That a fact?'

'They suppose to bring it, we suppose to take it. Turk look after his end, me and Sen look after the Brothers' end.'

'Suppose I happen to be in the middle?'

'You fucked, baby.'

Richie laughed out loud, bright blue eyes dancing at the way Lance had seen him off. 'I like it. Great. "You fucked, baby." Terrif.' Then, relaxing, changing the subject, Richie said, 'Here, you know that boozer,

Belsize Park?'

'What boozer?'

'Load a Hay. Was the Noble Art.'

'Yeah, they change it back.'

'Had a gym up there when I knew it, round the back.'

'Not no more they ain't.'

'No, I know. Some a your lads used to get in there, right?'

'So?'

'British West Hampstead International. What they used to call theirselves. Right? Had a cricket team as well.'

'How you know that?'

'Mate a mine used to hang out with 'em, play for 'em if they were short. Big Maori guy, Charlie Farr.'

'What about 'im?'

'Dead now, innee?'

Automatically, Lance looked across to see where Senda was.

'I said he's dead now, isn' he, Lance? Charlie Too-Far they called him. Some shit coke deal. He crossed them, right?'

'Who?'

'North London Brothers. Charlie thought he was dealing with blokes off the team. Got hisself clusterfucked. Right?'

'Stick a pin, man.' Lazily, as if his breakfast was weighing him down, Lance got to his feet. When Senda caught his eye, Lance beckoned him over.

Senda looked at Lance, then at Richie. 'Where we reach?'

Lance said to Richie, 'Say what you got to say.'

'Just talking about middlemen. People we know,

friends in common. Chewing the fat about this and that, as in Brothers.'

Senda said, 'You full a bull, kid.'

Richie, smiling his way over it. 'All I was going to say was, suppose I knew a way through all this shit –'

Senda said to Lance, 'Waste a fuckin' time, man –'

Lance shook his head. 'Listen, Sen. Go on, kid.'

'Right. Basically what I want is a cut, a share. I get you to the stuff, I get a cut, a share.'

Senda said, 'You sayin' if?'

'That's right. If.'

'Then what?'

'Then I want the Brothers to source me, goods and prices to be agreed, help me get set up, get established.'

'Where?'

'Here. Bristol. That's all, man.'

'In place a Julius?'

'Yeah, but working for and with the Brothers.'

'An' the Turk?'

'Fuck him.'

Lance glanced over at the two Turks. 'Keep you voice down.'

'He fucking burned me, I'll fucking burn him, the cunt.'

Senda said, 'Yeah, maybe. Why us, why the Brothers? You say you know the fuckin' way, why you don' fuckin' go for it, you so fucking smart?'

'Not fucking big enough, am I?' Then, to Lance, 'As the Man said, you can run but you can't fucking hide.'

'Yeah, that's right, Sen. He can run but he cyan hide.'

Senda said, 'You got a pitch, kid, you got a pitch it youself, you hear me?'

150

'Yeah, I hear you, Mr Senda, but you and Mr Lance could set it up for me.' Wondering if Mr was pushing it –

'Better'n sittin' here, Sen,' said Lance. 'What we got a lose?'

Senda sucked air through his teeth. 'What you got?'

'I got the kids who bought some of this fucking H and I got the woman who made the drop. The kids'll talk to me, she'll talk to me. All we got to do is track it back. Bingo. Fucking Bingo.'

Senda said, 'How you know it H?'

'It's all these kids do, man, all they fucking live for –'

'Yeah but how you know it this H?'

'They been gagging for it, been fuck-all about for months, suddenly Julius is walking round like a dog with two dicks.'

'OK. Nex'. How you know this woman talk to you?'

'You know I been checking Julius?'

'Yeah.'

'Last Friday I'm outside his house, she comes out, got this koala bear back pack on, he's with her, fussing away, she gets in the mini-cab, he gives the address, off she goes.'

'So?'

'So I follow her, don't I? I'm on the bike, she goes down to this fucking squat on the Feeder –'

'What Feeder?'

'Canal down by the docks. She comes out, no fucking backpack.'

'That it?' said Senda.

'Enough, isn' it?'

Lance said, 'You still ain't said why she talk to you, kid.'

'You know I told you he hates my guts?'

151

'Yeah.'

'Well, this woman is why.'

'How?'

Time to play the ace –

And hope no fucker's got another –

He could feel the sweat trickling down between his shoulderblades, running cold down the valley of his back.

'It's like she's his stepdaughter, lives in the house with him, does all his fetch-and-carry, knows all there is to know –'

'So why a fuck she talk to you, when he hate you guts?'

'She's got my kid, man.'

'What?'

'She's got my kid. The kid those two fucking no-no's on that fucking table there tried to fucking snatch.' Leaning forward, sweat running cold as ice, giving it all the edge he'd got. 'My fucking kid, man, and those fucking arseholes try to fucking snatch her –'

'Holy shit,' said Lance, looking past Richie.

'Yeah. My fucking baby-mother –'

Lance muttered, 'Look out, kid –'

Sabbahatin's hand smashed across the back of Richie's head, forcing it smack into the crockery-laden table.

'Fuck you, you fucker,' said Sabbahatin. 'Five kids. All fucking dead. All fucking dead 'cause of you, you fucker –'

People all over the restaurant were looking at the plates and cutlery clinking and rolling round the Duralay.

152

15

When Vic came out of the sluice room with Opal and Cromer, Ellie was waiting with the wood-grained formica drugs trolley. 'Thanks,' she said, and barged straight past them, shoving the trolley in front of her and kicking the door shut with the heel of her flat black shoe.

'You go on, John. I'll see you out the front.'

Vic pushed the door open and found Ellie spraying the sluice room with a half-litre can of Ozium glycolised air sanitiser. 'Place smells like a bloody knocking-shop.' She picked up the paper plates, clicked her tongue at the crusts Opal had left and threw the plates in a blue-lidded pedal bin. 'What do you want now?'

Vic could feel the ice forming so he said, 'I suppose a fuck's out the question?'

All he got was the cold blue stare. She threw the wood-grained lid up, squinted at the Blu-Tac'd drugs sheet and started pouring pills and capsules into small plastic beakers. There were about forty different containers ranged along the two white shelves of the trolley. 'Twenty minutes late, whole place is running with snotty-nosed kids.' Firing a look over her shoulder, 'Thanks to you.'

'Yeah, well, sorry about that –'

'Not the only one with a bloody job to do –'

'What I was going to say was, I'm taking this lot into protective custody –'

'Good. And bloody good riddance –'

'I don't know what time I'll be back tonight –'

'Nothing to eat there anyway.'

'I'll get a couple of Marks and Sparks –'

'Don't bloody bother.'

'What?'

'Staff O'Brien's off with her back again, they want me to do her four to twelve.'

'Oh.'

'Yes it is Oh, isn't it? Bugger –' A couple of red and white Tylex capsules bounced on the beige floor and rolled under the chipped enamel table. Vic groped around for them and handed them back to her. She shook her head and waved him irritably away. 'Just put them in the bloody bin and go, will you?'

'Right.' Vic let the blue lid clang down hard. 'I'll see you when I see you.'

She put a plastic beaker into its drilled hole and turned to face him. 'For someone who said last night he couldn't get out of the fucking Force fast enough and as far as he was concerned Sam Richardson and the rest could all go fuck themselves –'

'Yeah, what?'

'Doesn't take much of a sniff to change your mind, does it?' What he wanted to do was take her in his arms and calm her down. What he said was, 'Way it goes,' and turned for the door.

'Just don't come back smelling of that cow, that's all.' He went back through the waiting room. Nothing had changed except there were four more sad-looking people sitting there.

In the relative sanity of the fresh air with the April sun warm on his back, Vic found himself wondering what had gone wrong with Ellie: it wasn't like her at all –

she'd never gone on about any other bloody woman – black or white – and Jesus Christ – look at how many men's dicks she must have seen – black, white and every sodding shade in between – and on a daily basis –

'Vic!' Cromer was standing by the open back doors of an unmarked white eight-seater minibus. The uniformed driver and his mate wore black Kevlar waistcoats and crash helmets; behind them, two bench seats faced each other inside blacked-out windows. Opal, Nova and the three kids were already on board, looking out nervously at Vic and Cromer.

'Any sign of matey on his trail-bike?'

'Not so far,' said Cromer.

'Just as well,' said Vic. 'Whose idea was it to send an OSG wagon?'

'Sam's, apparently.'

'The fuck does he know we don't?'

'Search me.'

Vic hauled himself on board. As in other Operational Support Group vehicles, the last two seats were tip-ups to facilitate egress and access to the locked black steel boxes underneath. One, known as the bang-box, contained flares, smoke-bombs, stun grenades and CS cartridges; the other housed the weapons used to launch them.

When he and Vic were seated Cromer banged twice on the steel-plated rear doors and the eight-seater pulled slowly away from the NO STOPPING turning circle in front of Casualty.

With the women and children quiet, daunted by the brown mirror-glass gloom inside the minibus, Vic's thoughts went back to the row that, for some reason, he seemed to be having with Ellie.

155

It wasn't much on the surface, but then neither was a boil when it started: it was what was lay underneath that caused the trouble. What was it with women – what made them pick up on one thing and not another?

Tracing it back, she'd been pissed off from the moment he'd walked in. Yeah, well, he had been half an hour late. And, yeah, she was busy – but apart from that, what? She'd been OK over the toast, and as far as he could remember, they'd been all right the night before. Admittedly the police house he'd pulled on a temporary basis wasn't up to much, bare lino, damp and cabbage-smelling, but fuck me, it was only for a couple of months, and at least suburban Bishopston was quiet enough to have a decent kip in.

So, what had they done? More to the point, what had he done? They'd eaten – rump steak, tinned petit pois, sautée potatoes, bottle of Aussie red – he'd washed up, they'd watched telly, and then because they'd both got to be up early, they'd gone to bed, made love, gone to sleep. He went back over their love-making: nothing suspicious there. Nothing epic, maybe, but nothing mean about it either: he could remember her going to sleep with a smile on her face and feeling fairly pleased with himself as a result. So it wasn't as if she was underfucked or unloved or financially or emotionally insecure or anything, and as far as he knew it wasn't the curse coming on, so what was it?

Why so fucking ratty, for Chrissake?

He told himself that if he knew that much about women, if he knew the rest of the stuff that went on simmering away inside them and then suddenly for no apparent reason erupted and did its best to wreck, burn, twist and flatten everything that had been built up before – yeah, well, if he knew that, he wouldn't be a bloke would he? Not a normal bloke anyway – even old Sigmund, so it said in some fucking *Reader's Digest* he'd read on all-night obbo somewhere, ended up asking What Do Women Want?

So what chance have you got, Hallam?

Fuck all, mate.

Fuck it – if you removed every other possible explanation then what was left, according to old Sherlock, was the truth . . .

And the only thing left, as far as he could see, was Opal.

And she's Cromer's problem, mate, not yours.

'Fucking women.'

'Yeah,' said Cromer. 'Fucking right there.'

Vic listened to the combined drone, rumble and whine of the labouring minibus' exhaust, diff and half-shafts and decided their voices wouldn't carry if they kept it down, so he said, 'What's up with you and Louise then?'

'Eh?'

'No need to fucking shout, John – I said what's wrong with you and Louise?'

'Oh.' Cromer thought about it, then blew air out of his cheeks. 'Where'd you want me to start?'

'How about little Miss Fuckable sitting up front?'

Cromer shook his head. 'Goes back yonks before that.'

'What then?'

Cromer pointed to his short grapefruit-yellow haircut.

'This.'

'Yeah. I was wondering why you had that done.'

'Fucking hairdresser, isn't she?'

Vic nodded. 'True, O Mighty One.'

'Fucking abortion. Like a fucking celeriac.'

'That what you told her?'

'Fucking hell no. Wouldn't dare, would I?'

'Oh come on, mate, she's not that fucking terrifying.'

Cromer shook his head.. 'It's not that, Vic. Thing about Louise —' he stopped, then started again, 'trouble with Louise is she can't bear being in the wrong. I mean *she* knows it, and *I* know it, it's a right fucking abortion, but you tell her and she cracks up. Cracks right up. Can't take it, Vic, can't take fucking criticism.' He glanced up at Opal. She smiled at him, holding Esme on her lap, and made a slight finger-wave with her free hand. He gave her a wan, hangdog smile back. 'Louise was here now, she'd have my fucking eyes out. And yours —'

'Yeah, I've just had a fucking mouthful off Ellie.'

Cromer grinned despite himself. 'Have you?'

'Too fucking right, mate.' Vic frowned, trying to work it out. 'Maybe women like that have that effect on other women.'

Such a thing as being too good-looking for your own good, Victor.

Is there really?

Yes there is.

Cromer said, 'She seems to get on all right with Nova.'

'Nova's hard as nails.'

'Yeah.'

Vic said, 'But if you didn't tell her — if you didn't tell Louise what you thought about it — what happened?'

'We had a row about something else. In Ikea.'

'Fucking Ikea.'

'I bought this bathroom cabinet, she went fucking ape.'

'Yeah, they do that.'

'All it is, Vic,' said Cromer, reluctantly coming to the crunch, 'is, I leave my razor out – I got one of them Mach 3's, blades are a pound a time – I leave it above the sink, she fucking uses it, don't she, uses it to shave her fucking bits.' Looking at Vic worried stiff over this betrayal of their domestic intimacy.

'And?' said Vic.

'I come to use it, it's blunt as fuck.'

'Yeah, it would be.'

'I wouldn't touch her fucking scissors, would I?'

'No you wouldn't, John.'

'Go fucking spare.'

'So what happened?'

'I told her she could stick her fucking wedding up her chuff.'

'Jesus Christ, John.' Thinking, thank fuck the worm has turned at last.

'That was another nineteen nervous breakdowns.' Cromer, unable to help himself, fed himself another glance of Opal.

Vic said, 'So where are the pair of you now?'

'Like the First World War all over again. No advance, no retreat, just grinding fuck out of each other, day after fucking day.'

'So where does Opal fit in?'

Cromer shook his head again, then, as Vic surmised he might, youth being what it is, picked himself up off the floor, and gave Vic a big cheeky grin, 'Like being on leave and winning the fucking lottery at the same time.'

'Yeah. Makes a change from all this fucking death and fatality.'

Still grinning, Cromer said, 'Chance'd be a fine thing.'

'You young fucker.'

'Come on, Vic, you're only jealous.'

'Yeah,' said Vic, knowing he wasn't.

As he pondered the idea of Cromer marching cheerfully out of one set of whirling mincer-blades into another, the OSG bus ground its way into the razor-wired forecourt of Trinity Road Police Station.

Behind them the sheet-steel reinforced gates clanged automatically shut.

The last time Vic had been in Inspector Caroline Coombe's office, she'd had a couple of fading African violets on a shelf over a radiator. Now she had pot-plants, cacti and a Bonsai all along the windowsill, spider plants and a miniature variegated ivy thing trailing down from a bookshelf and a fucking great shiny spear-leaved aspidistra in a tall stoneware vessel on the floor.

Seeing Vic gaping at it all, she said, 'Everybody needs something to love, Vic.'

'Yeah, but why a fucking aspidistra?'

'Surprised you know what it is.'

'My gran used to have one, in the window in her front room. Spindly little table with a fucking doily on it. Scared to death to go in there – thing used to shiver as soon as you put your foot on the floor.'

'I hope it was north-facing –'

'Used to shiver and tremble as if it had seen you – like those big sepia portraits they had, eyes used to follow you round the room . . . Yeah, yeah, it was

160

north-facing, come to think of it. Blocked out all the light, like the bloody jungle in there –'

'They say they're supposed to put people at their ease.'

'Do they? My gran used to feed hers milk, wiped the leaves with it, said they drank it. Fucking scary to a kid.'

Caroline tugged the skirt of her uniform jacket straight. 'Good job we stopped when we did then, isn't it?'

Now she'd suddenly wrong-footed him.

What was it with women?

'How'd you mean?'

'If we're going to argue about aspidistras, doesn't give us much chance on the rest of it. Realistically speaking.'

'No . . . Not going about this very well, am I?'

'No you're not. Did you ever?'

'Caroline –'

'Yes?'

'Could you do me a favour?'

'You've got a bloody nerve.'

Vic grinned. 'Can you have a word – not, not a word, a chat – with young Opal?'

'Why?'

Vic waved a hand at the greenery. 'You say all this relaxes people –'

'You're not getting anywhere, are you?'

'No, I'm not.'

'Why?

All else fails, fall back on the truth.

'Cromer's besotted, I seem to rub her up the wrong way.

'What about Ellie?'

161

'What?'

'Cromer told me on the phone you'd tried to offload her on Ellie, and Ellie wasn't having it.'

'Putting it mildly, yes. Went right off her as soon as she saw her.'

'What makes you think I won't?'

'You get on all right with Nova, same way you did with Maelee, Maelee Thomas. I thought you liked these kids –'

'I respect the fact they've got a bloody hard life in front of them. Having children doesn't exactly help.'

'I can't even begin to get close to her.'

As ever, Caroline was weighing her options.

One more reason she's inspector and you're still sergeant.

'Chat to her about what?'

'Anything so long as it's not the case.'

'She's not stupid, Vic. If she's been on her own since her mother died – never mind old Julius – she'll be too smart to see a copper as a girl's best friend. Specially one in uniform –'

'Yeah.' Putting on a frown. 'Best leave it up to you then –'

She saw straight through it. 'You're a cunning old bugger, aren't you?'

'That supposed to mean?'

'Just tell me what you want me to get out of her.'

'Whether or not she knew these kids down the Feeder, for one. And how well.'

'Does she know they're dead?'

'No. No, I don't think so.' Wondering if Cromer had been shooting his mouth off, hoping he hadn't.

'What else?'

'See if you can find out who the father is. She told

me it was none of my business. At the time I thought she was right –'

'But not now?'

Vic stood up. 'It's a lead, that's all. I'll be down the Three Tuns, then back here.' He looked down at the aspidistra. 'You come up with anything, I'll buy it a bottle of milk.'

After Vic had gone, Caroline decided she would do better to talk to Opal and Nova together: that way it wouldn't seem so much like an interview and she could catch up on exactly what had been happening. She moved across the small greenery-shaded room, took three pale green cups and saucers out of her filing cupboard and switched on the coffee machine.

One thing she didn't want was the distraction of three small toddlers crawling all over the floor and in all probability pulling everything down and wrecking the place. She picked up the phone and asked the desk sergeant where they all were.

'In the interview room, ma' am.'

'Is it still in one piece?'

'Just.'

'What about the cells? Have they seen their new accommodation yet?'

As the Desk Sergeant hesitated, Caroline could hear the sound of children's voices. At least one seemed to be crying – or maybe it was laughing: hard to tell over the phone.

The Sergeant said, 'Hoping you'd take care of that, ma'am.'

'Right. In the mean time, could you bring the two mothers up to see me, please.'

'Yes ma'am.' The Sergeant sounded first relieved

and then worried. 'Er – what about the sprogs, ma'am, the children?'

'DC Cromer can look after them for a few minutes, can't he?'

Sounding even more relieved. 'Yes, ma'am. Thank you ma'am.'

As Caroline put the internal phone down her direct line rang.

'Caroline? Sam Richardson. Now listen. We're not having women and kids in your cells, Caroline. Not fit for blacks let alone little kiddies and the press'll go berserk. You understand?'

'For once I'm inclined to agree with you.'

'Well thank you, Caroline.' Sam's voice grated with sarcasm. 'Let me know what you come up with by way of an alternative.'

'I will, Sam.'

'No kids in them cells. Right?'

'Right.'

'Vic there?'

'On his way to the Three Tuns – Cromer's still here.'

'Well tell bloody Cromer to call bloody Parnes on his bloody mobile. Traffic have parked his bloody Escort in my forecourt and pissed off with the keys. Bloody thing's a bloody disgrace. Tell him to get his arse down the Bridewell and shift it.'

'I will, Sam.'

'Oh – and you'll need to call Parnesy as well. Re these bloody funeral arrangements . . . And Caroline –'

'Yes, Sam?'

'When you see Vic kindly tell him who's running this fucking show will you? Tarra.'

164

16

Whenever he got the chance Vic liked to take a look at the *Great Britain* – no reason, particularly, just the sight of the old ship seemed to buoy him up. He got the OSG driver to pull up a couple of hundred yards short of the Three Tuns and said he'd walk.

'Right,' said the helmeted driver. 'Don't want to make it look like a bust.'

'Our Billy's had plenty of them,' said Vic.

'Know him, do you?'

'Of old. Used to have the Kit-Kat before he went belly-up.'

'Beats me how he keeps getting a licence.'

'Fella like Billy Jewel pulls in all sorts of pond-life,' said Vic. 'Handy to have 'em all in one place.'

'Makes it easier for you lot, I suppose, yeah.'

'That's right,' said Vic. 'Look, just out of curiosity –'

'What's that, Vic?'

'Whose idea to kit you guys up and send a battlewagon?'

'Your Chief Super, Richardson –'

'Never told me.'

'Said he wanted a presence, on account of this funeral thing tomorrow.' The driver turned to his mate. 'What'd he call it, Keef? Containment and what?'

The co-driver looked up from the racing pages of

165

the *Mail*. 'Containment, visual deterrence and surveillance.'

'Yeah, that's right – surveillance.'

Vic said, 'How many's he got then?'

'All four divisionals plus some of your lot from the Pool.'

'You get half a dozen of these charging round St Pauls,' said Vic, 'more likely to start a riot than stop one.'

'Yeah, well, you know Richardson better than we do.'

'Don't I just.'

Vic made his way down the side of Macaulay's Restaurant. Two white-aproned middle-aged ladies were peeling and dicing carrot, turnip and swede into a big aluminium dixie. An old bakelite radio tuned to Atlantic 252 was booming out Tom Jones' 'Delilah' in the kitchen and the two young chefs, as chefs will, were shouting along with it.

The alley led past the rodent-proof blue waste-bins on to the crunchy cindered track where the docks railway used to run. Across the glittering water of the Floating Harbour, penned in the old dry dock that had once been her cradle and was now her grave, stood the *Great Britain*.

Vic stood with his hands in his pockets, breathed in, and found himself smiling at the sight of her: butter-yellow bowsprit breaking free of the dark stone walls, six raked masts cutting up into the blue sky, gleaming black white and gold in the morning sun.

Vic's father had told him their names when he was a boy – fore, main, mizzen, jigger, driver and striker – but when they went to look over the great hulk on its return from the Falklands in the summer of 1970 the hole where the rearmost mast had been was labelled SPANKER. Vic's dad, who was a mild-mannered man by and large, said 'spanker' was a load of book-reader's bollocks, and what the men called it, the men who worked her for a living out on the Western Ocean, was 'striker'. Vic, who had long since ceased to see his father as infallible – ever since Timperley, in fact – thought at the time that this was just another example of his father being wrong and doggedly insisting he was right.

Nearly thirty years later, typing a report and looking up how to spell something else he came across 'spanker'. 'Naut.' said the dictionary, 'gaff sail set abaft the after mast. Also known as "striker".'

Vic stood on the stone-edged dock wall, and the thoughts and memories he always had of his father when he caught sight of the *Great Britain* swam through his mind. After asking the old man's forgiveness for what he now saw as the ordinary resentments of boyhood, he went on gazing at the great old ship.

Feeling the lift of her, an idea took hold of him and he began to imagine her floating free of her old dry dock, swinging majestically round and sailing out down the Avon into the Severn; then, fully rigged and colours flying, surge on down to the Western Ocean.

Some reason, he heard his father's voice: *Go on, my son, you can do it.*

It was pleasantly warm walking along the water's edge until he came to the gap that isolated the Three Tuns from the buildings on each side. There, a cold easterly flattened the weeds and roughened the water; as Vic looked up, he saw, beyond the old marshalling yards on the opposite bank, a row of houses with boarded-up windows.

Foxes have holes —

The Gents of the Three Tuns was outside: a thickly painted black wall with a runnel of half-round brown vitreous pipe at its base; next to it, a surprisingly clean outside lavatory with – even more surprisingly – a working electric light. A white-painted plank door led into a short passage with the Ladies off to the right, and then you were in the main bar.

It was a four-square tattily comfortable room smelling of old beer, fags and polish. There was a dartboard on one side and a gas-flamed log fire in a fire-basket on a tiled hearth on the other. The furniture was red leatherette benches and bentwood chairs around cast-iron Victorian tables with fag-scarred mahogany tops.

As Vic entered, Billy Jewel was dipping a long spoon into the pickled-egg jar on the corner of the bar. He had grown ruddier in the face and stouter in the body since taking on the Three Tuns. Only his hair, white and thick and curly, remained the same and gave him the air of a fat but cheerfully fallen angel.

'Morning, Vic. Be with you as soon as I've got old Ted's glass eye out the jar.'

Old Ted, a sunken-faced cider drinker in an oversized brown car coat, made a gummy wheezing noise intended for laughter, then started hacking and coughing into his red-knuckled arthritic fist. The only other people in the bar were two punk girls, heavily made up to look pale and wearing short black skirts and leggings. They were sitting each side of the dusty log fire, hunched over the yellow gas flames, smoking very thin roll-ups.

Billy spooned the pickled egg on to a white saucer and stuck a couple of cocktail sticks in it. 'There you go, Ted.' He placed his hands on the counter in front of Vic; a Hong Kong Rolex dangled loosely from its bracelet on one wrist, a heavy red-gold identity chain hung from the other. 'All he ever eats,' he said to Vic. 'What can I do you for?'

'I'm working, Billy.'

'Large Vladivar then –'

'Better not. Tonic'd be nice.'

'Ice and slice?'

'Why not?'

Billy tossed the little bottle in the air, caught and decapped it in the same movement, shovelled ice into a tall glass, poured on the foaming tonic and slid a slice of lemon over the side. 'Straw?'

'No thanks.' Vic let the tonic fizz in his mouth for a moment. 'Get many kids in here, Billy?'

'Oh shit.'

'What?'

'It's that, is it?'

'What?'

'On the news every half hour –'

'What is?'

'Five kids OD'd on H, squat across the water. Brown bread, the lot of 'em.'

'Yeah, that's it, that's the one. They ever use this place?'

Billy glanced over at the two punk girls. 'Let's move round the corner. They can all fucking lip-read in here.'

Vic slid his glass round to the pickled-egg jar. When he needed to, he could see over Billy's shoulder to Old Ted and the punk girls by the fire.

169

Billy checked his eyeline. 'All right?'

'Fine.

'This your case, is it?'

'As much as anyone's.'

'Meaning what exactly?'

'I'm on it, yeah, but this is a biggie.'

'Yeah,' said Billy. 'So who's running it?'

'Sam Richardson.'

'Fuck.'

'What's the problem, Billy?'

'Cunt's been dogging me ever since the Moonglow.' Without looking, Billy put his arm out behind him to the Famous Grouse optic and jerked a double into his highball glass.

'What, personally?'

'Not that dumb, is he?'

'No, he's not.'

'He sends a couple of blokes in every weekend.' Billy patted the electronic till. 'Just when I've got the old piano up to speed, in they come, nine, ten, half-past. Seconds later the place is fucking deserted. Like the fucking *Marie Celeste* in here, pints on the tables, arrers still in the board, fruit machine going chunter-chunter-chunter, nobody here.' Billy took a big swallow. 'Ever since I got off pozzesh at the school.'

'Westminster Road?'

'Yeah, where that black piece got shot, nice kid, worked in the Moonglow.'

'Maelee Thomas.'

'Right –'

'But you got done for cocaine, Billy.'

'Fucking hell, Vic, I practically cracked the fucking case for you –'

'In the end, yeah. After a certain amount of persuasion.'

'Yeah, well, I told the wrong fucking bloke, didn't I?'

'You should have told Sam Richardson?'

'Yeah.' Billy glanced round the bar, came back to eyeing Vic. 'He doesn't go a lot on you. Thinks you're too fucking smart and too fucking idle.'

'He say that?'

'Not in so many words, no.'

'No . . . Look, Billy –'

'What?'

'He send any blokes in Friday night?'

'Friday?'

'You said the weekend. That include Friday?'

'Not half –'

'He send anybody in?'

'Hang about.' Billy reached under the till, took out a used till-roll with FRI written on it in black laundry marker, ran it through his fingers until he came to TOTAL ALL. 'No. No, he didn't. We had a good night, Friday.'

'Any of the squat kids come in?'

Billy looked at him, took another gulp before replying. 'How far is this going, Vic?'

'Not past me, mate.'

Vic felt no compunction in lying to Billy; in fact, it amused him that basically lawless but otherwise likeable punters such as Billy seemed to think they could beat the rap on anything from a parking ticket to a murder charge. They seemed to have an inexhaustible belief that influence carried more clout than the law.

Come to that, Vic thought, a lot of coppers were the same, inclined to think they could lean on villains and turn them into snouts instead of going through all the bother and rigmarole of charging them. It was as if both lots thought you had to play the system just to prove you fucking well existed: if you won, well and good, the Gods had smiled on you, and if you lost, well, fuck it, par for the course.

Billy said, 'You sure of that?'

'Mother's grave, Billy.'

'Right.' Another glance round the bar. 'We did have a few of 'em in.' Nodding over his shoulder at the two punk girls. 'They were with 'em.'

'Any names?'

Billy put his hand up to his mouth. 'Nearest's Emma, other one's Natalie –'

'No, you berk, the blokes, the kids.'

Billy lit a Benson's then offered Vic one. Vic shook his head. Billy took a drag and blew the smoke out luxuriously. 'First today.'

Vic looked at the half-dozen fag-ends in the ashtray.

Billy said, 'All I can tell you, names they use in here.'

'Go on.'

'There's Trozza, Diesel, Woolie, Neil and Blaupunkt.'

'Blaupunkt – what's he, German?'

Billy shook his head. 'What he nicks.'

'Oh, right.'

'Same as Woolie. They're all on the nick, mate. All day long. Expensive business, H, even when there's not much about.'

'What they on then? Methadone?'

Billy's chubby face went blank. 'I wouldn't know, Vic. Not my scene.'

'Time they stay?'

'Half eleven – ish.'

'Drinking much?'

'Fair bit. Like no tomorrow, some of 'em.'

'They had money then?'

'Oh yeah. Always on the look-out, Friday. Something for the weekend, isn' it?'

'Drinking what?

'Jack Daniels and Coke mostly. Fucking waste but there you are, blame fucking rock and roll. Girls on vodka and Red Bull chasers.

'Then what?'

'Drinking-up time, isn' it, and this dark piece comes in. Tall. Dark. Fucking gorgeous. Tits out here and arse to make your eyes water. Know what I mean?'

'Yeah, Billy, I know what you mean.'

'Not black but got that turn-to-shit look some of these black kids like to lay on you.'

Vic said, 'Right, Billy. No shit now. How does it work?'

'How does what fucking work?'

'Don't piss me about Billy, we'll both end up down fucking Bridewell –'

'Fucking hell, Vic, fine fucking friend you are –'

'I don't want it and you don't want it, so just tell me how it fucking works –'

'Fucking filth is fucking right –'

'No it fucking isn't, Billy. I'm still your mate –'

'Hoo-fucking-ray –'

'I'm still your fucking mate, you fat stupid fucker –'

'Less of the fat –'

'Trying to save you from dropping head-first into deep, deep shit, Billy. Now, either you want to face a charge of allowing licensed premises to be used for dealing Class A –'

'All right,' said Billy. 'Say no more.' Looking

nervously over his shoulder then back at Vic. 'You came through the alley, right?'

'Right.'

'Two of 'em go down there, out the alley into the Gents. The others all get round that table by the door to stop anybody getting through. If it's clear, one of the kids comes back, lets the dealer or the pusher or whoever out, and they do the deal in the Gents crapper.'

'Why the Gents, Billy?'

'Easier to do a fucking runner, isn' it? Two steps, you got the whole the fucking wharf to play with – no lights, nothing –'

'Scuse me,' said a slurred voice at Vic's elbow. 'You a copper?'

'No he's not,' said Billy.

'Yes I am,' said Vic.

'Fucking hell,' said Billy.

'How can I help you?'

The punk girl said, 'You can fuck off an' leave us in peace for a start.'

'Now that's enough, Emma,' said Billy.

'Anything else?' said Vic.

'Yeah, matter of fact, there is.' The punk girl swayed, and screwed up her eyes to keep focused.

'What's that?'

The punk girl smiled at him. Then she said, 'Drink my piss,' and threw the contents of her glass straight in Vic's face.

17

It took Vic a couple of seconds to get his breath back, first from the shock and second because it wasn't piss but warm white wine and soda.

When he finished mopping up with the bar-cloth Billy passed him, he said, 'Let's start again, shall we?'

The punk girl folded her arms, turned her head to smirk at her friend. 'Suit yourself.'

It was an attitude Vic was familiar with but not fond of. Either you got smart-arsed by the pair of 'em or you put the frighteners on straightaway –

He took out his pocket book. 'Right. Suppose I say you're under arrest for obstructing and assaulting a police officer in the performance of his duty. Now what have you got to say?'

'You what?'

'Fucking hell, Vic,' said Billy.

Old Ted quietly left his pint and pickled egg and started wheezing his way towards the back door.

'And furthermore,' Vic plucked a ballpoint from the spiral binding, 'this obstruction and assault took place in front of the following witnesses –'

Now the other punk girl came and stood in front of her friend. 'You lay a finger on her – you lay *one finger* –'

'And what?' said Vic. 'You'll call the police?' He took out his warrant card. 'Detective Sergeant Hallam, Bristol Central CID.'

175

'You bastard, you fuckin' bastard!' The second girl's eyes were glittering and she was waving her arms about. 'I'll have you!'

The back door banged shut behind Old Ted and then Billy was round the bar saying, 'Come on, ladies, that's enough, that's quite enough –' Billy took hold of the second girl's forearms, propelled her backwards to the nearest chair and sat her down.

'Fuckin' murderers! Fuckin' murderin' bastards!'

'Holy shit,' said Billy, appealing to Vic. 'Only just opened for Chrissake –'

Vic ignored him, moved between the two girls to cut off their eye contact and turned back to the first girl. 'Name?'

'Emma –'

'Emma what?'

'Don't tell him!'

'Emma Clarke.'

'Thank you. He swung round on the other girl. 'You?' She looked up defiantly. 'Your name please.'

'I ain't done nothin' –'

'Nobody's saying you have –'

'Oh go on, Nat, I had to –'

'Natalie . . . Natalie Forrester.'

'Thank you.' He pulled up a bentwood chair to the other side of the circular cast iron table and nodded Emma into it. 'What are you, students?'

'Yeah.'

'University?'

'Poly.'

He looked from one to the other. They were both young and skinny, and although neither had anything special going for them they both had that sullen fragility, that I-know-what-I'm doing-and-you-can't-stop-me bravado that intermittently lit up their lives like a strobe at a disco – and then, as with the kids in the squat, blipped out and left them either dead or pregnant.

'Why d'you do it, Emma?'

She looked down at her bitten brown-painted fingernails. 'Don' know.'

'She's upset,' said Natalie.

'The boys in the squat?'

'Yeah.'

'They were friends of yours, were they?'

Emma tried to speak and couldn't. She laid her head on the table, blurted something into her arm, and hiding her face, began to sob. Natalie put her arm awkwardly across Emma's skinny heaving back and tried to comfort her.

'What'd she say?'

'Said they're our mates.' Natalie glanced up at Vic for permission, shifted her chair to pull Emma into her arms.

Vic said, 'Any chance of a cuppa, Billy?'

Billy swallowed. 'Yeah, right.'

When he'd gone, Vic said, 'Now listen, I'm sorry I had to be hard on you. You help me, we'll forget it happened, all right?'

Emma's back went on heaving. Natalie kissed the top of her head and said, 'Come on, kid, he's not gonna do anything –'

Hoping the lie was worth it, Vic said, 'I saw those boys. If it's any consolation, none of them seemed to be in any pain – it was all too quick –'

Emma lifted her stricken face. 'Oh my God, oh my God –'

'Hush now,' said Natalie. 'Hush –'

Vic asked Natalie, 'Was one of them her boy-friend?'

'No,' said Natalie. 'Nothing like that. You don't get like that on H.' Biting her lip, but the tears kept rolling down her face. 'We were all just mates – they never –'

'Never what?'

'They wouldn' let us near them –'

'Why?'

'If they were doing H.'

'I see.'

'They used to say – they used to say, didn' they, Em? They used to say they couldn' – they couldn' raise a boner between 'em, didn' they, Em?' Shaking her gently, trying to raise a smile. 'Remember that?'

Emma slowly straightened herself up. 'Got a hankie?'

There were some folded paper napkins in a glass on the bar. Vic reached round and put the glass in front of her. Emma took one, wiped her eyes and nose, looked at the brown eye-make up on the napkin. 'Oh my God.'

'Don't worry about it.' Vic waited a moment. 'The name Opal mean anything to you? Opal Macalpine?'

The two girls looked at each other. Natalie said, 'Yeah, we know who you mean. Why?'

'How about a man called Spicer, Julius Spicer?'

'No, never heard of him.'

Emma said, 'Why, what's happened to Opal?'

'She's in custody.' Vic decided to leave it at that.

'Good,' said Emma.

'Why d'you say that, Emma?'

'Why d'you think? If it hadn't been for her –'

Vic nodded. 'Can you tell me what happened on Friday?'

178

'She comes in, he's called closing time, we're all laughing and joking – she just stands there, never says a word, does she, Nat?'

'Then what?'

'She's got this kid's back-pack on, like one of them koala bears?'

'Right.'

'Then her and Trozza an' Diesel are out the back an' she's never even said good evening, has she, Nat?'

Natalie said, 'You think she's stuck up –'

'I know she is. Walks round as if her shit don't stink –'

'I just think she's fuckin' nervous – know I'd be –'

Vic said, 'Trozza and Diesel?'

'Yeah,' said Emma. 'Terence Ross and Darren Linley.'

'Any idea where from?'

'Yeah, Leith.'

'It's in Scotland.'

'Always bangin' on about it – Leith this, Leith that –'

'How about the others?'

'All Bristol kiddies.'

'You know their names?'

'Yeah. Paul Wood, Neil Dacre, Brian Pitfield.'

'Out Kingswood somewhere.'

'Thanks.' He wrote the names in capitals. 'They ever say anything about Opal?'

'Used to call her Miss Ironpants.'

'Diesel tried to get off with her, dinnee?'

'He have any luck?' said Vic.

'Nah – she told him her man was away, din't she?'

'Meaning what?'

Emma shrugged. 'In the nick, isn' he? Double GBH, Diesel said. Put him right off.'

'Never cracked a smile, did she?' said Natalie.

'Never,' said Emma. 'Miserable cow.'

Billy came in with four blue and white striped mugs, two in each hand. He set them down on the scarred table top, reached into a trouser pocket and dropped a handful of white plastic spoons and sugar packets in the middle. 'Cheers.'

Cromer switched the radio off to retract the aerial and drove Parnes's metallic fawn Vauxhall Omega under the foot-thick concrete lintel into the underground car park.

Rufus James was sliding a wheeled alloy gurney out of a long black van and adjusting the telescopic legs. He led Cromer and Parnes to the 'Stretcher traffic only' lift and pressed the call button.

As they moved in and waited for Rufus to manoeuvre the gurney alongside, cold air sank down from above and filled the lift with its clammy chill. Cromer thought he could smell something like very old lamb fat, and felt it coating his tongue and the roof of his mouth. As they rose up, the air grew colder and tasted faintly of formaldehyde.

'Long time since I was down here,' said Parnes.

'Is how we all hend up, y'know,' said Rufus. 'Heh heh.'

'I don't think levity is called for, Mr James. Let's just crack on, shall we?'

One of the mortuary attendants pulled Maelee's drawer out of the wall and the other lifted up the stiff green sheet.

Rufus said, 'You will both have to formally identify the remains, gentlemen.'

'Of course,' said Parnes. He stiffened his back and

took a step forward.

'May not be as easy as you think, Chief Inspector –'

'I have done this before, Mr James.'

Cromer thought Parnes' voice sounded ratty; whether it was because Rufus was black or Parnes was feeling nervous was hard to say.'

Rufus said, 'What I mean is, due to length of time, certain changes will have taken place –'

'I'm perfectly aware of that, thank you.'

'All I am sayin' is we all have to be sure –'

'Of course.' Parnes beckoned – rather irritably, Cromer thought – to the attendant holding the stiff green cloth. The attendant lifted it higher and Parnes looked in. 'Good Lord. Poor woman.' Parnes remained bent over Maelee's body for several seconds. Cromer noticed Parnes' black leather gloves tensing behind his back. When Parnes sighed and stood back, a plume of warm breath rose and vanished into the cold air. 'Your turn, Cromer.' Parnes stood back and put a black gloved hand in front of his mouth to clear his throat.

Cromer looked into the drawer. Rufus was right: the big-built eighteen year old he remembered waitressing in the Moonglow was now a frail middle-aged woman. Her cheeks were sunken and the shape of her teeth and jaw was tautly prominent. In fact, her whole body looked wasted under the rough hospital gown, and the skin on her face and her feet – one toe tagged with her identity – had gone like old chocolate: brown with a faint bloom of grey.

'Have you positively identified the remains, gentlemen?'

'Yes I have,' said Parnes. 'The remains are those of Miss Maelee Thomas.'

'Constable?'

'I identify these remains as those of Maelee Thomas,' said Cromer. At first he was surprised to find his voice raw and unsteady, echoing inside his head, and he understood why Parnes felt the need to clear his throat: the presence of death, especially of someone you had known, no matter how briefly, always laid a cold hand on you, reminding you of your own inevitable change to come.

There was, thank God, a one-bar electric fire in the supervisor's office, and Cromer felt glad of its dull red glow. The supervisor, Mr Bowyer, a thin bent man in a brown suit with a bony face and a ferrety little moustache, looked up from his desk. 'All done, Chief Inspector?'

'Yes,' said Parnes. 'Thank you.'

'All satisfactory, Mr James?'

'As per usual, Mr Bowyer.'

Mr Bowyer pushed a thin manila folder across his desk. 'We do have these papers to sign, release of the body and so forth, so if you will all append your signatures, gentlemen, and write your name, rank or position in capitals, I'll do what I can to expedite matters for you. Excuse me.' Mr Bowyer stood up and moved to the door. Cromer noticed one of his shoes was built up a couple of inches or so and there was, through the heel, the glint of a steel caliper. Somehow, Cromer thought, it seemed to make the whole business ten times sadder and bleaker.

After Parnes had finished he held out his hand. 'Keys please, Cromer.'

'Oh,' digging his hand in his pocket, 'right –'

'What's the matter?'

'Nothing sir – I'm supposed to meet up with

Sergeant Hallam back at Trinity Road – neither of us have got any transport –'

'Not a taxi service, lad.'

'No sir.'

'I've got bodies to organise,' Parnes gave Rufus a thin smile. 'Got a procession tomorrow, haven't we, Mr James?'

'Yes we have indeed, Chief Inspector.'

'I want you to fax me routes and times from school to church and church to crematorium.'

'As I understand it, she is bein' interred.'

'Well, wherever.' Parnes took the keys from Cromer, swung them round his finger and pocketed them. 'I'm sure Mr James will give you a lift to Trinity Road, Cromer.'

'Sure, no problem.'

'Right. Best get on.'

After Parnes had left, Mr Bowyer came back in holding a thick blue file. 'Oh,' he said, looking round. 'No Chief Inspector?'

'No, sir,' said Cromer, 'he had to get on.'

'Oh. Right. I see.' The supervisor fingered his moustache for a moment, looked at Cromer and then held out the blue file. 'Perhaps you'd give him this, will you, Constable? It's all our duplicates, reports, findings, all the rest of the bumf that has to go with the body.'

'Yes sir, I will sir.'

'Good.' Mr Bowyer slipped a form out of the file. 'If you could just sign this release, and print as before, by the pencilled Xs.'

Cromer bent over the desk and wrote his name, rank and number.

'Jolly good,' said Mr Bowyer. 'All yours, Mr James.'

'Many thanks,' said Rufus.

Heading back to St Pauls in Rufus' long black van, Cromer opened up the blue file and riffled through its contents. Most of it was admin stuff, detailing Maelee Thomas' various movements: in situ paramedic reports from the school, transfers by ambulance from hospital to hospital, sheets of admissions, diagnoses and treatments, duplicates of her death certificate, mortuary transfers and subsequent examinations and statements in court. Poor old Maelee, he thought, moving from life to death down a staircase of paper.

He missed it the first time round because it was written on the back of a page in pencil and had failed to duplicate properly. Then, as Rufus retuned the black van's radio from Radio Bristol to Radio 3, it caught his eye again. It was a note from Calder on the reverse of one of the pages in his autopsy report and referred to the ballistics follow-up. The note identified the weapon used as a model 10/19 Smith & Wesson .38 six-shot revolver, serial number 1019SW386/0458, issued on the night of the raid to DCI Barnard, Bristol Central CID.

Underneath the initials 'RJC', someone else had written and underlined 'NFA': No Further Action.

18

When Vic walked in, carrier bag in hand, Cromer was sitting on the floor in Trinity Road interview room with the kids sprawled round his legs. He was reading out of a dog-eared rag book of Nursery Rhymes and getting the kids to do the actions.

'Don't mind me, John.'

'One last one, then uncle John's got to get back to work.'

Jamie, Maelee's kid, looked solemn and said, 'Catch naughty mans.'

'That's right, Jamie. Catch naughty mans. Now everybody ready? Here we go. "Little Miss Muffet, Sat on a tuffet –" '

The toddlers walked around, and then, as the penny dropped, sat down in turn.

'Very good,' said Cromer. '"Eating her curds and whey."' To help them out, Cromer mimed eating out of a bowl. As they followed suit, Cromer said, 'Yum yum yum. Lovely puddins. Yum yum yum –'

'Yum yum yum,' went the kids. 'Yum yum yum –'

Now Cromer put on a deeper voice: 'But then what happened?'

The two girls, Esme and Erin, started to squeal and clutch at each other. Jamie folded his arms and smiled nervously to show he wasn't scared.

Cromer leaned forward and made his voice go all

shivery. ' "Along came a . . . spider – And sat down beside her –" '

All three ran around yelling until they all fell over on top of each other screaming. Cromer waited until they stopped and then, in his normal voice: 'And she said, "Fuck off, hairylegs." '

The interview room door clicked open. 'Enjoying ourselves, are we?' said Caroline. She held the door open to let Opal and Nova through.

Vic watched for the look between Opal and Cromer.

There it was: their eyes meeting, displaying, then immediately concealing, a need as heavy and sick and weakening as flu, dragging at them, making them awkward.

Opal managed it better – women nearly always did, Vic thought – somehow it seemed to be the element they swam in, lived in, breathed in; Cromer stood like a leaden-footed lump, skin reddening, eyes hot and blue like a kid caught scrumping. Opal slid by him, smiling and saying hello to Esme, then as she passed letting her long lilac-pointed fingers brush Cromer's.

Vic felt first sorry for them, then irritable.

What a fucking time to pick, Cromer.

Maybe he was jealous, he thought, remembering how it had been what was it – fifteen years ago: him a newly promoted stop-at-nothing Detective Sergeant and Caroline an eighteen-year-old probationer – with a sweetly curved mouth and eyes that melted the ice inside you.

Oh shit.

This was an exact fucking re-run, right down to the illicit looks and fumbled touches, the continuous irritant when she was present, within reach, the balls-aching howling sense of loss when she wasn't.

Jesus, what a state to get into –

What was it Billy Jewel used to say –

It's only a hole with hairs round, but it sure made a cunt out of me –

He glanced over at Caroline. She had seen it too. There was the faintest of shrugs, dismissing him, Cromer and Opal all in one go.

She said, 'Can we have a word, Vic? And you, John.' She turned on her heel and left.

The blue file lay open on Caroline's desk next to a three-inch-thick Police Guide to Jurisprudence with a sun-faded spine and a fringed green leather bookmark stuck between the pages. She turned the file round to face Vic. 'I'm not sure what to do about this.'

Vic scanned through Calder's note.

Caroline said, 'Any ideas on NFA?'

Vic said, 'Pound to a pinch of shit it's Parnesy.'

'Why?'

'His handwriting for a start. Plus he always underlines things.'

'You sure?'

'Had enough fucking appraisals off him, haven't I? All signed AJP underlined.'

Caroline frowned. 'You think he'd have the nerve – on his own?'

'Always up the CC's backside. He could have mentioned it.'

'Even so –'

'Oh come on, Caroline that whole fucking job was full of cover-ups – you know that, I know that.'

Caroline turned to Cromer. 'What do you think, John?'

'What?' Cromer came back from wherever he was. 'Oh – I think Vic's right.'

Vic said, 'Anyway we can't ask the CC, he's dead.'

'So's Barney,' said Caroline.

Vic said, 'So's Maelee.'

Caroline looked at him sharply, then took the blue file back and weighed it. 'If she had any relatives, any relatives over here, there'd be a case to answer.'

Cromer said, 'She has got a relative, hasn't she?'

'Who?' said Caroline.

'Jamie,' said Cromer. 'Her kid.'

There was a silence.

Vic said, 'Where's the ballistics report?'

'There isn't one,' said Cromer. 'I've already looked.'

'There you are then,' said Vic. 'Nicked.'

'Let me get something straight,' said Caroline. 'None of us think Maelee was deliberately shot – or do we?'

Vic said, 'We weren't there. Parnes was. Ask him.'

Caroline closed the file. 'I think the best thing is to duplicate the whole file and then you, John, hand the original over to Parnes as if nothing's happened –'

'When in doubt,' said Vic, 'do nothing.'

Caroline glared at him. 'I didn't say that and for your information, Vic Hallam, that is *not* what I intend to do.'

Cromer said, 'What about Jamie?'

'Exactly,' said Caroline. She opened the Police Guide at the green leather marker. Embossed on it in gold was the candle-and-barbed-wire logo of Amnesty International. 'If there's any compensation to be had, which on the face of it the Fatal Accident Acts would seem to suggest –'

'What does it say?'

Caroline glanced down the double-column entry. 'Basically, it says no cause, no case. Incontrovertible cause, incontrovertible case.' She tapped the blue file. 'This makes the cause clear enough, wouldn't you say?'

'Hang on – you're saying a claim against the Force?'

'Yes,' said Caroline. 'I think it's right, and I think it's fair. Poor kid's got little enough going for him otherwise – no father and a dead mother –'

'Not going to make yourself exactly popular, you know that?'

'Never bothered you, has it?'

'No, but –'

'Why should it bother me?'

Vic shrugged. 'Your look-out.'

'Right, that's that. I'm glad we're all agreed.' Caroline pushed the file across to Cromer. 'There you go, John. Two doors down on the right –' As Vic and Cromer stood up, she said, 'Not you, Vic.'

They listened to Cromer's rubber soles squeaking down the corridor. Caroline said, 'What are you going to do about him?'

Vic shrugged. 'Let nature take its course.'

'He could have picked a better moment.'

'What I thought,' said Vic. 'What did you make of her?'

Caroline put her elbows on the desk, interlaced her fingers and leant her chin on them. 'I think she sees him as a way out. And she fancies him.'

'How d'you know that?'

Caroline gave him a frank, sexually knowledgeable smile; suddenly the rat inside him was scrabbling and thudding around desperate to get out and fuck her.

Caroline went on smiling at him. 'How d'you think?'

Vic cleared his throat and shifted in his chair. 'That easy, is it?'

'It is with you.' She leaned back in her chair, contemplating him, judging him. 'You had your chance, Vic.'

'Yeah, and blew it,' said Vic.

'Correct.'

The pause lengthened, and died.

Vic said, 'What else she say? She mention the father?'

'She said all that was over. Said he took off as soon as she fell pregnant.'

'He black or white?'

'I didn't ask.' She went on studying him.

'Now what?'

'You're living in the past, you know that?'

'Not PC enough for you?'

'Past all hope, more like.'

'Yeah, maybe,' said Vic. 'Maybe not.'

Caroline sighed, shook her head, said nothing.

'What I heard,' said Vic, 'she said the guy was away. The kids in the Three Tuns reckon he was inside. Double GBH.'

'I see. That makes him black, does it?'

'No, it doesn't,' said Vic doggedly. 'Apparently one of the kids in the squat tried to pull her.'

'And she told him her bloke was inside?'

'Her man was away, yeah. For double GBH.'

'This was one of these junkie kids?'

'Yeah. One of the ones that died. Scottish kiddy.'

Caroline considered a moment. 'I think if I was her, that's what I'd tell him. That or something like it –'

'To put him off, you mean?'

'Mmm. She doesn't go a lot on junkies.'

'Neither would I if I was looking at ten years possession and intent to supply.'

'Would you do that, lay that on her?'

Vic shrugged. 'It's a lever.'

'No wonder they hate us.'

'You got your job, I've got mine.'

'And you'd nail her?'

'I wouldn't, no. But Sam would. Why I'm talking to you.'

Caroline thought for a moment. 'Fair enough. Let's give her the benefit of the doubt.'

'How?'

'She came to you because Julius had whacked her. You didn't have to go after her.'

'Right. What she say about the Turks?'

'She said at first she thought that was Julius panicking – he'd never come up with that kind of deal before –'

'He had come on to her himself once –'

'Yes. She told me about that. Thinks you're a right pig.'

'Oh well. I only saved her kid, didn't I?'

'I told her that.'

'Thanks.'

'I told her they obviously think she knows where the stuff is.'

'What she say to that?'

'She said some time back, she thinks round about New Year, Julius came in late, dead beat but really chuffed with himself –'

'When he got hold of it?'

'He was even talking about buying her a place.'

191

Vic said, 'What's a two-up two-down round here? Forty-five to fifty?'

'Sixty and up for something liveable,' said Caroline. 'Days, weeks, months go by, he's getting more and more twitchy –'

'No more roses round the door for young Opal?'

'No way. Then last Friday he gets her to make the drop. The kids in the squat can't believe it.'

'Why's that?'

'She said they reckoned they'd got over a grand's worth for four hundred and fifty quid. Says they leapt at it.'

Neither of them said anything for a while.

'It all comes back to Julius, and he's dead,' said Vic. 'He have a lot of friends?'

'He knew a lot of people,' said Caroline.

'Yeah, I suppose that's more like it,' said Vic. 'Can you get your lot on it? House to house, starting Palmer Street and moving out –'

'We're already on it. Part of the murder inquiry.'

Vic said, 'You know Sam's putting his heavy mob in? Half a dozen OSG's?'

Caroline nodded. 'Brilliant, isn't it?'

Vic reached into the carrier bag and put a bottle of milk on her desk. 'Semi-skimmed was all they had.'

'Thanks,' said Caroline. 'One more thing –'

'You mean my luck's changed?'

'Hardly,' said Caroline. 'Sam won't have them here. "No kids in them cells."'

'Fuck.'

'He also said remind Vic who's running this fucking show.'

'Yeah . . . What you going to do with them?'

'All I've come up with so far is a couple of hostels.'

192

She pushed over a a Post-It with a couple of phone numbers. 'One's bad, one's awful.'

Vic folded the Post-It into his pocket-book and stood up. 'I think it's time I had a word with Sam.'

'Do that. Give him my regards.'

'Yeah. Good luck with this Parnes business.'

She looked up at him, surprised. 'Thanks.'

193

19

A dented white van sat in the corner of Trinity Road forecourt surrounded by traffic cones.

'What's this?' said Vic.

'It's a white van,' said Cromer. 'Ford Escort diesel one point eight.'

'Fucking hell, John —'

'All Traffic could spare.' Cromer moved a couple of cones aside, got in, leaned over to open the passenger door, failed, and then smacked it open with the flat of his hand. 'Lock's on the dodgy side.'

The passenger seat floor was covered in polystyrene cups and burger containers. 'What a fucking shitheap.'

'Been round the clock twice,' said Cromer. He turned the key in the ignition. 'Had a hard life.'

Vic looked into the back of the van: the whole of the inside was covered in dents and gouges where the cones and road signs had been piled in and out. 'You can say that again.'

Cromer said, 'You have to wait for the glow-plug to go out before you turn the key.'

'Ideal fucking getaway vehicle, then.'

Cromer started the engine. There was a death-rattle clatter and a cloud of thick brownish-grey smoke billowed off the wall behind. 'She'll be all right when she's warmed up. Mechanic said the injectors were a bit iffy.' Cromer crunched it into first.

'Holy fuck,' said Vic. 'Be lucky not to get arrested.'

Cromer grinned. 'Least nobody's going to nick it.'

They headed up Old Market for the Bridewell.

Vic said, 'What d'you make of old Rufus?'

'Gave me a lecture on the fucking slave trade. Bristol built on the backs and blood of blacks – all that shit you come out with. Good bloke though. Likes a laugh – need to in his job.'

'Yeah, not sullen like a lot of 'em.' When Cromer didn't reply, Vic said, 'Granville there?'

'Had to go training.'

'Who helped with the body then?'

'I did.' Cromer frowned at the memory. She was really cold, Vic. Really cold –'

'So would you be if you'd been stuck in a fridge for four months.'

Cromer glanced across at him. 'When we lifted her out, she was very light for a big woman. Rufus said they'd taken two stone out of her. Said they kept it in tupperware in the Path Lab.'

'Poor cow.'

'Fuck's sake, Vic, have some respect.'

'Bit rich, isn't it, coming from you.'

'What's that supposed to mean?'

'Not me fucking the chief witness, is it?'

'Not this time, no.'

'Cheeky bugger.'

Cromer grinned into the traffic. 'Chance'd be a fine thing.'

Vic took the Post-It out of his pocket-book and looked at the hostel numbers. 'Pull over, John, I can't hear myself think.'

*

Sam's office was on the corner of the second floor: grey carpet, grey walls, grey metal desk. One window looked out on to a square blank wall, and the other on to a square of tarmac where his maroon Saab 9000 Turbo was parked.

Sam was hunched over his desk, neck and shoulders bulging through his bright blue striped shirt, chin jutting out like Mussolini. He waved them to a couple of grey plastic chairs. 'You get my message?' He watched Vic take out his pocket-book and thumb carefully through the pages. 'Vic, I said did you get my fucking message?'

Vic looked up. 'The one about who's running this fucking show?'

'That's the one.'

'Yeah.'

'And?'

'Just wondered which fucking show.'

'All of 'em, Vic. All of 'em. What I'm fucking here for.'

'Right.'

'So why keep going behind my back all the fucking time?'

'Not going behind your fucking back –'

'Vic. Watch my lips.' Sam glanced down at the list on his desk. 'Calder, the Three Tuns, taking women and children into protective fucking custody, some kid on a fucking motorbike, slagging off the OSGs, wrecking a fucking vehicle and parking it where every fucker who comes in here can see it – and not a fucking word –'

Vic said, 'That wasn't us, that was Traffic.'

'Right,' said Sam. 'Start at the fucking kick-off, shall we? Why protective custody?'

'Because they'd been attacked,' said Vic. 'When they were discharged from hospital I didn't think it was safe for them to go home.'

'Why not?'

'Because I considered the attackers knew where they lived.'

'But you didn't think fit to consult me?'

'I thought you were busy with the kids in the squat.'

'You know what Thought did, don't you?'

'Yeah.' Typical Sam, waiting his chance to get his own back.

'And although you knew exactly what sort of a shit-hole Trinity Road was –'

'I don't think it is a shit-hole, I think Caroline Coombes –'

'Ah, the fragrant Miss Coombes –'

'I thought, she knows the women, she'll know how to deal with them, and the kids, and the whole fucking situation –'

'And what about the press, and the fucking telly?'

'Didn't bother me –'

'Exactly. You didn't give a fuck –'

'Thinking of the women and kids –'

'You didn't give a fuck, Vic, but I do. Part of my job. And I know you don't put kids in fucking cells unless you want to see the poor little bastards on the front fucking page of the *Sun*, the *Mirror* and the *Western Daily Press* . . . So, you should've told me, shouldn't you?'

'Yeah. If you say so.'

'You're a bolshie insubordinate fucker, you know that? This is a big fucking operation, getting fucking bigger by the hour – you're trying to do it on your fucking own as per fucking usual, and it doesn't 'fucking help. You should've told me, shouldn't you?'

'What d'you want me to do – write it out fifty fucking times?'

'Instead I had to find out, didn't I?' said Sam. 'And then what did I find out? I find out you've pissed off to the Three fucking Tuns, that's what I find out.' Sam put his thick fingers together to make a cage. He had expanding stainless steel cufflinks in and the hair on his forearms was ginger-blond. 'What I haven't found out, because you *haven't fucking told me*, is why. Why the fuck the Three Tuns?'

'Where I got the names.'

'What names?'

Vic flipped open his pocket-book. 'Kids in the squat. Terence Ross and Darren Linley from Leith, Scotland, known down here as Trozza and Diesel. Paul Wood, Neil Dacre, Brian Pitfield from Kingswood, Bristol.'

Sam's eyes shifted suspiciously from Vic to Cromer, who was doing his best to disassociate himself by concentrating on his own pocket-book, and back to Vic. He held his hand out for Vic's book, and glanced down the list of names. 'How d'you get hold of these?'

'Couple of girls in the Three Tuns. Names are in there.'

Sam pressed a call button under his desk. When the uniformed WPC came in, he handed her Vic's pocket-book. 'Copy these and get them circulated will you, Viv? No house calls till I say so, and nobody to come in here till I ring. Oh and Viv –'

'Yes sir?'

'Make sure Sergeant Hallam gets his little black book back.'

'Yes sir.'

When she'd gone, Sam said, 'You could have told me or one of my lads.'

'Billy Jewel's seen enough of you and your lads.'

'Cunt'll see a lot more an' all. Should've gone down the steps last time. What you go and see him for?'

'It's where she made the drop.'

'Who?'

'Opal.'

'I thought she went round their gaff.'

'Not according to Billy. Or her. Or the girls.'

'Right.' Sam added a query next to Opal's name. 'Now then, Cromer, you're next on the shit list.'

Vic could feel the heat coming off Cromer.

'Yes sir?'

'This kid on a motorbike –'

'Green and white trail-bike, sir.'

'Why no report? Not getting like Hallam, are we?'

'No sir. Haven't had time, sir.'

'Make time, Cromer, make time. You do a full report and you give it to me personally, you understand?'

'Yes sir.'

'And I'll get it out to my lads and Traffic.'

'Yes sir, thank you sir.'

'Now then,' Sam glanced at his list, then at Vic. 'Mr Calder.'

'What about him?'

'Said you went to see him.'

'That's right. I needed to ask him a couple of things about Julius.'

'Not the kids in the squat?'

'You told me you were handling that.'

'Go on.'

'All we'd got to go on was Calder's prelim –'

'Hang on. Who's "we"?'

'Me and John here.'

'See what I mean, Vic?'

'You put us on the fucking case –'

'It's just one long fucking argument with you –'

'I got Calder to tell me off the record. He said Julius had had a good going-over before they used the cattle prods. They stuck one down his throat and one up his arse –'

'And?'

'Struck me as a funny thing to do if you're trying to get something out of somebody. Testicles like fucking aubergines, according to Calder. Then they killed him. Calder said he needed to talk to somebody – one of his torture mates – and that's as far as it goes.'

'No it isn't,' said Sam. 'Half hour ago, Calder rings me looking for you. Good, isn't it? Who's running the fucking show, Vic? See what I mean?'

'Look, Sam, if I was going behind your back I'd have given him my mobile number, wouldn't I?'

'I don't know, Vic. I don't know what the fuck you're up to, do I?' Sam brought his thick red fist down hard on the desk. *Because you don't ever fucking tell me, do you?*

'What am I supposed to do? Ring up every time I want to go to the khazi?'

Sam looked up from his list. 'Why slag off the OSGs to the blokes driving 'em?'

'OSGs don't do any good. You ask anybody in St Pauls.'

'Such as?' said Sam. 'Caroline fucking Coombes I suppose.'

'Nobody feels safe – then the ordinary punter starts feeling fucking intimidated and the toerags and the rest start chucking bricks and bottles of petrol.'

For a moment it looked as if Sam was going to take them into his confidence. Then he thought better of it. 'Well, Vic, you know and I know.'

They had reached an impasse; all three of them watched it growing wider and higher in the silence.

Then Vic said, 'What did Calder want, anyway?'

Sam stood up, moved from behind his desk and walked over to the window to see if his Saab was still there. It was. He stood looking down on it for a while, admiring it, then turned round to face them, arms folded, brick-red face giving nothing away.

'Look, Vic, two things I can do. One is take the pair of you off the case, put you both on suspension and charge you with insubordination, lack of cooperation, all the rest of the shit, none of which will do your pensions or your prospects any fucking good at all . . . Or you can keep me informed, do as I ask, let me know of any developments on the Opal–Julius front which will affect this fucking heroin business – because as you know and I know, Vic, the two fucking things are interlinked and we've got six fucking bodies to prove it – and that's only so far.'

Another silence.

It's as much as you're going to get, Hallam.

'All right,' said Vic. 'It's a deal.'

'That go for you too, Cromer?'

'Yes sir.'

Vic said, 'What's Calder come up with then, Sam?'

Sam reseated himself and took a rolled-up telephone transcript out of his right-hand desk drawer. 'First I thought it was some bollocks about Turkey and how they kosher the fucking lambs, and then Calder says it's not fucking kosher it's halal because Turks are

Muslim, so that put me in my fucking place didn't it?' Sam pulled the fax-roll of transcript up through his fingers. 'Then he starts telling me about fucking astrakhan – you know what astrakhan is, Vic?'

'Some sort of fur?'

'You Cromer?'

'No idea, sir.'

Sam gave them his lipless got-you smile. 'Right. Now according to Calder and his torture-specialist mate, astrakhan is the fleece of baby lambs. It's black and very tightly curled, and used to be a big favourite on bookies' and old ladies' coat-collars. Now then, according to Calder's fucking mate, the reason it's so black and fucking curly is because it's the skin of the fucking unborn. Foetuses, as you might say – still with us, Cromer?'

'Yes sir.'

'So, because these foetus skins, or fleeces or whatever they're called, are fucking valuable, to stop the little foetuses ripping theirselves to fucking pieces in what Mr Calder calls an unnecessarily prolonged birth trauma, the mothers are killed, halaled or fucking koshered, Vic, by slitting them up between the ribs, slipping your hand in and holding on to their fucking hearts until they fucking stop. That way, neither the mother nor the poor unborn fucking offspring know they're dead.' Sam leaned back, thick pale-gingery hands gripping the chair arms. 'And that, according to Calder and Calder's mate, is what happened to friend Julius. Without the astrakhan bit, of course.'

Viv knocked and came in with Vic's pocket-book. 'All done.'

'Thanks, Viv,' said Sam. 'Any calls?'

'Four so far. None that can't wait.'

'Thanks, Viv.' The WPC smiled and closed the door quietly.

Vic said, 'So Calder and his mate reckon it's the Turks?'

'Makes sense, doesn't it? They know how to do it, it's quick and it's quiet apparently.' Sam shrugged, 'Goodbye, Julius.'

'Yeah,' said Vic reluctantly.

'Don't fall over yourself, Vic,' said Sam.

'Two things –'

'Go on.'

'How would a Turk understand what Julius was saying?'

'It's all fucking English, Vic. Julius has been over here twenty years. They didn't coco they'd fucking hit him till they did.'

'All right, why kill the fucking goose?'

Sam said, 'Perhaps he's told them where he's laid the golden egg. He's been done over enough. They're not going to want him telling anybody else now, are they?'

'Why ransack the house?' said Vic. 'Why go for Opal's kid?'

'Fair enough,' said Sam. 'Have you asked her?'

'I've interviewed her, so has John, so has Caroline.'

'Interview her again then.'

'Yeah.'

'Threaten her.' Sam eyed them both. 'Possession and intent to supply. Tell her she'll be bringing her kid up in nick. What's the matter, Cromer?'

'Nothing, sir.'

Sam went down his list with a silver propelling pencil, putting a line through each heading but the last and carefully ringing the query round Opal's name.

'Now then. Last thing. These fucking hostels.'

Vic said, 'I spoke to Caroline –'

'So have I –'

'She reckons one's bad and one's hopeless.'

'That's right,' said Sam. 'In her opinion.'

'So on the way over I spoke to both of 'em.'

'So have I,' said Sam. 'What d'you reckon?'

Vic flipped open the pocket-book. 'This first one, the Fishponds one, the DSS and Social Services place, sounds a real no-room-at-the-fucking-inn joint. They can't do this, they can't do that, no own money over a fiver, no smoking inside the house, no mobiles, no phone-calls outside hours, only one hour's visiting six to seven and no men in the rooms, no drink, no loud music, no singing, no dancing, no running in the corridors, all food parcels to be shared between residents and staff, lights out at ten, up at six, no children in bed with their mothers –'

'What about the other one? This Montpelier place?'

'Complete fucking bedlam,' said Vic. 'Woman in charge said any child or woman at risk would be welcome and the rules were no women fighting and no men in the bedrooms. When I said it sounded like there were already several riots going on, she said that was the kids expressing themselves. Mrs Macarthy. Said she knew your missus. Great supporter, she said.'

'I know.'

'Said it was all voluntary so any donations gratefully accepted.'

'I know.'

'So what's the problem?'

'It's the DSS one, Vic.'

'Fuck sake, Sam –'

'We can't go outside the system –'

'Fuck the system.'

'We all know your motto, Vic. Just do it, will you?'

'Even your missus –'

'Look, Vic, we can't go outside the fucking system, Social Services'll go fucking spare. So never mind the fucking niceties, just do it. It's fucking Fishponds, got it? F-I-S-H-P-O-N-D-S.'

'Fine,' said Vic.

No Fucking Way.

'Place has got bullet-proof windows, CCTV and ram-raider bollards for fuck sake – and don't you fucking dare quote my wife at me.'

'Right. OK. Got it. No problem. Come on, John.'

As Vic and Cromer stood up, Sam said, 'Vic –'

'Yes, Sam?'

'I want you and John kitted up and carrying for this one.

'The fuck for, Sam?'

Sam leaned forward, forearms on his knees and hands clasped. For a moment, he looked weighed down, genuinely concerned. 'Job could change any fucking minute.' Straightening up, jutting his chin out. 'All I can tell you, mate, so why don't the two of you just fuck off and do as you're fucking told, for once.'

20

After Sabbahatin's slapping, Richie stayed with his head hung in his hands for a full minute. Lance looked over his shoulder at the next table but one. In between silences Sabbahatin was muttering and swearing at his two punks. It sounded to Lance like he was saying the same thing over and over. Lance pushed a big dark-knuckled fist against Richie's upper arm. 'Hey, you OK, kid?'

Richie's head moved between his two hands.

'Look like you fucked up, kid. Look like you fucked up good.'

Richie raised his head and grinned.

Senda said, 'What the Shabba guy sayin', you want a walk out a here, you got to get you shit together.'

'Yeah.'

'You don't, he say they take a 'lectric drill to you kneecaps and you goin' a crawl out. Seen?'

'Yeah. Seen.' Richie pushed himself to his feet, shoved both hands through his short fair hair and walked over to Sabbahatin.

Sabbahatin said, 'Go fuck yourself.'

Richie stood where he was, hands clasped behind his back. 'I understand that, Mr Sabbahatin –'

'So fucking do it –'

'What you got to understand,' said Richie, 'is this. We got a result –'

'Result? The fuck you talk about, result?'

'We got a result shows this is the stuff. Uncut.'

'Result? I tell you what a result we got. We got a result you watch this black piece a shit selling my stuff, mine, you hear, you little fuck, mine – and all you do is fucking watch –'

'No Mr Sabbahatin –'

'You got a result, you got two thousand cop looking for my fucking stuff, looking for you, me, every fucker –'

'Listen, I know Julius –'

'Fuck Julius, fuck him, you hear?'

'Yeah, sure, but listen. Julius, the dumb fucker, he's scared, minute he knows you're coming he's scared, so he sells it on uncut. He hasn't dared fucking look at it let alone cut it, so he sells it on uncut. These kids, they don't know, nobody told them, they don't know – they don't know this stuff is ten, twenny times pokier than their usual shit – and they blow it. Nobody tells them – I don't fucking tell them, she, the girl, the mule, she don't fucking tell them, Julius, he don't fucking tell them – they fucking blow it.'

'So?'

'So,' said Richie, spreading his hands wide open, 'one phone call, the stuff's ours. Untouched. Un-fucking-touched, Mr Sabbahatin. Julius had've known, had've had more time, he'd have cut the stuff to fuck. Makes sense –'

'One phone call?'

'Yeah.'

'To?'

'The girl.'

'What she fucking know?'

'She's got my kid, Mr Sabbahatin.' Richie looked over at Lance and Senda. 'I didn't want to tell you that, but these guys, they said it was important –'

'Why you didn't want?'

'Puts me in a –' Richie hesitated, shook his head. 'Puts me in a position of weakness with you – with regard to you.' Trying a wan grin. 'Fucking weak enough already –'

Sabbahatin looked past Richie to Lance and Senda. 'He tell you she got his kid? He say that?'

Lance nodded. 'That's what he said.'

'Yeah,' said Senda. 'Little girl you two fuckin' shitheads try an' snatch.

Sabbahatin looked at Richie. 'You fucking . . . *loufara*.' The two Turks slid grins at each other. 'You try fuck me, you get fucked –'

Richie shrugged. 'One call. All we need.'

'OK. I tell you what you do. You get out my fucking sight, OK? Right out my fucking sight, yes? I think what you say, maybe I tell you. Maybe not. Maybe something else happen.' Sabbahatin's mobile chirruped. 'Now you fuck off, you fucking *loufara* –'

As Richie headed back to Lance and Senda, Sabbahatin started barking rapid guttural instructions into the mobile.

Lance and Senda stood up. Lance said, 'Keep walkin' kid.'

'My jacket, fucking bike helmet –'

Senda said, 'You wanna keep walkin', keep walkin'.'

Heading for the door, Richie said, 'Fuck have I done now?'

Senda sucked air between his teeth. 'This Shabba guy, maybe he don' like him cha-cha boy 'ave a baby mother.'

One each side, running him down the stairs. 'You what?'

Lance said, 'You too normal, kid.'

'Ain't just that,' said Senda. 'Him their Ganja Lee an' you mek him look a buguyaga.'

'He their bossman and you made him look a no-no.'

'Trying to fucking help –'

'Heh heh heh. Him gonna lass off you number nine.'

'He going to cut your dick off, kid.'

'Oh shit –'

'Cut you dick off, stick 'im in you mout'. Heh heh heh.'

Outside, in the car park, the kid driver had the back of the Ford Explorer open and was hauling the voluminous black chador hand over hand out of Senda's zipped leatherette bag.

Coming up the ramp towards them was a white Lux-U-Hire minibus full of dark short-haired sallow-faced young men.

Senda said, 'He after we fuckin' matics, man –'

Lance said, 'We been fuckin' set up, Sen –'

'Fuckin' right –'

Lance shoved Richie round the front of the big Ford. 'You fuckin' drive, kid –'

'What?'

'Get the fuck in an' fuckin' drive!'

Senda grinned at the driver. 'How you doin', son?'

As the driver looked up, Senda chopped him down. One short backhand slice to the side of the neck, then he grabbed the doubled-up driver by the scruff and hurled him in the path of the minibus.

'Go-go-fuckin'-go!' shouted Lance.

Richie jumped into the driver's seat, grabbed for the ignition key, twisted it. A thud as Senda crash-landed in the back then a roar as the four-litre V8 burst into life. Tyres squealing, four-wheel-drive howling, the big black Ford lurched towards the exit, swerved round the prostrate kid driver, smashed wing-mirrors with the minibus and careered off, front tyres smoking, back door banging and swinging, down through the crowded ranks of the car park.

'Shit!'

'Whass matter, kid?'

'Left my fucking bike –'

'Fuck the fuckin' bike!'

From behind Senda jammed the ugly screw-thread barrel of an even uglier twelve-hundred-rounds-a-minute Ingram MAC 10 automatic into the back of Richie's neck. 'Keep fuckin' drivin'!'

'Where fucking to?'

'Any fuckin' where!'

Richie took them back four miles to the M4–M5 interchange. All the way Senda was lying angled against the rear door, MAC 10 in hand, keeping a look-out through the tailgate window.

'They comin'?' said Lance.

'They fuck,' said Senda.

'Where we going, kid?'

'Almondsbury interchange,' said Richie. 'Like a six-lane racetrack, fifteen fucking exits, they won't know where the fuck we've gone.'

'Holy shit –'

Overhead gantries – BRISTOL NORTH EAST – SOUTH – WEST – SOUTH WALES – LONDON – AVMTH BRIDGE – EXPECT DELAYS – as eight lanes converged

210

into six and split again into threes and twos – sixteen-wheeler trucks and trailers thundering past and shoving the bulky Explorer sideways with their air pressure. Then a big sign saying HYPERMART IST LEFT and Richie peeling off out of the rush into a glittering mile-wide oasis of parked cars round a blank hangar-like brick building about a quarter mile long.

Lance said, 'We in a fuckin' car park, kid –'

'Yeah,' said Richie. 'Change of vehicle.'

'What?'

'Mondeo, Cavalier, Vectra. M reg and up. Darker the better, tints for preference –'

Half a mile in, Block 11G, furthest away from the hangar, Richie found what he was looking for: a dark green P reg Primera with tinted windows. 'Fuck me, they've even left us the parking ticket –'

Richie hoiked a six-inch hardened steel screwdriver out of his pants pocket. 'Do serious damage with one of these –'

By the time Lance and Senda had their kit out of the back of the Explorer, Richie had screwdrivered the Primera's door-lock, snapped the steering wheel lock, wrenched the alarm and ignition wiring from under the dash, ripped it apart, reconnected it and shorted the Primera's engine into life. 'In the back, lads. If we're stopped, we're fucked, so keep your pieces handy under your kit –'

Richie slipped the ticket into the metal slit; the barrier lifted; they were away.

Senda said, 'Hey, stick a pin, man. How come you know all that?'

'Learn it all in nick, don't you? Used to do a bit. Taking and Driving Away. Any wheels you want, supplied to order. Good little number till some cunt gets stopped and shops you.'

Senda frowned. 'Thought you said you was in the fight game.'

'Yeah, well. You ask Lance. Can't live on fucking prize money, can you, Lance? Specially if you don't win no fucking prizes –'

'Fuckin' right, kid.'

Richie followed the M5 towards Bristol as far as Junction 17, swerved off on to Cribbs Causeway and doubled back under the motorway into the narrow, twisting lanes heading towards Severn Beach and the New Severn Crossing.

Senda, shifting in his seat, saying, 'Fuck we goin' now?'

'Scene of the crime,' said Richie. 'Something to show you.'

21

Close to the motorway the river country and its old single-track lanes had been hijacked by builders. Passing places had been carved out of the hawthorned banks, rutted roads resurfaced, and bijou new developments built in the maze of lanes.

Richie said, 'Way I see it we need to keep our heads down, stay out the game for a couple of hours.'

'Seen,' said Lance.

With that agreed, Richie said, 'Can I say something else?'

Senda said, 'Why? You got somethin' on you mind?'

'No offence, mind, not trying to tell you your business –'

'Shit, kid, we take you out any time – hear me nah?'

'Yeah I know.'

Lance said, 'Spit it out, kid.'

'Right. OK.' Glancing in the rear mirror. 'They were coming at you team-handed back there.'

'So?'

'My point is you should've fucking known that.' Keeping an eye on them in the mirror, getting ready to back off and arse-lick if he went too far. 'This fucking deal, shit, they were always going to blow you away – I mean, I could see you thinking three or four against you two, no problem – but all they were doing was fucking waiting . . . Now there's a dozen of these guys, they're going to gyp you, tip you, ship you out in bags, man . . . I mean, this deal, you're going to see nothing, no return, nothing. Nothing-nothing-*nothing*-nothing-nothing –'

Senda said, 'If we ain't, you ain't neither, kid.'

'Yeah, I know that, but –'

'Man got hair up his ass, he better pull it out fass.'

'OK,' said Richie. 'Way I see it, Mr Senda – no offence now – the fucking Brothers set you up, man. They knew these Turk guys would get you to do the dirty work and then fuck you out the game. You got enemies, man, enemies you don't even fucking know you got –'

Senda hissed air in through his teeth.

Lance said, 'Go on, kid.'

'It's either that or these fucking Turks reckon they're hard enough to take on the Brothers full out and macerate you guys for a pastime – means we're all going end up fucking bluterated for sweet fuck all . . . Well, I don't know about you, but to put it fucking mildly, that's what I'm trying to avoid.'

'That it?' said Senda.

'Yeah.'

'Right. Now shut up an' fucking drive.'

'No offence.'

In the back, Lance put his head down, kept his voice low. 'Kid right 'bout one thing, Sen.'

'You reckon?'

'Got one posse shootin' up another posse, too busy on they own turf, they don't see these fuckin' Turks comin'. We lose this one, we say goodbye to the whole fuckin' H trade.'

'Fuckin' kid need watchin'. He tell us this, he tell us that – he slippy as a sack a dogfish, man.'

'Yeah.' Lance said, 'Hey, kid –'

'Hello.'

'What you lookin' for out a this?'

Senda leaned forward, close to Richie's neck. 'An' get fuckin' real, boy.'

'Now, you mean? What I'm looking for now?'

'You got it, boy.'

'OK. Right.' Richie slid a battered red and white pack of Beaumont Superking Lights from the side pocket of his camo pants and pulled a bent cigarette out with his teeth.

Senda said, 'Didn' know you was a smoker.'

'Nervous, aren' I?' He pushed in the cigar lighter. 'You guys, make anybody nervous –'

Senda turned his head to Lance. 'See what I mean? You axe him one ting, he slippin' us somethin' else.'

'Yeah.'

Richie lit the cigarette. 'Way I see it, seventy-three k uncut, we're looking at three, three and a half million. Cut and on the street the stuff's worth five, six times that, but we ain't looking at that, we're looking at one pop, offload and go, right? Say a million each –'

'If.'

'Yeah, sure. Always a fucking if – but me, all I'm looking at as of now, is this one deal. One deal and out –'

Lance said, 'You don' want the Brothers set you up no more?'

Senda shook his head. 'Too fuckin' slippy, man –'

Richie said, 'Job's changed, hasn' it? Changing every fucking minute – Jesus Christ man, you fucking ask me, I'm fucking telling you –'

'OK kid,' said Lance. 'Is cool.'

'One job and out. All this shit's too strong for me – be a bag a fucking nerves do what you guys do –'

'You slippin' us again, kid –'

'OK, you want the fucking truth, it's one deal and out, shit on the fuckers who shit on me, take out a contract or two – you guys if you fancy the work – then get out and live nice. No flash, just the lady and the kid. Got it now? Me, my lady, my kid, somewhere nice, somewhere quiet, not Spain. Maybe somewhere out your way. Somewhere like St Lucia, quiet, nice, off the fucking hassle-map –'

Senda said, 'Full a shit, kid.'

'You fucking asked, I fucking told you –'

'Caribyan, ain't nowhere quiet,' said Senda. 'You take Castries, Castries San Lucia, every fuckin' day four, five big fuckin' cruise boat full a fat white dudes, woman a sixty an' seventy wantin' a piece a black man's dick – four, five thousan' every day, man – ain't nowhere quiet no more.'

Richie ground the cigarette out. 'Got to be somewhere – got to be fucking *somewhere*.'

'Yeah,' said Lance. 'Somewhere.'

They drove deeper into the maze of lanes and rhines, ditches and dykes that ran like capillaries off the broad artery of the Severn.

Breaking the silence, Senda said, 'Hey man, fuckin' trees got flowers on 'em.'

'Yeah,' said Richie. 'Cider country.'

In between the bungalows and the fawn-brick brown-tiled houses there were remnants and stretches of the old apple and pear orchards where some old-style farmer or smallholder either couldn't be arsed or was too fucking cussed to grub them up for subsidy. Like them, the low trees were arthritic with age, twisted and mossy, all on the lean away from the southwesterlies that came rampaging up the Severn. Here and there among the barren grey heads there was the odd live tree leaving drifts of red and pink and white blossom massed on the wet roads as if a wedding had just gone past.

Senda shook his head. 'This is Inglun?'

'Was,' said Richie.

'Yeah, you right, kid,' said Lance. 'Was.'

'Jesus,' said Senda. 'What fuckin' 'appen?'

The Primera breasted a low rise on the edge of the lime-green and ploughed-chocolate flood plain. Richie said, 'Over there on your right.'

Four or five miles to the north stood the round copper-green keep of Oldbury Nuclear Research Station; five or six miles further north, the paler, prison-square pile of Berkeley Nuclear Power Station.

Richie said, 'When I used to come out round here as a kid, the power station blokes used to pull fish out the warm water outlets. Then the fucking salmon started coming out with four fucking eyes or none at all, so they said no more salmon-fishing, by reason of preservation. Preserving fucking what, though?'

'Yeah,' said Lance. 'Fuckers.'

'Fucking land's poisoned, cunts call us fucking villains.'

'Heh heh heh.'

'Wait'll you see Severn Beach,' said Richie. 'Then you'll fucking laugh.'

Time was, before the New Severn Crossing, when Severn Beach was nothing more than a dirt lane. It wound its way through a spindly wood scattered with whitewashed plank huts raised on brick and concrete block piles against the spring and autumn floods. The huts had black-tarred mineralised-felt roofs with rickety verandahs, and some had neat pocket-handkerchief gardens fenced off to deter the wandering black and white Friesians let loose to graze the lush summer pasturage.

Pre-war, people said, you could drive your car down by the Severn, park, go for a picnic and come back to find your Morris Eight or Standard Flying Nine up to its axles in thick black bog. Other people said that was a story put about by the chalet-owners to warn off the gatecrashers, thieves and vagabonds who, to their minds, comprised the rest of the population.

With its thin birch woods and its thick black soil, Severn Beach looked more like the outskirts of Moscow than the fringes of Bristol, but to the families of the prosperous tidy-minded bank and factory workers of Filton and Bristol, the place was summer heaven; more than that, it was theirs.

Then came the big yellow machines, the drag-lines and the eight-wheeled earth-movers and the diggers with their hanging-gaping dinosaur jaws, and after the Second Severn Crossing was built, Severn Beach had all but ceased to be.

Richie pulled up by one of the last remaining stands. Half-hidden in the trees, burned and rusted bright orange, was the tyre-less shell of a Leyland DAF 400. 'This is it, man. This is where it happened.' Richie got out, walked over to the DAF 400.

Senda said, 'You believe this guy?'

Lance said, 'What else we got?'

'We get the girl we home free –'

'Yeah, and who gonna get us to the girl?'

Senda's lined and seamed brown face split in a grin like an axe splits wood. 'Yeah. Irie, man.'

'Way I'm thinkin'.'

Richie smiling, saying to himself, Come on you dozy black fuckers. They ambled over, Senda hands deep in his dark blue fleece, Lance stretching his long legs till his kneecaps cracked.

'OK?'

'Sure.'

'Right. Now what you got to remember is, time this happened, there's a whole fucking riot going on, cops have teargassed the school and some black kids have firebombed a joint called the Moonglow. Ambulances, fire engines, battlewagons, cops everywhere – and there's old Julius, middle of all this, calm as you like getting into his Honda minivan. Meanwhile, this mush here –' Richie pointed to the cab of the van – 'falls out with his black mate, his black mate tries to slot him then gets slotted hisself, while matey here, blood all down his face where his black mate has creased him, has it on his toes out to Avonmouth – you with me?'

'Yeah,' said Senda, 'Avonmout'.'

'Where matey here meets up with the Turks. This selfsame Sabbahatin –'

'This Shabba guy after you ring?'

'Yeah, him . . . Anyway, they're all tooling off in convoy up to the bridge there –' Richie pointed up at the swoop of concrete and cables cantilevered across the Severn – 'Granada in front, matey here in the van with the stuff, Scorpio behind so he's well fucking sandwiched isn' he, and what happens? Fucking roadblock. Cops all over. Traffic tailbacking right off the fucking bridge – and matey sees his chance, dives the van off the road, in and out the pilings and the pipes and the storm drains, all that shit – and he's off and away, isn' he? Well fucking chuffed with with himself because he's got three and half million quidsworth of H under a load of manky old Christmas wrapping paper. First chance he gets he's off the road and he's ducking and diving down in here, isn' he? Only half a mile off the bridge but, night, it's a fucking jungle. Bats, badgers, owls, rats, all sorts. So he's sitting here, going fuck me, that was close, and rolling hisself a joint and thinking holy shit, I'm a fucking rich man when up comes Julius with his fucking fireaxe –'

Lance and Senda, well into the story now, but still searching Richie's face for clues, mistakes, anything to get a grip on.

'Old Julius is in no hurry, is he? Fucking sirens and blue lights all over the bridge, but he's down here, waiting, waiting by the cab door here –' Richie took up a position by the burnt-out cab door, flat against the bodywork. 'The guy finishes his spliff, tosses it out the window, thinks he'll have a quiet slash, ponder his next move, gets out and *wallop*.' Richie slammed the flat of his hand against the orange metal, gave his manic crooked grin as Lance and Senda both jumped. 'And down goes matey, still thinking he's fucking rich, with a hole in the back of his head size of a fifty-p piece.'

'Shit,' said Lance.

'Yeah,' said Richie. 'Rough, innit? Anyhow, Julius unloads the stuff into his fucking Honda, shoves matey back in here, spikes the fucking gas tank, pours some over the fucking paper, strikes a match, whumpf, up she goes – and old Julius is out a there like a longdog.' Richie dusted the rust off his hands and cocked his head at them. 'Then what?'

'Yeah, then what?' said Lance.

'Stick a pin, now, stick a pin,' said Senda. How come you know all this, boy?'

'I'm waiting for him, aren' I? I keep my fucking eye on Julius, don't I? Morning he comes back, nackered, goes in his place dying for a fucking kip, I give him twenny minutes, then I do his van, right?' Another lopsided grin. 'Nothing there but the fucking fireaxe wrapped up in a pair of old underpants old Julius uses to demist the fucking windscreen. Underpants covered in blood and snot, grey bits, yeller bone, all kinds of shit . . . And that's it, basically.' Richie dug out another cigarette, struck a match on the bodywork and pointed to a gap between the wire remains of the tyres. 'Where the tank was, before Forensic took it away.'

Senda stuck an Interdens between his teeth and chewed. 'Yeah, but how come you know all this shit?'

'In the paper, innit? Front page fucking news down here –'

'Not all what you say, kid – spliffs, gettin' out to take a leak, all that shit.'

The lopsided grin again. 'Got to make it interesting – give it a bit of colour –'

Senda's straight fist, with only the top two joints clenched, struck out, hit Richie in the solar plexus and slammed him back winded against the burnt-out van. Senda looked at Richie. He was doubled over, in the perfect position for a down-chopping rabbit-punch.

'Easy, Sen.'

'You gettin' soft in the belly, boy.'

'Fuck – you do – that for?'

'Fuck you bringin' us here for?' Senda looked at Lance. 'I say waste him, get the fuckin' train out a this shit-heap.'

Lance said, 'You hear what the man sayin', kid?'

'Yeah,' Richie still gasping for breath. 'Yeah, I heard.'

'Well, then, kid, ' said Lance, 'you tell us something we don' know, 'stead of all this baby-mother–Julius crap.'

'Waste him.'

'You hear that?'

'Yeah –'

Lance shrugged. 'Up to you, kid.'

'OK, just don't fucking hit me – OK?'

Senda stared at Richie, clicked his tongue and shook his head.

Richie said, 'Listen, I know Julius –'

Senda, yelling at him, 'You fuckin' white piece a shit!'

Richie screwing his face up like a kid fighting not to cry: 'No – please – listen, listen –'

Lance said, 'You las' chance, kid.'

'Right, OK – oh fuck . . .' Richie pulled himself up straight, arching his back against the pain in his stomach. 'Julius – he wouldn't – he wouldn't stash it – where he couldn't keep an eye on it . . . same time, he's too fucking canny to go near the stuff himself . . .' Looking from one to the other, pleading, wondering where the first blow was coming from. 'The girl. She fucking knows – she's fucking got to know – he'd send her. Got to – fucking *got to* –' His voice broke; he put his hands in front of his face, bent his head, and waited.

Lance looked at Senda. Senda turned his head away in disgust. Finally Lance said, 'OK. No more fuckin' bullshit. Get her.'

'What?'

'You woman, kid. You get her.'

22

In the lift going down from Sam's office to LG2, Vic said, 'Something's not right, John.'

Cromer said, 'I thought we were bloody lucky –'

'You saw old Sam at the end. He looked almost fucking human. What'd he say? "Job could change any minute." What's that supposed to mean? "All I can tell you, mate." "Mate" – Sam never calls you mate unless he knows he's going to drop you in the shit.'

'Always looking for the downside,' said Cromer. 'Just because you don't fucking like him –'

'Not that.'

'What then?'

'I don't fucking trust him.'

'You don't trust any fucker.'

'Correct,' said Vic. 'Still here though, aren't I?'

The lift went past LG1 and juddered on down to LG2.

Cromer said, 'We going to play this by the book or not?'

Vic said, 'Yeah.'

'That supposed to mean?'

'Meaning do we tell Sam or not? Meaning do we tell Sam every move we fucking make?'

'Yeah, basically –'

'Yeah, we'll tell him.'

'But.'

'What d'you mean, but?'

224

'Oh come on, Vic, know you by now, don't I? You left out the "but". "We'll tell him, but –"'

'All right, John, say it. Go on, say it.'

'Say what?'

'Say, "It's all right for you, Vic, you're leaving."'

'Fucking difficult not to,' said Cromer. 'Thing is, I'm starting, you're finishing –'

'Feel better now?'

'Do I fuck.'

'All right, we'll tell him – we'll tell him every move we make.'

'Good. Thank God for that.'

As the lift stopped, Vic said, 'Question of when, really.'

Cromer grinned despite himself. 'You bugger.'

Sergeant Leatherbarrow was an ex-Guardsman, grey-haired, uniformed and ponderous, a real bigfoot, and like stores pros all over the world he gave the impression of knowing everything and believing nothing except stores were there to be stored, not issued. He had red rheumy eyes and big shaky hands; improbably, above his head hung a framed certificate proclaiming that Sgt George Arthur Leatherbarrow, 2nd Coldstream Guards was a Fully Qualified Firearms Instructor. Handwritten in red italic at the foot of the certificate were the words 'Passed with Distinction, 1965'.

'Morning, George.'

'Morning, Vic. Chief Super rang.'

'Nice of him.'

'Said he wants you kitted up-and carrying.' Looking at Cromer. 'What's this?'

Cromer said, 'DC Cromer, sarnt.'

'You don't look old enough, son.'

'Twenty-three, sarnt.'

'Done the course, got a ratin'?'

'Yes, sarnt. Marksman, sarnt.'

'Know what this is, then, won't you?' He slid a thick transparent plastic bag containing a dull grey automatic pistol across the counter.

Cromer knew enough to look at it without picking it up. 'Yes sarnt. Nine millimetre Glock, sarnt.'

'Anything else, son?'

'Yes sarnt. Lightweight durable polycarbonate body, 17-shot magazine, self-loading, half the weight of the standard .38 it replaces. Oh – and it's made in Austria, sarnt.'

'Very clever. Now get these vests on.'

The lightweight covert body armour Leatherbarrow plonked down in front of them looked more like a bodywarmer padded with strips and squares of Kevlar than a vest, but you still had to wear it under your shirt. On the short indoor range, Vic and Cromer were issued with two magazines each, one for rapid-fire and one for opportunity-shooting as soon as the targets flashed. 'All you've got to remember, Vic –' Sergeant Leatherbarrow had clearly decided that Cromer was too much of a smartass to be spoken to, '– is that if you can hit a bloke with a cricket ball at seven to ten yards, you can hit him with one of these.'

There was still a kick to the Glock, and on rapid-fire it still made all the muscles under your arm and shoulder shake as if you were trying to use a hammer-drill one-handed, but it was nothing like the bucking recoil of the .38: you fired that and it was like someone was trying to kick the thing out of your fist.

After the signing and countersigning and pro-longing the whole business as much as possible before returning to the comfort of his memories and a fake coal fire, the old Sergeant regretfully let them go: 'Just remember, every Yank cop carries a gun, but after twenty years' service most of 'em'll tell you they haven't so much as drawn it, let alone used it. On the other hand, look upon it as you would your prick: if you do pull it out for fuck's sake use it. Good luck, Vic – and you, son –'

In the Escort van going to pick up Opal, Nova and the kids, Vic had to open up his baggy suit jacket and let his trouser belt out a notch or two to accommodate the vest and the black nylon shoulder holster. 'Can't fucking breathe – how about you, John?'

Cromer had his elbows out wide to steer. 'Doesn't make it any easier, does it?'

'What you fucking grinning for then?' said Vic.

She was waiting on the steps by the door. Vic began fiddling with his safety belt adjustment to give Cromer a moment with her. Cromer was off like a flash and Vic was left reflecting that if telepathy existed at all it was something to do with the state those two were in. Whatever you called it, being in love or just fucking dick-happy, the obsession seemed to grow on its own, without the other person being there, so when you finally did meet, the pressure was so intense it was like being smacked back together by a bloody great elastic band. It wasn't an emotion, it was a force, like a dam being breached and carrying all before it – no blame attaching, no normal rules applying – and whether it did more harm than good was neither here nor there, matter of luck really, because if it was going to happen it was going to happen, and fuck-all anybody could do about it, least of all the two poor sods involved.

And anyway, Hallam, you slept with Ellie, didn't you?

Yeah, but that was different.

Always is, Hallam, always is.

Some reason, Vic thought of an old song his Uncle Ernie used to sing at Christmas and weddings:

> If I could plant a tiny seed of love
> In the garden of your heart
> Would it grow into a great big tree
> And blossom while we're apart –

Uncle Ernie would sing it after he'd had one or two, often as not tears rolling down his thin peaky face, openly making spaniel's eyes at Vic's mother, whether Vic's dad – his own brother – was there or not, openly admitting he'd married the wrong woman, and nobody, not even his wife, Vic's Auntie Val, seemed to mind. It was love, they all knew it was love, and there was nothing poor old Ernie could do about it. He was pitied, as if he'd got a stutter or a birthmark, which in a sense he had –

> Or would it shrivel, fade and die,
> And leave me with love's memory?

Vic slammed the door hard on the Escort van to give them a a warning; the way they pulled guiltily apart as soon as they saw him he could tell they'd been embraced in their own oblivion: razor-wire all round the yard and they'd been gumsucking.

Fuck, fuck and double-fuck.

'John, can I have a word please?'

'What? Oh – yeah –' A glance at Opal and she moved quickly back inside the door. Cromer came trotting down the steps trying not to smile.

'What's up, Vic?'

'You're a cunt, that's what's up.'

'What for?' Sounding innocent, aggrieved even.

'Supposed to be fucking working –'

'Wasn't doing anything –'

'Not fucking much – John, you're wearing a gun and a fucking flak jacket and you're sticking your tongue down the fucking chief witness's throat –'

'Wasn't –' Cromer flaming red from his neck to his ears.

'Yes you were, you cunt.'

'Chrissake, Vic –'

'Suppose she fucking felt it? Suppose she put her arms round you and said, "John, why are you wearing a fucking corset and what's this fucking hard lump under your arm – not your dick is it?"'

'She didn't –'

'What would you fucking say? "Oh don't worry Opal, it's only a gun and a flak jacket so if some fucker shoots you and your kid I won't get fucking hurt –"'

'Being fucking stupid now –'

'No, John. I'm not the one who's being fucking stupid, am I? Am I? Suppose she's fucking lying, stringing you along, up to her neck in this shit? Is that being stupid?'

'No – but –'

'What? But what?'

'Well – she only had her arms round my neck –'

'Oh, did she?'

'Yeah –'

229

'John, I don't want you on this case. Am I getting through now?'

Cromer nodded, began to look hunted, miserable.

'Right. Now then, I don't want you on this case if half your mind's between her fucking legs. Is that clear?'

'Yeah. Sorry Vic.'

To rub it in and make sure that daft fucking smirk didn't return, Vic said, 'Repeat after me, "I, John Cromer, am a cunt."'

'I, John Cromer, am a cunt.'

'Right,' said Vic. 'Now let's get a fucking move on.'

It took an unbelievable two hours to get two women and three toddlers packed and ready, and because Vic had to tell them their stay in the Fishponds Hostel could well be indeterminate and not just overnight, there was barely a moment when the two women were in the station together. Either Opal or Nova would be off out down the town, in patrol cars and escorted by plain-clothes WPCs, plundering Mothercare, Boots, Marks & Sparks and, as far as Vic could tell, the whole of the rest of the main downtown Broadmead Shopping Centre. And the worst thing of all was, because they didn't have any credit cards of their own, they had to use Vic and Cromer's Visas and PIN numbers. By the time they'd finished, Vic thought, looking at the mountains of baby gear piling up in the interview room, the fucking cards would be so fucking irradiated even if you cut them up they'd glow in the dark. At first he checked the foot-long till receipts that came back with the bulging king-size plastic bags to make sure they weren't milking every sodding hole-in-the-wall in Broadmead, then he just said fuck it, let 'em get on with it.

In between sessions on the multi-link computer system – Cromer was at least trying to keep himself away from Opal – he said to Vic, looking at the accumulating piles of stuff, 'What's Louise going to say?'

'Finally fucking remembered have you?' said Vic. 'Don't worry, John, you'll get reimbursed.'

'No fucking consolation, is it?'

'Why's that?'

'Joint card, isn't it? Louise goes to use hers, machine'll either swallow it or spit it back in her face.'

'Yeah, could be awkward.'

'Awkward? She sees the fucking charge sheet for forty-eight thousand Pampers, Tommy Tiddler pisspots and crates of fucking arse-wipes, she'll go fucking apocalyptic. One thing she hates it's snotty-nosed kids –'

'What about you, John?'

Cromer shrugged.

'You going to tell her about Opal?'

'I don't fucking know . . . Got to haven' I?'

'Up to you mate. Lot of blokes don't – how long you been living with her?'

'Three years, off and on.'

'You love her?'

'I don't fucking know – I used to . . . Anyway, love's one thing, money's another.'

'Hope for you yet, my son.'

'Fuck am I going to tell her?'

'Tell her you did it for the woman you love.'

'Thanks, Vic, you're a real mate.' Hands in pockets, head down, Cromer slouched back to his keyboard.

Vic looked at the bags and boxes of baby gear: over a vanload, if you included the packaging – and that'd mean another OSG for the mothers and kids. He started tearing the packages apart. Every one had a picture of a cute and cuddly baby on the front, usually in the arms of a happily smiling nicely made-up thoroughly unstressed young mum.

Vic thought about Ellie, and confronted by the mass of apparently indispensable impedimenta, found himself going off parenthood at a rate of knots. What was it she'd said?

Whatever you do don't come back smelling of her.

This rate it'd be more like Baby Oil, Nappy Cream, Milton, Wobble Topper Bubble Bath, Dry Nites, Nappy Wrappers – No Smell No Germs No Mess – Tixylix, Bickiepegs, Colic Drops and all seventy-nine different varieties of bottled yellow baby puke.

Plus a Boots Bear Nipper Gripper, whatever that was.

By the time he'd finished the room was knee-high in packaging and the pile of stuff was half the size. Cromer stuck his head round the door. 'Got something, not much but something.'

Vic heaved and scrunched the interview door shut over the rubbish and followed Cromer into a small room containing a scanner, printer, Xerox and terminal. Cromer swung the monitor so Vic could see and tapped away at the keyboard. 'According to Traffic and Swansea, hundred and fifty-eight trail-bikes in the Bristol, Avon and Somerset areas – some green and white, some not – some stolen, some not –'

'Hooray fuck.'

'Give us a chance.'

Cromer paged down through screeds of TDAs, Accidents and Incidents until he came to an M4 motorway patrol report: 'Motorhispania 50 cc green and white m/c. No previous owner reg. No DVLA trace.'

232

Cromer said, 'I phoned the M4 guys and they said it had a photocopied tax disc, a rear plate made out of sticky-back numbers and had probably been brought into the UK unregistered.'

'Lot of fucking trouble for a fifty cc dirt bike.'

'What they thought. Then one of the Severn View catering managers came out and told them there was a helmet and jacket left behind and there'd been a bit of an altercation. A white kid, two black guys and three blokes he said looked Greek or Italian. Then a guy off the pumps came up and said the white guy and the two blacks had thumped an Arab-looking kid and driven off at speed in a black 4 by 4 and smashed the wing mirror off a white hire bus full of more dark-haired blokes. Then the white hire bus picked up the three blokes and the kid who'd been thumped and then *they* went tear-arsing after the 4 by 4.'

'All in all,' said Vic, 'sounds like a-bit of a cock-up.'

'Reckon it's the Turks?'

'Possible. More than possible. You ring Sam?'

'Not yet.'

'Ring him now. Give him something to do, something to think about, get him off our backs.'

'Right –'

'Say about fifteen blokes altogether, not counting the two blacks and the white guy.'

'Right.'

By quarter past four Vic had booked Opal, Nova and the three kids into the Fishponds hostel. Fifteen minutes later his mobile rang: Nova, screaming blue murder down the phone, pleading with Vic to come and get them out before some fucker got killed –

233

23

According to Nova, what happened was that after Vic and Cromer had left them all at the Fishponds hostel with the ram-raider bollards and the CCTV cameras, the other women and children had offered to help them in with their gear. Needless to say, within ten minutes half of it had gone missing.

'Well, I lost my rag, didn't I? People like that you got to lay it on 'em fast – you got to let 'em know straight off or they'll fucking walk all over you. So there I was, calling 'em everything I could think of, bunch of fucking slags and wankers and pisspot-thieving-fucking-lesbians, and our kids are all crying and all them other little bastards, they're all going "Ner-nar-nee-nee-nar", and then the mothers, they're all gathering round, the fucking matron's watching all this, mind, she's got this grey nylon prison thing on with a big fucking black belt with all keys on, and the so-called fucking care-bear assistants, all in dark blue like fucking warders, and they're penning us in, in this fucking circle, all linking arms, Mr Hallam, and then the fucking mothers and their kids are pointing at our kids one after another – and they're going, "One black one, one white one and one with a lump a shite on –". Kids are fucking terrified, and the mothers are grabbing and poking at us so I goes to Opal, 'I'm not fucking having this,' so I belts one, don' I? With this bag I got in me hand, one of the fucking care-bears, got her hand in me fucking hair trying to pull me down . . . Anyway bag's got a bottle a Ribena in it, that smashes, and down she goes yelling and screaming she's bleeding to fucking death then the matron's coming over to have a go and Opal smacks her one with her handbag – they're all screaming blue murder, so we get the kids into the vestibule, and they've locked us in haven't they, locked us in between the two sets a doors, an' they've got this unbreakable glass in, so the kids are howling and yelling and this fucking matron, her eye's all come up like a miner's Friday-nighter, she's saying we can stay there all fucking night all she cares – so that's when I phoned you, Mr Hallam –'

'How you do that, Nova, haven't got a mobile, have you?'

'Fucking pay-phone innit? In the fucking vestibule –'

'Right.'

'Course, when you an 'im come, they're all fucking gone aren't they? And all our fucking stuff. Fucking ratbags. Not going back there again – sooner be in fucking jail –'

'Could well come to that,' said Vic. He looked at Opal. 'The kids all right?'

'So far.'

'And you?'

'Yeah. So far.'

'You should a seen her whack that fucking matron,' said Nova. 'One wallop, bang, down she went –'

'Pull up here, John. I want to give Sam a ring.'

As Vic climbed out of the white van he heard Nova, still high on the adrenalin from the punch-up, saying, 'Ey, John, you don' want to cross her, mind, lay you flat soon as look at you –'

Sam listened to Vic's account without saying a word. When Vic finished, Sam said, 'Well, least it tallies.'

'What d'you mean?'

'Just had that Fishponds supervisor on, bending my fucking ear. Any chance to chuck shit at us, they're queuing up with both hands full.'

'So what d'you think? Where to now, Sam? Back to Trinity Road or what?'

There was a brief silence. It passed through Vic's mind that Sam was recording the conversation, and had paused to watch the red LED on the voice-activated Sony blink on and off. Then Sam said, 'Looks like you've got your own way again, Vic. Montpelier it is – has to be –'

'Nowhere else, is there?'

Another pause, then: 'Not at this stage of the game, no. Good luck, Vic, and keep in touch. Tell us when you get there –'

'Will do.'

'Oh, Vic –'

'What's that, Sam?'

'You kitted up and everything?'

'Yeah.'

'Good. Take care, mate.'

The line went dead.

When Vic opened the van door, Opal was sitting next to Cromer and Cromer had Esme sitting on the steering wheel. They were making faces at each other.

'Excuse me, Opal.'

'Oh yeah, sure.' She took Esme from Cromer, passed her over to Nova, then hoiked her long black skirt up round her hips and clambered into the back of the van. She was wearing stockings held up by black

236

suspenders and glimpsing the flash of ivory thigh between stocking-tops and suspender belt Vic found himself thinking, Jesus, what a gorgeous fuck she'd got to be –

Cromer's voice broke in: 'How'd you get on?'

'It's Montpelier, John.'

'You tell him about the punch-up?'

'Briefly.'

'What'd he say?'

'He called me "mate" again.'

As Cromer made a U-turn to head west for Montpelier, Vic found himself wondering what sort of a woman it was who gets walloped by a bloke at five in the morning, goes upstairs and puts on stockings and suspenders.

Maybe she'd run out of tights.

Maybe.

The hill running up from St Pauls to Montpelier was ringed with small steep Victorian and Edwardian terraces and many of the tightly-packed houses had been gentrified with white-painted windows, brass door furniture and cleaned stone frontages. There were still a few boarded-up derelict industrial buildings covered in overlapping posters for albums and dance nights by groups and DJs Vic had never heard of, and here and there cul-de-sacs and alleys lined with lock-ups for one-man plumbing, electrical and motor repair businesses. Cars were parked on both sides of the narrow roads and from a driver's point of view Montpelier looked a lot easier to get into than out of.

The Women's Refuge, near the top of the hill, had been a group-practice doctors' surgery: a double-fronted stone-faced Edwardian house, shuttered bay windows on ground and first floors with sash windows above, standing at the foot of a car-lined cul-de-sac.

Mrs Macarthy, a tall ruddy-faced woman in her forties with a loud cut-glass voice but a friendly gap-toothed smile, was waiting for them in a wide black-and-white tiled hall crowded with buggies and pushchairs. She was wearing a tartan skirt and a green Barbour bodywarmer and sounded more Berkeley Vale than Bristol: maybe a farmer's or a vet's wife, Vic thought, who'd brought up her kids and then decided she wanted to do something a bit more real than gymkhanas and charitable works. Whatever it was, Vic decided, she'd got the right blend of warmth and authority to run a joint like this.

All around was the noise of children's voices and feet echoing in empty wood-floored rooms. She welcomed them all in by name and seeing Vic stiffen at a burst of footstamping and shouting, she said they hadn't been open long and the grant didn't run to carpets so pieces of underlay was all they'd got at the moment. 'Plus of course we've all had our siestas and we're feeling rather lively.'

'I see.'

'Look, why don't I take care of the registration and all the bumf, and you can use the caretaker's office to call your Mr Richardson.'

'He rang here, did he?'

'About five minutes ago. Sounded rather terse, I thought.'

The caretaker's office was no more than a boxroom with a heavy-duty upright vacuum cleaner, a floor-polisher, a stack of wooden fruit-boxes full of cleaning fluids and cloths, buckets, mops, a scarred plywood office table and a phone.

'Sam? It's Vic –'

'Fuck have you been?'

'On the way –'

'What's the place like?'

'OK – I think they'll be OK here – Mrs Macarthy –'

'Never mind Mrs fucking Macarthy, what's the place like?'

'Biggish, down a cul-de-sac, was a doctors' surgery before they built the Health Centre –'

'What about the windows, they got bars or anything?'

'Shutters at the front –'

'What about the back?'

'Haven't had a chance to look –'

'Jesus Christ, Vic –'

Vic felt the heat rising up the back of his neck. 'Look, Sam, I'm telling you what's going on – every fucking move we make – how about you telling me something for fuck sake?'

'Fair enough.' Vic heard Sam draw in breath as if he'd just lit a cigarette. 'Basically, as you well know because you were fucking there, Vic – they've tried it once and my best guess is they'll try it again – unless we get to this fucking stuff before they do.'

'Which "they" is this, Sam?'

'Wish I fucking knew, mate. Way I see it, it's all down to this woman of yours, what's her name, Opal.'

'Why don't I just bring her in then? Be safe enough in the fucking Bridewell, surely to Christ.'

'Not with kids, mate. And we're not splitting them up now. Vic heard Sam shuffling papers. 'Listen, Vic,

239

you'll like this. This woman, Mrs Washburn, goes into Thornbury station with her two kids, says her Nissan Primera had been nicked out the mall car park, Cribbs Causeway. The desk sergeant says he saw her pull up in a bloody great Ford Explorer – and she says she wasn't going to carry two kids and all her week's shopping home, was she? Turns out the Ford was parked in her space with the keys still in it.'

'The two blacks and the white guy?'

'Yeah, green Primera, reg RIW 5769.'

'Northern Irish plate.'

'Yeah, you can buy 'em for about hundred quid. Her husband's initials, she got it for his birthday.'

'Anything about the Turks – anything on them?'

'Hang on, somebody on the other phone.'

Vic heard Sam start to talk, heard him say something about Fishponds then Sam's phone crashed down.

24

While Richie was off recce-ing the Fishponds place Lance and Senda decided it was time for a little blow. The Primera was parked in a row of other cars and vans in front of the narrow red-brick church so nobody was overlooking them. There was a tarmac'd alley with a couple of green plastic wheelie-bins, then a wall between the church and the hostel. The road was straight, lined with trees just coming out in new leaf, and they could see down both sides of it for a hundred yards or so before the houses and gardens finished and the shops and main-road traffic started.

Lance said, 'Could be a nice one, Sen.'

'Bout time.'

'Nice and quiet. What you reckon?'

'Kid come out with the woman, we drop him in the alley.'

'Way I'm thinkin'.'

'Way we go with long tall Sally. Pick up the H, back to the smoke.'

'Yeah. Is cool.' Lance reached up, pulled the front passenger vizor down, looked back at Senda. 'We got time?'

'Sure we got time.' Senda dug his fingers into the mesh lining of his dark blue fleece while Lance ripped the vanity mirror out of the foam-backed passenger vizor. Senda laid out four lines on the mirror and straightened them with the blade of his four-inch

241

fisherman's clasp-knife. Lance gave Senda the vanity mirror to hold and rolled up a crisp twenty. After they'd both hoovered up a couple of lines Senda held the resealable plastic bag of cocaine over the mirror again.

'You reckon one for luck?'

'Sure, why not?'

After a couple more lines, Lance stuffed the mirror loosely back in the vizor lining and shoved it up towards the roof. He relaxed back in his seat and stretched his legs till his knees cracked. 'Yeah, could be a nice one.'

At first Richie was too high on his own buzz to notice theirs. He slipped back into the driver's seat and said, 'Right. She's there – I saw 'em all having tea. This is what we do –'

Senda nudged Lance and pointed to Richie's left leg. It was going up and down like a treadle-machine. When Lance let out a manic high-pitched giggle instead of his usual deep chuckle Richie said, 'Fuck sake man, what's so fucking funny?'

'Nothin' – ain' nothin' funny is there, Sen?'

Richie looked at them both. They grinned back at him. He sniffed the air for spliffs. Nothing. Then he saw the passenger vizor drooping from the roof lining. He pulled it down, saw the mirror, took it out, held it up to the afternoon sunlight, saw the line-tracks left across it.

Senda said, 'Jus' passin' time.'

'Oh yeah –'

Lance said, 'Go on, kid.'

Don't fuck up now.

'OK, right.' Richie smiled, dropped the mirror in the door pocket, pulled a creased manila envelope out of his camo pants. There was a sketch on the back of it; he used his biro for a pointer. 'Car – church – alley – hostel front – hostel back – hostel garden. Right?'

Senda shrugged. 'You say so.'

'I recce'd all these places, right? While you two, you're sitting in here getting coked up to your fucking eyeballs –'

'Heh heh heh.'

Lance said, 'Go on, kid.'

After he'd told them about the lines full of washing in the back garden they could use for cover, Richie said, 'Now then, shooters. Just the sight of a fucking spray-and-pray should be enough – they're only women and kids. If not, just give it a double tap up in the air, not a fucking squirt – right? Give me ten and go.' He slipped out of the car and began his bouncy unconcerned walk up to the front porch of the hostel.

Lance began counting on his fingers. 'Fuck's a double tap?'

Senda said, 'Kid full a shit.' He leaned forward in his seat. 'Hey man, he took the fuckin' starter wire –'

Lance finished counting. 'OK let's go.'

Senda, shaking his head. 'Took the fuckin' hot wire, man.'

Lance climbed out. 'Ain't so fuckin' dumb. Let's go.'

Senda handed him the leatherette shopping bag. 'No rush.'

It was a nervous twenty yards from the single yellows where Richie had parked the Primera to the front porch and by the time he got to the ram-raider bollards surrounding the porch his thigh muscles were jumping and his mouth was dry.

He checked back over his shoulder and saw Lance

leading Senda down the alley by the side of the church. All they had to do now was drop over the brick wall into the garden.

All he had to do was ring the fucking bell.

His heart was going like a fucking road-drill.

He drew out his mobile, dialled, said, 'We've got her Mr Sabbahatin. She'll talk to you later –' He cut himself off, dialled again. This time his message was even briefer: 'Game on.'

Now ring the fucking bell for Christ sake.

He looked through the porch and the bay windows: nobody.

So ring the fucking bell.

Then he saw the two CCTV cameras – one in the porch, one in a bay window – red LEDs blinking, hooded metal boxes turning, black lenses widening, pulling him into close-up.

Fuck it. Too fucking late now.

He pressed the old china bellpush. Someone had sellotaped a note to it: YES IT DOES WORK PLEASE WAIT.

Seconds passing, everything going into slow-motion. His nerves screwing him tenser and tenser. *Answer the fucking door!* Noticing things like flakes of paint, dried-out putty; looking at his distorted reflection in the porch and vestibule doors; feeling himself shuddering, wanting to pee, to piss himself endlessly, warm and wet and free and out of it.

'Yes?' A dumpy pale-eyed woman in a dark blue nurse's coverall was on the other side of the wired Triplex glass. 'What do you want?' Her voice was harsh, coming through the sort of tinny door-security intercom they had in blocks of flats.

Still in his hyped-up state, he noticed that if he

moved his head slightly from side to side the flaws and ripples in the glass seemed to detach parts of her face and body into pink and dark-blue blobs . . .

He said, 'Sorry, I can't hear you.'

The woman dipped her head closer to her side of the door. 'This is a Women's Refuge, you understand? Women and children only.' Then slowly mouthing the words at him: 'What – do – you – want?'

Making himself sound helpless, thick but harmless, scared and in a mess: 'I – I was wondering if it was possible to speak to my – my wife – for a minute.'

'You know you're here outside visiting hours?'

'Yeah, I know – sorry – I tried phoning.'

'When?'

'Hour ago? All I got was Engaged.'

'I can't help that. You should have waited.'

'I – I know, but – I come all over here from Knowle West.'

'You could have saved yourself the journey. This is mothers' and children's rest period.'

'Yeah, but – it's about the rent, see, my missis' rent.' Hangdog, he pulled out the creased manila envelope, showed her its cellophane window. 'She don't sign this paper, housing people say they'll have to – what they call it? – kick us out, like.'

The woman tried to peer at the envelope through the glass. 'Are you saying you've had an eviction order?'

'Yeah, that's right, eviction . . . What they do, see – what they told me, down the DSS.'

'The DSS people told you? I don't think so.'

'No, no, they don't want to, but they say they might have to. Place is in her name, see – they pays the benefit –'

245

'Now you're saying you're on housing benefit?'

'Yeah, right, housing benefit . . . I've offered to pay, like, to show, well, you know, show I'm willing – show – I'm serious about getting her back, but she's got to sign as well, see, showing she's the real tenant and this is only temp'ry, me showing goodwill to get her back like, not trying to take the place over, while she's . . . with her being in here.

'What's your position now?'

'On bail aren' I? An' bound over – can't get a job nor nothin' –'

'So how are you going to pay the rent?'

He shrugged. 'Get it somehow.'

'Get yourself back in jail more like.'

Richie stood there, head down, arms hanging loose, saying nothing. The dumpy pale-eyed woman was shaking her head at the fecklessness of men in general and Richie in particular.

'What's your wife's name?'

'Opal. Opal Macalpine.'

'Yours?'

'Gordon Kendrick – not married, see, more partners – but she's my missis – she's got my kiddy.'

'Child's name?'

'Esme.'

The woman looked at him hard, every last vestige of sympathy and concern drained clean away. 'Just wait here a moment.'

She moved back through the vestibule door.

Fuck sake don't shut it.

The deep stuttering hammer of an automatic MAC 10 at full chat. A shocked silence. Another shattering blast, shorter but closer. Again, silence.

Dumb fuckers – told you a double tap, not a fucking squirt.

246

Through the warped greenish glass he could see dust and flaky white emulsion falling from the porch's wooden roof.

Shit – fucking go for it – only thing –

He took three steps back and launched a double-footed flying kick at the centre of the door panel. The locks and reinforced glass held, but the plywood centre panel, weather-rotted over the years, splintered inwards. As he leopard-crawled through, keeping his weight on his elbows, he heard the start of it.

Women and children, screaming.

Shit – clusterfucked – the whole job clusterfucked – you stupid coked-up fuckers – you fucking deserve to fucking die –

Senda was on the broad cast-iron-balustraded staircase at the end of the brown and green tiled hall, his head and face hidden in a face-mask balaclava and a black Kangol, MAC 10 cradled in his arms, black gloves holding the muzzle pointing at the walls, feet set wide apart..

Dumb fucking poser.

'They all down?'

Senda nodded, pointed the MAC 10 at the dining room. 'In there.'

The dining room ran the full length of the building. Stacking chairs and tables were piled at one end. The walls were green and cream and there was a highly coloured Victorian print of Christ in Glory framed above the fireplace. It looked as if He had impaled Himself on a gilt sunburst mirror. Lance was standing in front of it, MAC 10 dangling from his gloved hand. He too had a face-mask and beret. Being Lance, he had added a pair of black Aviators.

What a fucking twat-head.

Above Lance the moulded ceiling was sprayed with

bullet holes, some still leaking faint drizzles of plaster.

'They all here?'

'Everybody here, man, kids an' all.'

The women and children were lying face down all over the floor. Some of the women had an arm thrown out to protect their kids. Some of the kids were still whimpering and being shushed by their mothers. All in all, he thought, it looked like the fucking massacre had already taken place.

Richie went round each mother in turn, stepping carefully between them, bending down to look at their faces and their children's faces, until finally he came round to Lance again.

He kept his voice low, trying not to let it tremble. 'She ain't here.'

'What you mean, she ain't here?'

'What I'm telling you –'

'What a fuck, man –'

'Yeah –'

'She got to be here. They all here.'

'She ain't.'

'We done every fuckin' room.'

'How?'

'Me down here, him up there.'

Shouting at him now, the splittle flying from his mouth. 'She's not fucking here! I oughta fucking know! She's not here so go and fucking find her! And tell that cunt out there to fucking look this time! Fucking roll on.'

As Lance ran stumbling out, Richie shouted at the women and children, 'Stay down! All of you stay down! On the floor! Look at the fucking floor!'

He went to the door, saw Lance and Senda racing up the stairs. He shouted after them, 'Every room –

and the fucking roof-space! And get a fucking move on!'

Plunging back into the room. They were all still face-down on the floor. 'Who runs this place?'

A woman with short iron-grey hair in a grey coverall with a black elastic belt was being helped to her feet by the dumpy woman. He strode over to them. 'Get them out! All of 'em!'

'What –?'

'Don't fucking argue – fucking do it! Get them out! Now!' He went back to the door, took up position at the side of the cast-iron balustrade and stared upwards. All around he could hear women silently rushing, their feet slithering on the tiles, until he felt, rather than saw or heard, that all life had leaked out of the building.

Footsteps on the stairs. He turned and ran for the porch. Both MAC 10s hammering and resounding like the clappers of hell in the empty hall. Chips of floor-tile and ricochets humming and whanging all round him. Getting kicked in the back by something that felt like a flying rugger boot.

Then he was out. Breathing fresh air – praying he could get the Primera to start first go. Clambering in, fiddling with the wire, shorting it across the screwdriver.

For the first time seeing the dark red stain spreading across his groin down the inside left leg of his camo pants.

Fighting the nausea, right foot hard down, engine yowling, shoving it into gear – oh shit, no feeling in his left leg – shoving the leg down on the clutch with his hand.

The car clutch-jumping, bucking and kangarooing

all over the road, tortured engine screaming.

Useless fucking leg wobbling all over the place –

Catching the first flat hammer of gunfire in the open air.

The Primera's rear window shattering.

That fucking rugger boot again –

Kicking him in the back of the head –

25

It was gone five before Vic and Cromer got around to lunch. They sat in the Escort van outside the Montpelier refuge eating Pot Noodles and egg-and-bacon baps. From the passenger seat Vic could see the outline of PC Lever behind the refuge door; WPC Bradley was inside with Opal, Nova and the kids, and there were a couple of plainclothes guys round the back. Vic didn't know whether they were all carrying or not but by the bulky look of them in their Goretex jackets and chequer-banded police baseball caps, it was almost certain they were.

Yeah, well, that was between Sam and Caroline.

He wondered what she was doing.

Then what Ellie was doing.

It was what the job did: left you feeling cut off, isolated.

Cromer had egg running down his chin.

Now he was licking and wiping it off.

Down the hill the main road overhead lights were coming on.

After a sunny day the air in the streets had turned cold and condensation had formed on the screen of the Escort van. Cromer was clearing it with his leather glove when Vic took the all-units ARV call. When it was finished he gave himself a couple of moments to review their options, then put the lid on his Pot Noodle and dropped it in the footwell.

251

Cromer had already started the engine and put the fan up to full blast. 'What's the SP, Vic?'

'Put your foot down John, they've shot a copper.'

'Where?'

'Fishponds. That fucking hostel.'

As the van tyre-squealed out of the cul-de-sac Vic reached over and switched on the flashers, light-bar and siren. With the diesel's clattering roar, the yip-yip-yip of the siren and the difficulty of negotiating the traffic-filled rush-hour streets, the bad news left them with plenty to think about, not much to say till they hit the main A432 to Fishponds.

'They give a name?'

'No. Guy was undercover.'

'He dead?'

'Yeah.'

'Fuck.'

'They're still there.'

'Who?'

'Two black guys.'

'You reckon it's the two from Severn Bridge?'

Vic nodded. 'Yeah. Now they're in the fucking church, John.'

The DO NOT CROSS tapes and crowd barriers were already in position. A good hundred yards of the straight tree-lined road had been sealed off. A traffic cop in reflective silver and yellow let them through. Forty yards further on, close to the floodlit church and hostel, were the two black Range Rovers of Specialist Firearms Operations and Sam's maroon Saab. A dark blue surveillance helicopter circled and clattered over the steeply-angled church roof, searchlight coning in and out. Cromer pulled in behind the Saab. Sam was talking to the SFO team leader, Sergeant Steve Humphries. Although it was a cold evening and he was a tall athletic-looking guy in his thirties, he was sweating under four stone of full assaulter kit: ballistic helmet and goggles; Bergen backpack; blue coveralls; heavyweight black Kevlar body armour and leg protectors; belt rig strung with respirator, stun grenades and his Glock SLP. His pockets were bulging with spare mags and multi-burst distraction devices and he was carrying a retractable-stock Heckler & Koch MP5 sub-machine-gun slung across his chest. When Steve Humphries turned away to speak into his covert radio rig, Sam caught sight of Vic and Cromer.

'Fuck are you doing here?'

Vic said, 'We got the ARV call.'

'Not a fucking armed response vehicle.'

'Call was for all units.'

'Give me strength – who's looking after the women and kids?'

'Four guys from Trinity Road.'

'Armed?'

'Far as I know.'

Sam breathing in and out, trying unsuccessfully to contain himself. 'Hadn't been for you, Vic, none of this would ever have fucking happened.'

'In what way?'

Here we go, thought Cromer. Same old fucking truculence – fight on sight, like two black dogs.

As Steve Humphries came lumbering back, Sam said, 'Let's leave it at that for now.'

Vic shrugged. 'Whatever you like.'

Cromer, manoeuvring himself out of the firing line between Vic and Sam, caught sight of two paramedics running low, stretchering a body away from a green car into an ambulance. The face and chest were covered with a bloodsoaked green sheet but the camo pants and para boots were clearly visible.

'Vic –'

'Not now, John –'

Steve Humphries was saying, 'Chopper guys have a problem, Sam. Place has got a lead and copper roof. Heatseeker doesn't want to know.'

'Fuck.'

'No thermal imager, no way we know where they are.

'Gas?' said Sam. 'Fill the place with CS, gas the fuckers out –'

'Too tall, Sam. Nave's got to be sixty feet high, you'd never fill it. Probably get us before it ever got them. Stuff'd just come pouring out, ground level. They get somewhere like the pulpit, up in the organ loft, even behind the altar, they've got all three entrances covered.' He shifted the retractable stock under his armpit. 'Fact is, if you wanted a defensible building, a safe house, you'd have a job to beat a church.' Showing his even white teeth in a non-smile. 'Short of bombing it, of course.'

'Vic –'

Vic ignored Cromer. 'Tried talking?'

Sam said, 'Steve's tried his negotiators, we've tried ours.'

'And?'

'Some fucking rubbish about seeing the vicar and saying they were claiming sanctuary.'

Vic said, 'Where is the vicar?'

'Tenerife,' said Sam.

Some reason, Vic and Steve Humphries both grinned.

'Not fucking funny,' said Sam. 'Four months' work and a fucking good kid's life down the drain.' Then, unable to resist it, 'Thanks to you, Vic.'

Vic said, 'I hope you heard that, Steve.'

Steve said, 'Heard what?' He turned on his heel and strode back to his stick of five armed SFOs. Sam said, 'Cheers, Vic,' and took off after the SFO Sergeant.

Cromer tried again. 'Vic –'

Ripping off his car coat. 'May as well fuck off out of it –'

Cromer took hold of Vic's arm. 'Listen for fuck sake –'

Vic, wrenching it away. 'Fuck you think you're doing?'

'Vic, you know who this kid is don't you?' Waiting until Vic looked at him. 'It's the kid on the trail-bike.'

'How?'

'Saw his camo pants and para boots – they were stretchering him out. Same kid I saw at the hospital, same kid was at Severn Bridge –'

Vic stopped the ambulance at the barrier, showed his warrant card. 'Sorry lads – need to confirm ID on the deceased. Can we have a look?'

The paramedic took them round to the back of the ambulance, opened up and lifted up the soaked green sheet. The left half of Richie's head looked like a kicked-in blood-coloured football; the right half was comparatively unmarked.

'Oh shit –'

'Is it, John?'

'Yeah. It's him.'

The paramedic locked up, led them to the ambulance cab, took a clipboard off the dash. 'All it

255

says here is Richard Warren Bell, UC, SO 11 – whatever that is.'

'Met Surveillance,' said Vic. 'Any address, rank –?'

'Not so far.'

'Right. Thanks, lads.'

Cromer drew the crowd barrier aside to let them through. Vic watched them drive slowly away.

No need for sirens now.

'You know what I think, John? Anybody's fault that kid died, it's Sam Richardson's. He was pulling that kid's strings same way he's trying to pull ours –'

'Jesus Christ, Vic –'

'I fucking phoned him, he fucking knew we pulled 'em out – that woman supervisor must've told him – I told him – I stopped the fucking van and fucking phoned him . . . I phoned him again, Montpelier, that caretaker's room. He's on the other phone, says something about Fishponds, slams the phone down on me. Cunt was telling the kid to go to Fishponds while I was telling him we'd just pulled the women and kids out.'

Cromer took his time replacing the metal barrier, then turned to face Vic. 'Not the point, is it? Not any more.'

'Is if you don't want to end up like Sam Richardson.'

'Maybe they didn't want to risk the women and kids.'

'Bollocks.'

'You're as sick as he is.'

'Who?'

'Sam.' said Cromer. 'Fucking bloke's dead for Chrissake, half his fucking head blown off, you and Sam bickering like a pair of fucking schoolgirls.'

Vic waited, then he said, 'Sorry, John.'

On the way back to the Escort van, Cromer said,

'You're going on and going on, and everything seems all right and you're getting somewhere, doing something useful, even if it's only looking after women and kids – and then something like this and it all comes on top . . . I used to play round here, Vic. Now this.' Cromer shook his head. 'Maybe I should've gone shelf-stacking at Safeways like the old man said.' Trying to force a smile. 'I could have been at the cutting edge of retail by now.'

'You used to play round here?'

'Yeah. Dark nights we used to dare each other, walk through the graveyard. Used to say to some poor kid, you do it and Shirley Withers will give you a kiss and a feel. Then the rest of us would tear-arse round in front of him, hide behind a fucking gravestone, jump out and scare the shit out of him.'

Vic said, 'What happened to Shirley Withers?'

'Got married. Had to.'

'Figures.

'One night – me and her –'

'What? One night me and her what?'

'One night me and her found out where they kept the communion wine, all the candles and stuff. I thought we'd get in there, get pissed like – and do it.'

'You bugger.'

'No, she was all for it – I'd got the corkscrew, packet of three, everything –'

'What happened?'

'We got down in there, all quiet, lit a couple a candles, I open a bottle, she has a swig, I have a swig – she has another, I have another – get through one bottle – on to the next –'

'Fuck sake, John –'

'Tastes like dried blood only, you know, sweeter.'

'Sounds about right.'

'Then it's all metallic, got after-taste like iron filings, that metal stuff they put in your teeth – fucking horrible, only I'm not going to tell her that, am I? I'm saying it's fucking gorgeous, and she's fucking gorgeous, and all that, and I'm getting her tits out and she's getting my knob out – and – and –'

'What?'

'I come all over her face and hair and she throws up all over me best fucking strides.'

'Jesus Christ, John –'

'Yeah. She said it was God.' Cromer opened up the Escort driver's door. 'You're the first person I've ever told that.'

'Not surprised. Where did all this happen then?'

'In the crypt, round the back. They had those sort of double metal covers you get in the pavement outside pubs – you open 'em up, roll the barrels down a sort of ladder –'

Vic and Cromer, looking at each other across the silver frost forming on the roof of the Escort van.

Steve Humphries let Cromer maglite him and his stick through the crypt to the brick steps that led up into the back of the vestry. Two of the team had Steyer 7.62 sniper rifles with stubby telescopic legs and night sights. Nobody said anything until they lined up close behind each other and started numbering off at the foot of the steps and then Steve Humphries was whispering to Cromer, 'You don't want to see this, son, so fuck off now, all right?' As Cromer made his way back, he heard Steve Humphries say, 'Right lads – across the pavement. Game on –'

Outside, the metal covers of the crypt entrance felt

cold enough to freeze-burn skin. Cromer stood on one side, Vic on the other. For ten or fifteen minutes nothing happened and Cromer found his mind had gone blank and taut at the same time. Then there was a brief inconclusive double burst, muted by the thickness of the brick crypt to the 'brrrp-brrrp' of a two-stroke motorcycle; another longer burst; four or five sharp cracking shots like twigs being snapped.

Then a radio call for 'casevacs' and it was all over.

Cromer found he was shivering so much his teeth were chattering. Vic slapped him on the back and said, 'All down to you John. Just don't expect any credit.' They went round the front with three plainclothes guys Cromer didn't even remember seeing. They were ribbing each other and laughing as if they'd just come out of a football match.

The two black guys were being stretchered out fully covered in bright green sheets. Sam, bareheaded in his navy blue crombie, was rubbing and clopping his black-gloved hands together, congratulating Steve Humphries and his team. 'Well done, lads. Good result. Well done. Good result. Nice one, Steve.' He looked briefly under the sheets at the faces of the dead men. 'Excellent. Perfect.' After the bodies had been slid into the ambulance and the back doors slammed and locked, Sam stood in front of them and addressed the SFO team and anybody else who gathered round. Vic and Cromer stood at the back of the ragged group.

'Just to say, well done everybody. First class team-work. Now then, let's get the rest of the bastards –'

As he walked past Vic and Cromer he said, 'You two come with me.'

Cromer said, 'What about the van?'

'Fuck the van.'

26

Sam drove so fast it was fucking frightening: lunging and jerking and booting the big Saab through roundabouts and into overtaking situations that would have had a police driving instructor foaming at the mouth and screaming to get out.

At first Vic, sitting in the heated front passenger seat, thought Sam was either showing off to scare the shit out of them or the events of the night had shot his adrenalin-aggression levels off the scale.

Time and again Sam would push the Saab up behind a bus, van or truck, hang it out in the middle of the road with traffic blazing towards them – and for a couple of seconds Vic was so sure they were going straight into a head-on he could see glass shattering, smell rubber, flesh and metal burning – then the Saab would gather itself, howl and whoosh up the rev band and, front tyres struggling for grip against each other, catapult itself forward against a blare of oncoming lights and horns – and, last minute, Sam hauling away, heave itself back into safety.

Vic was burying his right foot in the carpet so hard he could see it going straight through the footwell into the fucking engine.

Finally, after Sam had overtaken a builder's Transit at sixty in second, going into a roundabout on the outside and coming out on the inside, tyres scrabbling through the roadside grit, Vic cleared his throat.

Sam said, 'Don't worry, touch of turbo lag.'

By the time they hit the M32 at Eastville Junction, Sam seemed to have got it out of his system and settled for a steady eighty-five in the outside lane.

'You're a jammy fucker, you know that?'

Vic said, '*I'm* a jammy fucker?'

'Fucking lucky we got a result or you'd be up shit creek.'

In the back, watching the curved black fascia bristling with red and green and orange LEDs, Cromer thought here we go again.

Instead, Vic said, 'What's the story on the kid, Sam?'

'Richie?'

'Yeah. How long was he undercover?'

'UC since last Jan. Smart kiddy, had it all about him –'

'You were his contact were you?'

'Who the fuck told you that?'

'Makes sense,' said Vic. 'No other fucker knew did they?'

'Rules of the game, Vic, you know that. One on one, no fucking leaks – until you stuck your fucking nose in.'

Vic let it ride. 'Sheet said he was Met Surveillance.'

'The fuck you see that?'

'Paramedics,' said Vic. 'Long-term infiltration's more MI5's bag –'

'Yeah, well –' Sam booted the Saab past a red BMW and shook a finger at it, '– we've all been trying to crack this North London Brothers thing for yonks. Idea was for us to pick up all three in the hostel, but the blacks lost it, went fucking trigger-happy. They hadn't, Richie would have set up a meet with the

261

Turks, saying he'd got the girl and the H and we'd have had the lot. Only life doesn't work like that, does it, Vic?'

'Sort of background this kid Richie have?'

'Before the Met he was a para. Did a bit as middleweight for the United Services. Made Sergeant but thought he was being used as the organ-grinder's fucking monkey because he could box a bit. So instead of doing a second stretch he joined the Met. So he said. From Bristol originally – Barnardo's kiddy. Why they put him down here I suppose.'

'Makes sense.'

'What – putting him down here?'

'No, him coming from Barnardo's.'

After that Sam gave up on Vic and switched on the navigator. From the back seat Cromer saw the Montpelier Women's Refuge was already keyed in. Time to time a woman's voice with a faint Swedish-American accent suggested calmly that Sam should make a left or a right. Sometimes Sam said, 'Thank you Greta.'

Vic said, 'Who's Greta?'

'Greta fucking Garbo. Before your fucking time.'

'This Fishponds thing –' Vic began.

'Good result, mate. Rest is history. Doesn't exist –'

'I phoned you, Sam. Phoned you fucking twice to say we'd pulled the women and kids out the fucking place.'

'Doesn't work like that.'

'You could've told him –'

'Fucking hell – what did I just fucking say?'

'You said it doesn't work like that.'

'That's right.'

'So how does it work?'

'You listening?'

'Yeah.'

'Words of one syllable, Vic –'

'Go on.'

'He phones me, I don't phone him.'

'Why?'

'Not so fucking clever now, are we?' Sam, smirking to himself, swung left off Parkway, then third left on Lower Ashley Road into St Pauls and Montpelier. 'He phones me, Vic, I can't phone him, can I? Case he's surrounded by fucking scumbags – which he almost certainly fucking will be, ninety-nine per cent of the fucking time. Got it now?'

'Yeah. Fair enough.'

'Fuck me. Phone the *Evening Post*. Vic Hallam almost apologises.'

'Yeah, but how'd he get on to Julius? I mean it's not as if Julius is on twenty-six arrests and no convictions. No sheet and nothing on him – Julius is clean as a whistle.'

'Think back, Vic. It's just after Christmas, right, and there's nowt about. No H, no coke, grass is long gone and there's sweet FA on the street. Julius is the only dealer going round with a smile on his face. Not selling the stuff, too canny for that, but not weeping tears of blood either. So our kiddy keeps an eye on him, finds he's using Opal as his mule. So he keeps an eye on her as well. Not exactly rocket science, is it, Vic?'

'Then five kids die and some cunt kills old Julius.'

'That was the black guys.'

'How?'

'We found their happy bag. Cattle prods, trans-formers, roll of butcher's knives, the lot.'

'Thanks for telling us.'

Sam smacked the side of his fist hard against the steering wheel. 'Fucking hell Vic! Telling you fucking now aren't I!'

Cromer leaned forward. 'Excuse me, sir –'

'Fuck do you want?'

'Refuge is back there on the left, sir.'

Sam pulled in behind a black Range Rover. 'Fuck did he get here?

After he'd satisfied himself Caroline had people out front and back, Sam led Vic and Cromer through the downstairs rooms. The kitchen, cloakrooms and dining room were empty; Sam went round checking the windows.

In the sitting room WPC Diane Bradley, black Kevlar waistcoat over her white shirt, was perched on a stool at a small drop-leaf oak table just inside the door. Opal, Nova and the kids were noisily watching *The Simpsons*. The gas fire was bright red and they were crammed all together on a big old-fashioned green damask settee drinking tea or orange juice and helping themselves to a tin of Quality Street full of broken biscuits. Vic caught a brief burn of a glance between Opal and Cromer; then as soon as Sam stepped forward she shrank back into her role of passive, quietly sullen motherhood.

Caroline introduced Sam to them all. He asked the mothers if everything was all right and the children if they were having a nice time but he was just too brusque and overcoated to get through. He drew Caroline aside; the mothers and children went on watching *The Simpsons* in silence.

Sam said, 'Where's the rest of them?'

'Upstairs packing. We're bussing them out to B & Bs.'

Sam nodded, looked over at the now-silent couch. 'Who's the blonde again?'

'Nova Perrott. She said she'd stay here with Opal –'

'Did she?'

'Yes.'

'And you let her?'

'Yes. Why?'

Instead of answering Sam went to the bay window, drew back the lined and weighted bamboo-patterned curtain. The cream shutters were closed and the drop-over black locking bars were in position. Sam pulled at the bottom edge of one of the shutters: it gave an inch or two. He looked back over his shoulder at the group on the settee, calculating lines of sight between the shutters and the fireplace. 'I'd be happier with the kids upstairs.'

'Right.'

Sam drew Caroline past Vic and Cromer into the hallway and closed the door. 'The black officer carrying?'

'Diane?'

'Is the black officer carrying?'

'Yes she is.'

'Should she be?'

'I think so. She's qualified –'

'Fair enough.'

'Look, Sam, if you're not happy, say so –'

'Thinking about the Turks. I can't see them backing down in front of a woman, let alone a black woman – gun or no gun.'

'I see,' said Caroline. 'You want me to tell her that?'

Sam looked up at the big scallop-shell fanlight over

265

the sandblasted-glass outer doors. There was another, plainer fanlight over the reeded-glass inner door. The outline of PC Lever in Goretex jacket and baseball cap was visible between the two. 'Not yet. Where's Steve Humphries?'

'Checking the attic rooms and the roof. I asked him to wait till the women had gone, but –'

'We need to talk. All of us. Got a room?'

'Dining room, through there.'

Sam started heavily up the stairs. 'Tell Vic to get a table set up, will you?'

Sam was at one end, Caroline at the other. In between Vic and Cromer sat opposite Steve Humphries and his number two, Roy Harvey, one of the guys Cromer had seen with a Steyer 7.62.

Surprised, Sam said, 'Still with us, Roy?'

Roy Harvey, a sharp-featured sandy-haired guy whose attention was definitely elsewhere, said, 'What? Oh yeah, Chief, with you till end-ex.' He said nothing after that, just looked at the wall, through it and out into the distance, frowning, hunted, trying to make sense of something that had no sense.

Steve Humphries said, 'Rules are, you slot somebody, you don't go on automatic suspension till end-ex.' Looking at Caroline. 'Until the operation's over and the inquiry starts.'

'Thanks.' She was smiling at him.

'No problem.' He was smiling back.

Sam said, 'Right. Good. Glad about that, Roy.'

Roy Harvey showed no sign of having heard.

Sam put his elbows on the rickety wall-papering table the refuge was temporarily using for meals and let his temples rest on his fingers. He glowered at the grease-marks on the hardboard surface as if they were withholding vital information.

The silence lengthened.

Vic could hear feet, women's and children's, moving around above their heads. Cases were being picked up, put down, pulled along uncarpeted boards.

Sam brought his head up, looked from Steve Humphries to Caroline to Vic. 'It's not going to work.'

Caroline nodded her agreement.

Steve Humphries followed her lead.

Vic scraped his chair back from the table: to Cromer, a sure sign he was getting pissed off. 'What's not going to work? I mean, I know me and John here, we're only the poor bloody mushrooms in the cellar waiting for the next load of fucking fertiliser –'

Caroline said, 'Leave it out, Vic –'

Steve Humphries nodded his approval.

Vic said, 'All I'm asking is what isn't going to work? I mean, is there a plan?'

Sam said shortly, 'Plan's the same, same as it's always been. 'Tice the buggers out and bluterate 'em.'

Vic said, 'Oh, right. Thanks for telling us.'

Cromer, under his breath, 'Chrissake, Vic –'

As if neither had spoken, Sam went on, 'Nothing wrong with the plan, straightforward enticement-entrapment – it's just that it won't fucking work *here*.' Sam put both fists under his chin, jutted it out. 'And that, I put it to the meeting, is a bastard.'

'Any particular reason?' said Vic.

Steve Humphries said, 'Basically, Vic, it's too good. I know you and John found it, mate, and, yeah, it looks perfect, just the hammer –'

'So?'

'It's got trap written all over it. Cul-de-sac, narrow

streets, cars everywhere, big back garden, houses overlooking – trap. All it wants is a big sign saying MICE THIS WAY.' Looking at Caroline to see if she found him amusing.

She did.

Fuck it –

For fuck sake grow up, Hallam.

Sam looked up at the ceiling, listened to the noise of feet and cases on the floor above. 'Better tell the good ladies to start unpacking again.'

'Right.' As Caroline stood to leave, she said, 'Oh, Vic – Lever and Diane have got the house-to-house stuff on Julius.'

'That all right, Sam?'

'Yeah, for what good it is. You come up with anything let me know.'

'Sure.'

Outside the dining-room door Cromer said, 'You and Sam getting very chummy all of a sudden.'

'I know,' said Vic. 'Makes you sick, doesn't it? Thing is, John, they told us all about fucking entrapment, fuck-all about enticement. How's that supposed to fucking work?'

'Vic –'

'What?'

'Any chance of a quick word with Opal?'

'You cunt. What are you?'

'I, John Cromer, am a cunt.'

'Get this house-to-house out the way I'll think about it.'

'Thanks.'

WPC Diane Bradley unrolled a computer print-out across the drop-leaf table and dropped a couple of laser-copied Enprints of Julius at a wedding on top. 'These are the most recent photos we could find, these are the questions we asked and this is the percentile response.'

'Forty-three per cent,' said Vic. 'Not bad for a working day.'

'Lot of people here don't have a working day, Sergeant.'

'Vic – call me Vic.'

'Right.' She spread more of the roll across the table. 'This is the analysis we came up with.' She showed him a couple of pie-charts, two area maps scattered with coloured dots and a sunburst graph like a Test Match Special chart showing where a batsman got his runs.

'You do this?'

'Yeah.' Looking at him sideways. 'We ran out of cowrie-shells.'

'Here John, this is your dap-off.' He moved aside to let Cromer in. 'What about personal stuff, Diane?'

'We can't get all of his bank account details yet but we know he spread it about from his paying-in books.'

'Much cash?'

'Julius was a gambling man – made sure it was all recycled.'

'Figures.'

'We did get one thing.' Diane sorted through the papers in her document case, took out a shiny travel agent's folder, opened it up and showed Vic the silver and blue envelope inside. 'He bought himself an open BWIA ticket to Barbados. Club class.'

'When was this?'

'Last week. Saturday afternoon. Paid in cash.'

'Single or return?'

'Single.'

'Hear that, John?'

'Yeah.'

'Opal mention it to you?'

'No.'

Vic flipped open his notebook. 'All she said to Caroline was just after Christmas Julius talked about buying her a place, but when he started getting twitchy all that went by the board.'

Cromer looked up. 'I can ask her again.'

'Do that – ask her how often he went back.'

'He never went back,' said Cromer. 'Some sort of trouble.'

Vic nodded. 'Then all of a sudden he changes his mind. Opal does the deal at the Three Tuns on Friday, Julius buys the ticket on Saturday. What about his habits, Diane?'

'Julius was a night-owl. Get up around four, go to bed around five, six in the morning, depending on the action.'

'Kind of action?'

'Mainly cards, mainly with mates or the Chinese. Plus the evening dogs, sometimes horses, occasional nights at the clubs.'

'Whiteladies?'

'Now and again, but he preferred downtown. Places like La Soufrière, Dennery's. Typical night would be the papershop first, the bookies, the Crown, other pubs depending who he'd got to see. Then the barber's or Rufus's. After twelve if there was nothing going down, he'd be at the Cat on the Roof. Sometimes he'd eat, but most of the time just ganja, scotch, poker and dominoes.'

'You got that written down?'

'It's all on the starburst. 'Places he was seen. The thicker and longer the line –'

Vic nodded. 'Like a wind-rose.'

Diane shrugged. 'If you say so.'

'Let's have a look, John.'

The line leading to Rufus James was fifth or sixth in length and thickness. Vic said, 'Why so often?'

Diane smiled, but whether it was because he'd asked the right question or because he was just showing his ignorance was hard to work out. 'Julius was like a lot of black people, Vic, specially the old ones. They want to be buried back home, have a good nine-night and a big send-off. You pick the biggest most expensive coffin you can afford from Rufus's catalogues, you pay your money every week – Rufus does the rest.'

'And Julius went for all that?'

'Oh sure. Him and Rufus were Bajans from way back.'

'Bajans as in Barbados?'

'Yeah.'

'What's a nine-night?'

'A kind of wake. Back home you can't leave a body lying round too long so you have the party later.' Her mobile went. She listened, then said, 'Caroline wants me upstairs.'

'Right. Thanks Diane.'

'Vic –'

'Yeah, go on, John.'

'Thanks.'

'Oh, John – when you see Opal –'

'What?'

'Tell her from me I think she's lying, will you?'

'Eh?' Cromer growing pink again. 'What about?'

'Just say I think she's lying. See what happens.'

27

The attack came in at 4.10 a.m.

Before that, out of everything else that had happened – the hours going through Sam and Richie's reports, the briefing, the prepping, the get-in, that bizarre fucking wake, the waiting, the feeling of being mentally tense but physically knackered, wanting it to happen, not wanting it – imagining the worst – Vic reckoned the hardest part had been getting Opal to make the phone call.

Vic had tried, and so had Cromer. Both of them had been calm and reasonable with her and neither of them had got anywhere at all.

The way Vic saw it, sooner or later he'd have to come down hard on her; hard and vicious. Trouble was, apart from telling Cromer he thought she was lying, and hoping that would prey on her mind, he'd got precious little to go on except what hard and vicious might dig up.

The question was when to come down on her: hard and vicious could go both ways – she'd either break down completely, or clam up – and what Vic needed was cooperation: she had to make the phone call or the job was fucked before it started.

Pressure, yeah, but how much?

At the moment, as far as he could judge, she'd terrorised and traumatised herself into inactivity: cornered, she felt every move she could make was fatal, so her best option was do nothing, stay still . . .

Vic had an image of a mouse under a cat's paw, bright dusty eyes not even daring to blink, hoping the cat doesn't notice you even though it's got you, hoping it will lose interest, lift its paw and slope haughtily off, bushy tail lashing . . .

But cats weren't like that, were they?

They lifted one paw to pat and clamp you down with another, to play with you and play with you, tossing you bleakly this way and that, until the last pounce and the spine-cutting relief of teeth in the neck – and then, only then, soft and pretty and inert, bright dusty eyes finally closing, was it over.

Something like that anyway.

Behind that, and backing it up, he thought, was the fact she felt betrayed; not just by the way she looked, wholly desirable, wholly vulnerable – but by her whole fucking life so far.

Yeah, if what she said was true.

You lose your father, your mother, your stepfather – even a stepfather who comes on to you then gets you running out his dope for him because you made the mistake of getting yourself pregnant by some fuckwit whose first thought was to fuck off – or so she'd told Cromer . . . You lose all that and you're bound to think some of it's got to be your fault no matter how good-looking you are.

And that was as much a curse as a blessing, singling you out like a birthmark, making you an automatic target of exploitation for every passing prick-for-brains. Result was, she'd shut herself off, denying not only who she was and what had happened, but the shit she was in.

Yeah, if what she said was true.

*

They were sitting in the kitchen of 14 Palmer Street. Vic, Cromer, Nova and Opal, with the thick chalk outline of Julius's body on the varnished cork tiles between them. Upstairs they could hear Diane Bradley and Don Lever with the kids. The two of them had turned the slit mattresses good side up, remade the beds and put the cot back together; now Diane was reading them a Little White Duck story while Don sluiced out the bath. The hot water and steam made the whole house smell of lemon and pine.

Not that the kids would be staying there – they'd be moved over to number 25 for safety once they were asleep – but what the fuck else could they do? You had to act normal for their sake.

Through the wall they could hear feet tramping up and down next door's stairs. Number 12 was the mirror-image of number 14: the way they built these terrace houses was in pairs, for economy, with the chimneys, fireplaces, staircases and outhouses stacked up against each other. Sam, Steve Humphries and his team were recceing the place, boots echoing, voices occasionally laughing through the empty rooms.

Opal was sitting on a bentwood kitchen chair, forearms on her knees, staring at the cork tiles, voice a low monotone. 'What's the point? Is no point. Nobody going to stop.' She listened to the boots and voices next door. 'They ain't going to stop. And if they ain't, you ain't. I can feel it – everythin' heading for a big bang-up collision, all you want me for is mek it start. Why should I? Ain't my fault – why should I risk my life, my kid?' Going silent a moment, shuddering. 'I ain't that guy on the bike am I? Just as much a fuckin' victim though –' Cromer tried to put an arm round her shoulders. She shrugged him off. 'I trusted you, I thought, least he'll help me. You say you love me, want me, not true, is it? You don't mean it, no more'n they do. Nobody wants me.' She looked up at them, cold and accusing. 'Only for abuse – all I'm for –'

Time to go for it.

He gave Cromer a warning look. The kid's eyes were hot and blue, his face stolid with rejection. Vic hoped he'd have enough sense not to butt in, start riding to the rescue.

'You're a fucking liar, Opal.'

She looked at him and nodded her contempt: Vic was always going to be the one to stick the knife in.

'You're a fucking liar because basically this is all your fault and you know it.'

Eyeing him, keeping her voice low, warning him: 'Fuck off.'

'You know what I mean, don't you? Julius didn't whack you because you wouldn't go with the Turks for five hundred quid –'

Watching him, a faint infuriating smirk on her face.

'There never was no five hundred quid, was there?'

Still that superior you-can't-touch-me look.

Two goes left, he thought. One a fact, one a fucking guess. Play them wrong, or in the wrong order, and the whole fucking house of cards comes clattering down and the job's fucked.

'It wasn't five hundred was it?' Deliberately hardening his voice, bullying her but keeping half an eye on Cromer: '*Was it Opal?* It was four fifty – wasn't it?'

Her mouth curving down, still contemptuous, still amused.

'It was four fifty you took off those kids in the Three Tuns, and then you went back to the squat with them –'

'You shit –!' Out of nowhere the squall breaking, lilac nails lashing for his face. 'You fuckin' shit!'

He caught both her hands in his and pulled her close. 'And then you went back to the squat with them – yes you fucking did – because you were fucking followed, Opal – the kid on the bike –'

Struggling with him, glaring at him, hissing at him.

'The kid on the trail-bike, Opal – he followed you to their fucking squat – where you took the poor buggers for another four fifty, five hundred, whatever – didn't you?'

Pulling herself together, fixing the smirk back. 'Fuckin' pigs. Them *an*' him –'

'Where'd he keep the stuff, Opal? You found it, didn't you?'

Her contempt open now, knowing Vic was guessing. 'Julius, he ain' t that dumb. Said a bag was burst, one a the bags was burst an' he kep' it back. Said the rest was already gone.'

'Where?'

She shrugged, uncaring, turned her face away.

Fuck it, Hallam – you're losing her.

Trying another angle: 'What about the kids in the squat, Opal? What did they do? Tell Julius?'

That got her back. There was no smirk now: Vic had a feeling he could be on the right track at last. 'They rang Julius, didn't they? Told him you'd rushed 'em for a few hundred more.'

A pause, then: 'That fucker – that mean fucker – he wait until he about to go – then he tell me I got no place to live, because he goin' back 'ome an' the place going up for sale an' beside I been robbing his money, stealing him blind he don't know how long . . . An' then he fuckin' whack me –' The truth glaring out of her, fury pouring out of her. 'That fucker. Deserve to die.'

Vic waited a few seconds. 'They're all dead now, Opal.' Glancing down at the thick white chalk outline 'Julius. The five in the squat. And the kid on the bike –'

She stared back at him, defiant. 'Good riddance.'

'That kid on the bike was one of our lot, you know that?'

Opal shrugged.

'You know what he told the Turks? He told them he was the father of your child –'

Her expression did not change. 'So?'

Nova stood up. 'I've had just about enough of this,' and walked straight across Julius, picked up the electric kettle, filled it and plugged it into the power point on the wall. She swung round on Opal. 'Look, kid, never mind them – we'll all be fucking dead, me and you and the kids an' all, 'less you pull your fucking finger out and phone this bugger – because the fucking Turks aren't gonna stop now, are they? This Richie bloke's told 'em – told 'em you fucking know where this stuff is so it doesn't matter whose fault it is –' She began hunting and banging through the overhead cupboards. 'Fucking coppers won't be here for ever, will they? Then these fucking Turks'll be back and it won't be Julius getting one up the arse, darlin', it'll be you . . . Where's he keep the fucking tea-bags anyway?'

Quiet and resigned, Opal said, 'On the left, over the stove.' She straightened herself up. Cromer

277

offered her a bunch of white tissues. 'Thanks.' She wiped her eyes slowly, frowning at each soiled tissue, until every trace of make-up had gone, then she said to Vic, 'What's the number?'

Vic pushed over his mobile and a page out of his notebook.

'What's his name again?'

'Sabbahatin.'

Opal said the name quietly to herself a couple of times, then to Vic, 'I can't do this with you here.'

'Fine.' Vic stood up. Cromer began to follow suit. Opal said, 'Not you, John. Him.'

Vic went into Julius's sitting room. There was a telly and a sofa with a baize-topped folding card-table next to it. On the table was a reading lamp, a glass of water and a yellow-green packet of max strength Lemsip. Beside it was a copy of yesterday's *Western Daily Press* open at the racing pages. Julius had circled three horses in red. Vic wondered if any had come in.

Life's not like that, is it Julius.

Nova banged herself through the door, eyes shining. 'She was fucking terrific – you should a fucking seen her Mr Hallam, she was fucking brilliant.' She's, you know, all fucking pissed off and choked up like she was, and she's going, "They fucking killed him Mr Sabbahatin, fucking cops killed my man, killed the father of my child, I loved him and they fucking shot him down in cold blood – I'm fucking done for, Mr Sabbahatin, help me, help me –" Then he says something, and she goes, "That ain't no fucking help – you don't fucking help me, I'll fucking top meself, I don't care, I don't fucking give a shit, I can't take any more – have the fucking stuff, take it – oh, please God, help me –"' Nova brushed away her own tears, looked at Vic seriously. 'She said Julius kept the stuff in the empty house next door, number twelve, and she'd be there. She was fucking shit-hot, Mr Hallam.'

Vic nodded, thought about it. 'She ask for anything?'

'No, not right out –'

'What then?'

'Said he'd give her a grand. Said he'd ring back.'

Back in the kitchen, Cromer was standing with Opal in his arms. She was making heaving-croaking noises as if she was trying to be sick but couldn't.

Cromer said, 'He rang back. He wants Esme to be there.'

'Why?'

'He didn't say.' He put his hand on Opal's head, drew her close to his chest. 'Guess though, can't you?'

'Yeah.' They looked at each other. 'Oh fuck –'

Cromer said, 'I've told her I'll be there with her.'

'Have you?'

'Yes I have.'

'Not up to you, John.'

'Isn't it?'

'No.'

'Right. Thanks.' Cromer refused to be faced down. 'I mean it, Vic.'

'Yeah, you do, don't you.'

Then the briefing in the Bridewell and Sam in his element. 'Right everybody, listen up, this is it, here we go.' Besides Vic, Cromer, Caroline and Steve and his team of SFOs, there were about forty people in the ops briefing room, half a dozen women, the rest men, all AFOs – Authorised Firearms Officers – in various stages of kitting-up. The overhead projector threw a grid-squared image of St Pauls on the pull-down screen. Sam was using an old pool cue as a pointer. 'This is number twelve Palmer Street – Ashley Road at the top – Newfoundland Street here at the bottom. Two battlewagons at the top of Palmer Street here, two at the bottom here. Your objective – seal off Palmer Street – once the buggers are on the plot.' Sam paused. 'Try not to do it before, or we'll all have to come back next week.' A scatter of laughs, mainly nervous. Sam moved the pointer from the bottom of Palmer Street along Newfoundland Street: 'Passing on to Newfoundland Way, Parkway and the M32, which may well be their favoured get-out route, we shall have the other two battlewagons, roadblocks, pursuit vehicles and ASU eye-in-the-sky.' Sam rapped the pointer back on Palmer Street, 'But this is where we see the job starting, progressing and finishing – here, number twelve.' He drew the pointer in a circle with Palmer Street for diameter and number 12 for centre. 'This, if you like, is the Wheel of Fire. Thank you. Steve –'

Steve Humphries came forward and took hold of the pool cue. 'Plan, please.' The screen image changed to a plan view of ground and first floors of numbers 12 and 14 Palmer Street. 'What we're using here is the standard formula.' Running the letters downwards on the wipe-clean marker-pen wallboard, he wrote: I I M A C. 'This is not, contrary to what some of you may be thinking, the stuff we put on our legs in SFO –' Another scatter of forced laughter. 'What it is, the tried and tested MO used in firearms operations up and down the UK.' Pointing to each letter in turn, he said, 'Intention – Information – Method – Admin – and Comms, for Communication. To go through this backwards, which some of you may be thinking is how we operate in SFO –' Another pause, this one met with complete silence: 'Comms is basically radio. We use what I might as well call a big set and a portable. The big set, which is encrypted against scanners, goes between the OP, or HQ Ops, and the SFO individual on the ground. The portable, which is still hard to crack on account of frequency shift, communicates between individual SFOs. So if some Zulu is bashing your head in with a brick, you can call up your mucker and tell him to come and persuade said Zulu otherwise.' This got more of a laugh; any mention of stuff like Zulus always did. To counter it, and keep himself on top, Steve Humphries said, 'I should point out that Zulu is SFO radio code for Hostiles, and does not refer in any way to that fine upstanding race of black people.'

And so it went on through each letter until Vic said, 'Fucking hell, John.

'What?'

'Every copper a comedian.'

Seeing his chance, Cromer said, 'Inspector Coombes seems to like it.'

'All I need.'

'And lastly,' said Steve Humphries, 'Intention. Quite simply our intention is to blag, cuff and otherwise spoil the day of as many of these Turkish gentlemen as possible. With, and I stress, as little as possible risk to ourselves and the public at large.'

Strangely enough, at least to Vic's way of thinking, everybody clapped. Caroline's face was, he noted, quite warm and pink with pleasure.

Afterwards, Sam came over and said, 'Looking for volunteers, Vic.'

281

'Sorry Sam, haven't seen any.'

'Very funny. I can only ask you to do this Vic –'

'What?'

'We need somebody in number twelve.'

'With Opal?'

'And whoever.'

Vic tried to look as if he was giving it some dispassionate thought and his best objective judgement but what was actually going through his head was, *Here you go a-fucking-gain, Hallam – another fucking situation you can't fucking well walk away from because you fucking well won't let yourself, will you, you stupid fucker – all because you're too much of a fucking coward to actually behave like one –*

What he said was, 'What made you think of me, Sam?'

Sam said, 'Don't be a cunt all your life, Vic. You and Cromer know her, don't you? Only ones that do.'

'Yeah well, you've made Cromer's day. Not sure about mine.'

Sam's lipless grin. 'Thanks, mate – you're a star.'

Sam was already turning away when Vic said, 'Sam, do we get any back-up?'

The grin went on a little too long. 'Sure. Talk to Steve. His dap-off now.'

'Yeah. Right.'

'Good man. Take care, mate.'

'And you.'

As usual, Cromer had moved himself out of the firing-line. Now he came back. 'That all about?'

'You got your way, John.'

'Thanks. Great.'

'Yeah. Just don't ever call me mate, will you?'

After that, Vic walked around trying to shake off

the feeling that somebody had put a full stop after his name.

He found Steve Humphries supervising the gear being loaded into the black Range Rovers. Beside the bang-boxes carrying the launchers, flash-bangs, stun grenades and gas, there was a whole pile of kit looked like it was burglars' big night out – heavy chains, crane hooks, sawn-off Remington pump guns, abseil ropes, bolt croppers, hydraulic and manual door-ramming devices, axes, sledgehammers and crowbars.

'Sam said I should see you.'

'Oh yeah. You're strapping as inside man, aren't you?'

'Something like that,' said Vic. 'I was wondering about back-up.'

Steve Humphries giving him the non-smile. 'Shouldn't worry about that. Plan A is we pick 'em up on the way in. You shouldn't ever see them.'

Vic said, 'What about Plan B?'

The same non-smile. 'What Plan B?'

A voice from the Range Rover: 'Plan B's the usual clusterfuck, mate.'

Steve Humphries said, 'Anything does go wrong –'

'Yeah?' said Vic, 'What?'

'If by any chance it all does come on top and you get the Bandits signal, hit the floor.'

'Thanks.'

Steve Humphries moving away. 'I was you, I'd get hold of a couple of black flak jackets – ones with ceramic upgrades –'

Ten p.m. Mist thickening to fog around the streetlamps. Tops of punters' cars white with frost. Curtained front windows lit yellow from within. Here and there the bluish glow of colour TV. A figure in a Jimi Hendrix fedora and dark overcoat down to his ankles walking down Palmer Street. Using both arms to carry something like a car mechanic's toolbox. The toolbox wrapped in cloth. From the Observation Post established in Nova's darkened upstairs front window at number 25, radio crackle:

'Oh-one-two. OP two-five.'

Cromer's voice: 'OP two-five.

'Suspect India Golf Three to Golf Two, carrying large box.'

Vic moving to the unlit curtained window, looking through, nodding back to Cromer. Both sweating now, wearing heavyweight black Kevlar flak jackets as well as their lightweight vests.

'Oh-one-two. We have him, OP two-five.'

'Suspect India crossing road, your side.'

Vic tightening the thick Velcro straps, nodding to Cromer.

'We have him. OP two-five received. Oh-one-two out.'

Knock on the door. Cromer glancing into the back room. Opal and Nova watching Julius's nicked telly. No other light showing.

Vic moving to the front door, shifting the Glock from shoulder holster to the waistbelt at the back of his trousers, keeping his hand on the safety. Opening the door, pulling it towards him, standing behind it. 'Yes?'

'Hey man, what 'appen, you got no 'lectric?'

'Fuck sake Rufus, get inside 'fore you get slotted.' Vic closing the door, holding Rufus against it. 'What's the box?'

Rufus took the dark grey army blanket off a brown

bakelite box about two foot long and a foot square. He spun it round in his long-fingered hands and showed Vic a double-octave keyboard and half a dozen white chord buttons. A length of black rubber flex with a 13-amp plug on the end was knotted round the box. The keys and buttons were all numbered and labelled in metallic gold 50s lettering and on the space where the fold-down music stand had once been, the same lettering read: MAGNUS 300 ELECTRICHORD ORGAN MADE IN USA.

Rufus said, 'I bought her in Galveston, workin' ship on the way over. Was secon' hand then, and she's a semitone out on the chords here and there, but she does.' Looking round the darkened room. 'On the other hand if you ain't got no 'lectric.'

Vic said, 'We got power, no lights. Put it down somewhere will you, Rufus.'

Rufus sniffed at the cold and damp coming out of the walls and up through the floorboards, folded the blanket and laid the Magnus 300 reverently on it.

'Now then,' said Vic. 'How d'you know we were here?'

Rufus looked directly at him and began unbuttoning his overcoat. Underneath he had a black alpaca jacket and a pastor's black shirt and white collar. 'Folk on the street tol' me.'

'All supposed to have been warned or evacuated –'

'Yeah, well, y' know what folk are like – somethin' like this 'appens, they all start guessin', want to 'ave their say –'

'Shit. Better get on to OP, John.'

'Right.' Cromer lifted the mic. 'OP two-five, oh-one-two.'

'Oh-one-two.'

285

'Suspect India recognised as Mr Rufus James, undertaker and community counsellor.'

'The device, oh-one-two?'

'Mister James's organ.'

There was a pent-up silence. Even Rufus started to grin.

Vic said, 'Fuck sake tell 'em, John.'

'Mr James has information our presence known on Palmer Street.'

'Oh-one-two received. Will check. Detain suspect India pending. OP two-five out.'

Vic said, 'Sorry about that, Rufus. They're going to have to house-to-house the street again and set up Choose to Refuse over the whole area to put the block on anyone calling the Turks or the Turks calling them. Could take some time.'

'No problem.'

'Care to tell us why you're here? While we're waiting —'

'Sure. I come by to harsk if the ladies want a see Maelee, see if they satisfied what I been able to do for our poor young sister.'

'I see.'

'Is quite important, Mr Hallam.'

'Yeah, I know,' said Vic. 'Trouble is, so is this.'

'Of course.' Rufus inclined his head: in the diffused light filtering in from the street and aureoling his hair and beard, he looked more than ever like Haile Selassie. 'Also I come to harsk if they want a hold a watch-night for our sister Maelee. Is too late for a nine-night, even a forty-one night, but I just had a feelin' I should harsk, you know?'

'Look Rufus, you go in and have a word, we'll try and sort it out here.'

'Tank you.'

'And keep it light, will you, they're both pretty fragile.'

'The word of God is always a comfort in time a need.'

'Yeah. Just stick to that, OK? No leading questions, all right? You're in deep enough shit already.'

'I been there before, Mr Hallam, I been there many time in this countree.'

'I bet. Just don't count on going home tonight.'

What seemed like half an hour and a lot of faffing about later, the decision was that Rufus should do his business, whatever that was, because, they said, it was good cover: any bandit sweeping the plot and hearing fucking organ music would think that was more normal, or more normally fucking abnormal, seeing they were in St Pauls, than a woman sitting in a blacked-out house all alone except for her kid and seventy-odd k of fucking heroin under the upstairs floodboards. Afterwards, they said, for reasons of operational security and his own personal protection, Rufus would be escorted as soon as possible to a place of safety until end-ex. Meanwhile, he was under arrest.

When Cromer told Vic what the decision was, Vic nodded and said, 'Hear that sound, John?'

'What sound?' All there was, static crackling on the radio as messages were passed back and forth.

'That, my son, is the sound of your superiors saving their fucking arses.'

Then the lights came on.

Rufus's long elegant fingers sped over the keys and

chord-buttons like pond-skaters. He sang with his eyes closed and his head back, giving the floor an occasional stomp to keep the rhythm going from his head to his feet. The organ made a reedy, breathy, front-room-harmonium kind of sound and the fact that the notes and chords were a semitone shy of each other, either sharp or flat, made it even more plaintive, even more hair-on-the-back-of-the-neck shivery. The young women were natural movers, hand-clappers and shakers, Nova more angular and staccato, whereas Opal's long lithe body flowed and swerved, to Vic's way of thinking, like the fucking Mississippi.

Cromer, who had a lapsed Methodist background, had a clear tenor voice and knew a lot of the words, not that that was altogether necessary because Rufus had years of practice in belting out the next line just before the congregation got to sing it, and even Vic, a natural growler, felt it would be fucking churlish not to join in, so before long they had a small but energetic revival jump-up going on.

They had 'Let's All Gather at the River', 'By the Rivers of Babylon', 'Guide Me Oh Thou Great Redeemer', 'The Twenty-third Psalm', with Cromer soloing away over a low hummed backing from Opal and Nova with Vic trying to keep up and thinking, *If you're going to make a prat of yourself you might as well go all the way.*

Then, because Rufus said it was a piece they always had on a nine-night back home, Cromer, looking like the choirboy he once was, sang 'Oh For the Wings of a Dove' with all his heart and soul, and had Rufus, Nova and Opal in floods of emotional tears; even Vic, who had always hated the fucking thing even when his Auntie May used to sing it, had to admit to being

288

moved – but when Rufus asked him if he didn't feel a better man for it, for opening up his lungs and his heart, Vic said Yeah, but he was glad they hadn't had 'Nearer My God to Thee'. When Rufus asked why, Vic said, 'Too much like the fucking *Titanic*'.

Then, judging they were warmed up, Rufus said he had a short prayer to say for the soul of our dear sister Maelee and asked them to bow their heads and put their hands together and make of themselves a church that Jah's spirit might more easy enter in.

In the stillness before Rufus began, Vic felt the damp and cold once more rising up round his ankles from the gaps in the uncarpeted boards. Place had that unlived-in, dank, claggy, wet-rot smell – as if the last person to live there had died and never been found.

Rufus was saying, 'Death is nothin' to be afeard of, nah, because look, a seed, even a seed of herb of Jah, have to die before it quicken again. Like you put a seed in the dark before you plant him out in a light, so Jah put us in the dark, and same way the herb grow into a mighty five-finger flower the heighth of a man, an' no longer look like the little-bitty speck a seed a man put in, so we all shall grow, as sister Maelee growin' now, up an' up an' up an' up until we raise our head into Glory-Hallelujah. For behold we all start as seeds growin' in the dark of our mother's womb, an' then we come out an' make our way in this cold unfeelin' world with only Jah's love to keep us warm. An' when Death come an' we cut down, all that 'appen is, we go back to Mother Earth an' become part of another seed, another child, an' we too, like the stars that fall like rain upon the earth, shall rise an' shine again an' again an' for ever, a testamen' to the glory an' incorruptible face a Jah Himself –'

289

A heavy knocking like somebody using the butt of a gun. A key snicking the lock back. Cold air and boots entering the house. Then Steve Humphries' voice, not unfriendly: 'Come on Pops, got your squeezebox have you?'

Eleven, then twelve midnight; Vic and Cromer taking hourly shifts to sit up in thick chrysalis-shaped khaki sleeping-bags next to the dark green radio in the front room. In the back room, Opal and Nova, also in sleeping bags, lay head to foot on the sofa brought in from number 14, watching Julius's telly.

At 12.30 a voice said, 'Oh-one-two. OP two-five.'

Vic said, 'OP two-five.'

'Lights out, oh-one-two.'

'OP two-five received.'

Vic climbed out of the sleeping bag, checked round the upstairs rooms, came down, put the hall light off, sat by the radio in the dark.

Five minutes later: 'Oh-one-two. OP two-five.'

'OP two-five.'

'Turn the fucking telly off – CCTV can see you from the fucking garden.'

'OP two-five received.'

Vic went into the back room, switched the TV off at the socket. The screen blipped and faded. Neither Opal nor Nova moved. Cromer's whisper: 'Anything?'

'Fucking telly', said Vic. 'They've got CCTV out the back, John. In the fucking garden.'

'Oh. Right.'

'No one to go near any windows, John. Longer this lasts, more fucking trigger-happy everybody gets.'

Cromer did from one a.m. to two. From time to time the house creaked and settled. Every fifteen minutes he did a round of the house and made a check-in call.

'OP two-five. Oh-one-two.'

'Oh-one-two.'

'No change, repeat, no change.'

'Oh-one-two received. OP two-five out.'

Cromer sat hunched over in his sleeping-bag, knackered, dying for a kip, watching his breath plume out and keeping himself warm by thinking about Opal sleeping in the next room.

He couldn't get over what a fantastic stroke of luck she was – like being resurrected into everlasting sunlight from the cold, dark grave of his relationship with Louise. What did old Rufus call it? 'Glory-Hallelujah'.

Yeah, that was about right.

He could feel every nerve, every cell, every drop of blood in his body, singing out in praise and thanks for his good fortune in meeting her, loving –

Oh God, please God, don't let her come to any harm.

He even caught himself feeling sorry for Louise – for everybody, really, who didn't have an Opal to love and wonder over – and hoped Louise would meet a bloke who was more interested in hairdressing than he ever was . . . Barrie seemed the right sort of name . . . they could set up a unisex together . . .

And as for that miserable old cunt Vic trying to give her a hard time, saying she was a fucking liar, well, what the fuck did Vic expect? As far as he, Cromer, was concerned, she was as brave as a lion and he was fucking proud of her for standing up to Julius and trying to shaft him for a few quid. Why the fuck not? Julius had shafted every other fucker.

Only thing was she was so fucking vulnerable,

291

being on her own and all that. Well, all that would change for good when they they got set up together.

Him and her and little Esme, bless her – get set up somewhere well away from St Pauls, somewhere nice with a garden – like one of those neat little Victorian terrace houses on the hill above Westbury-on-Trym . . . Life, when he thought about it, suddenly became a broad sunlit highway through fields of ripening corn, and they were floating above it, entwined in each other's arms, for ever . . .

He wondered whether he should have the last half of his Bounty bar and wished to Christ it was all over – to lie at peace, deep in a warm double bed, sleeping, next to her – to wake up and watch her breathe, to inhale the calm of her sleeping face – oh Jesus . . .

'Thanks John.'

Sitting bolt upright. 'What?'

'Don't think I'm giving you an extra ten 'cause I'm not.'

Cromer focusing on his watch-face: 2.12. 'Sorry, Vic.'

Three fifty, just after Vic had done his third round, made his third 'no change' call, Nova came shuffling in, barefoot, sleeping bag bulked up round her skinny form, yawning, not looking at him. 'Couldn't sleep. Wanna cup a tea?'

'Better not.'

'Got a fag?'

'Yeah.' Shielding the lighter, touching her hand, feeling it tremble: 'What's up?'

She shook her head, drawing deep on the cigarette, still not looking at him.

Making his voice kinder: 'What's the matter, Nova?

You don't have to be here you know.'

She shook her head again. 'Not that.'

'You worried about the kids?'

'Bit.'

A sound of movement from the other room, like someone turning over, making a slight murmuring noise before settling down again. Nova's eyes flickering at him, then away.

Vic saying, 'No need, you know, they've got Don Lever and Diane with 'em – number 25's packed out with coppers –'

Then Nova, seeming to want to keep Vic talking: 'What d'you think this Sab bloke's going to do when he finds no kiddy?'

Vic saying, 'What's he going to do when he finds no heroin?'

From the back room another murmur, a floorboard creaking.

Vic starting to get up, still inside his sleeping bag.

Nova whispering, 'Don't –'

'What?'

'Don't, Mr Hallam.'

Now Vic was whispering. 'Don't what? What's going on?'

Nova looking at him like a kid trying not to betray a secret, knowing it's going to come out anyway.

Oh shit – all we fucking need.

Nova trying to stop Vic getting out of his chair and sleeping bag: 'No, Mr Hallam. Don't, it's not their fault –'

Oh yes it is. I'll crucify the cunt –

The sort of noise people make when they're trying not to make any noise: swallowed-up murmurs, whimpers, rustlings.

Nova hanging on to him, her thin arms round his knees, his feet still in the. sleeping bag. 'Please, Mr Hallam, don't stop them, give 'em a chance –'

You cuntstruck fucking idiot, Cromer –

'Please, leave them alone.' Her eyes huge and dark in her pale pinched face. 'Please, Mr Hallam, please. Let them be –'

Sitting down to free himself from her, pull the bag off his feet. Glancing at his watch: 3.54. Standing up again, Nova standing up with him, putting herself between Vic and the door through to the back room. More creakings; then more, getting into a rhythm, then slowing. Vic and Nova looking at each other, each knowing exactly what was going on.

'Fucking hell, Nova –'

Nova starting to crack up, eyes starting to glitter, putting a hand over her mouth, suppressing laughter into a muffled snort, wiping her nose with a peach tissue, her mouth grinning, her eyes dancing. 'Oh, Mr Hallam –'

'Nothing to fucking laugh about –'

'Oh Mr Hallam –' As if she couldn't get any further without cracking up altogether.

'What?'

'I never seen a bloke look so – look so fucking baffled –'

More noise, unmistakable now – old Julius's sofa getting a right pumping and pounding.

'Yeah, well, I'm the bloke gets fucking shot – while he's fucking shagging –'

'Oh come on, Mr Hallam – give us a hug.'

'What?'

'Give us hug.' Looking lost, anxious, scared of rejection.

Vic took her in his arms. Her chin barely came up to the top of the ceramic plate in his flak jacket. Holding her reminded him of picking up a damaged seagull once: so light that one squeeze, you felt, and the whole fragile bone structure would be crushed flat. He felt her relax against him and sigh. Then she pulled herself away. 'Oh,' she said, 'that's better. Thanks.' Stubbing her cigarette in the paint-tin lid ashtray.

In the back room, the humping going like a train, grunts, creaks, moans, little sharp aahs and cries like small nocturnal animals, and overall a sound like someone trying to hammer a punchball off its hook, slowing to a series of grunting thuds like punches being socked into the heavy bag, then accelerating again.

Vic thinking, *One sofa, hardly used.*

Looking irritably at his watch: 3.57.

Nova saying, 'Oh come on Mr Hallam, you must know what it's like, how it all starts, you ain't that fucking ancient.'

'Thanks.'

'Only like choc'late innit? You think oh I'll only have a little bit, then you have a little bit more, and a little bit more – before you know where you are you're fourteen-stone and brain-dead, or pregnant.'

'Wish he'd fucking hurry up.'

To take his mind off it, Vic did a final round, checking every room, even looking in the roof-space. When he came down again all the thudding and grunting had stopped. Nova said, 'Peace at last.'

'Not for fucking long.' He picked up the mic. 'OP two-five. Oh-one-two.'

'Oh-one-two.'

'Zero four hundred hours no change. Repeat, zero four hundred hours, no change.'

'Oh-one-two received. Stand by for stand down. Repeat, stand by for stand down.'

'OP two-five received. Oh-one-two out.'

Instead of the relief he anticipated, the dead weight of tension lifting, all Vic felt was totally worn out, incapable of either thought or action, legs and arms like waterlogged lumps of wood, brain flickering on empty.

When Cromer came in, grinning, flushed, scruffing up his hair and doing up his black flak jacket, Vic couldn't even summon up the energy to bollock him. All he said was, 'Better now, John?'

'Yeah, why, what's happening?' Turning to Nova, 'Thanks, love.'

Vic said, 'Standby for stand down.'

Cromer grinning, rubbed his hands. 'Fucking great –'

'Was it?' said Vic wearily. When Cromer went on grinning like the fucking village idiot, Vic felt a dying spark of irritation fan itself back into flames. 'Just as well it is fucking stand-by-for-stand-down, because otherwise, if I didn't know you better, John, I would swear that Detective Constable Probationer-in-brackets Cromer had just walked in here in grave dereliction of his duty and smelling of cunt.'

Before Vic's words had a chance to sink in and wipe the smile off Cromer's face, the radio crackled and burst into life: 'All units, all units, bandits on the plot, repeat, bandits on the plot –'

28

'Hit the floor!' Blood starting to pound and thump in his ears, his voice sounding thick like it was coming through layers of kapok; then adrenalin surging, turboing through his senses, leaving everything sharp, clear, up to speed. Grinning like a wolf, looking down at the Glock already in his hand, safety off.

The fuck did that get there?

'John?'

'Yeah –' Cromer was up close against his back covering the doors while he crouched at the window. Lifting the curtain with the dark grey barrel of the Glock, peering out. The road empty, balls of fog round the streetlamps, needles of softened orange light raying out; ears straining at thick damp silence . . .

'Nova?'

'Yes, Mr Hallam.'

Glancing down, seeing her curled up behind Cromer, huddling the bulky sleeping bag round her; in the diffused light from the street she made a shape like a sheep with all four legs tucked under.

'Opal?' No reply. 'Opal?' Looking out under the curtain edge down the street: nothing. 'Fuck is she?'

'Think she's gettin' dressed Mr Hallam –'

'Fuck.'

'Want me to get her?'

'No. Fuck sake stay where you are –'

'Yes, Mr Hallam.'

Cromer saying, 'Shall I –?'

'Shhh –'

Headlamps making fans of light, fog-lights stabbing out in front: a big black car, silent except for its tyres sucking at the wet tarmac. Coming closer – Vic looking for open windows – passing, everything closed up, but then slowing as it moved past the entry between Julius's place and number 16. Vic straining his ears – something like the soft double-click of a door opening. Then the black car accelerating away far too fast for fog; and this time a definite thud as a door was belatedly pulled shut.

And then two sets of feet planking up the entry between 14 and 16: that distinctive echo you got running between two blank brick walls.

'Couple going down the alley, John.'

'Right.'

'Back door locked?'

'Yeah. Key's in the lock.'

Now, coming the other way, another fucking car. No, a van, driving on fucking sidelights but the sidelights too high for a car, even a Transit: more like a three-and-a-half tonner. Now the sidelights going off – now the fucking engine cutting out for Chrissake –

Tyres squealing along the kerb, mounting it, graunching the suspension – and then, the big square body of the van sliding past the window less than six inches away, slowly cutting off all Vic's light –

Right outside the fucking front door for Chrissake –

Then a silence lasting several seconds.

Vic thinking the driver had judged the distance well, Turk or no Turk: wasn't easy with no lights, brakes, power steering –

Feeling his bladder contracting, sending a shiver right through him.

Fuck it fuck it fuck it –

Whispering. 'John.'

'Yeah.'

'Too fucking close, they'll never open the fucking doors –'

And even as he spoke realising the big centre door-panel was moving out slowly towards him, inch at a time, and then the whole door panel was sliding slickly back on its greased rails towards the rear of the van.

Nobody visible inside, no sound or movement.

Now another fucking wait.

Right outside the fucking door. Fuck was going on?

Feeling the polycarbonate grip going slippy in his hand, shifting it quickly from right to left, wiping his hand down his trousers.

Why the fuck didn't number 25 open fire – at least a dozen blokes in there, all with Remingtons, Steyers, MP5s – fucking things were lethal up to two fucking miles for Chrissake: this was less than thirty yards, they could blast the fucking tyres to rubber-crumb, riddle the fucking inside till everything was fucking dogmeat . . . Then the answer sailing out of the blue:

Because they want the fuckers inside, you silly cunt, they want them fucking hands-on, don't they?

All that Steve Humphries' shit about picking them up on the way in, and 'You'll never fucking see them –'

No, not fucking much.

This is a stake-out and you're the fucking steak, mate.

Grinning, digging his elbow in Cromer's ribs: 'Hey, John.'

Turning his head, grinning at Cromer until Cromer grinned back. 'What?'

'I don't like it Tonto, it's too quiet.'

Cromer grinning even more. 'You cunt –'

The quickly cut-off trill of a mobile. The scintilla of its green light inside the van. Two or three guttural words. The green point of light going off. Now the first sign of movement: the van rocking slightly on its tyres.

The thought flashing through Vic's mind they'd be better off top of the stairs, taking the fuckers out as they came up –

Too late –

Behind them, coming from outside the back room, the muffled pock-pock pock-pock of a silenced automatic. Glass breaking –

The radio screaming, 'Hit-hit-hit! All units. Hit-hit-hit!'

Somewhere off in the fogged-out distance sirens cranking up.

Closer, the blaze of a halogen flood lancing over from number 25 washing the street and fog white –

A bullhorn bellowing, 'Armed Police! Armed Police!'

Vic thinking, *Thank fuck for that* –

Then chaos as reality shatters into a dazzle of unrelated images –

The hammering blatter of heavy automatics –

The facade of Number 25 erupting in yard-long rushes of orange sparks, white smoke –

The bullhorn, 'On the ground! Armed Police! On the ground!'

The deep repeated bark of a pump-action Remington 870 thudding powdered-lead-and-wax Hatton rounds into the body and tyres of the van –

Mind-blinding, ear-cracking blasts of stun

grenades and multi-bursts, 'mothball' distraction devices –

Black-clad bodies piling out of the van, yelling and screaming, stabs of orange fire in their hands –

Glass shattering all round Vic's head –

A black baseball boot coming through the window –

Squeezing the trigger of the Glock at point-blank range –

The boot going limp, dangling from the ankle, the body falling back screaming –

More bodies, squirming over each other out of the belly of the van, all in black, like some grisly reptilian birth –

Jesus Christ how many more –

Riot guns slamming away – gas canisters whanging into the van –

The heat-fizz-smack of a round passing close to his head – a smell of burnt hair – his hair –

Too fucking close –

Vic, half-standing, half-crouching, dragging Nova's sleeping-bagged form away from the window bay into the angle of the wall: 'You all right?'

'Fuckin' hell, Mr Hallam –'

Her face and head disappearing into the sleeping bag –

A black-clad arm holding a gun – snaking and feeling its way – edging round the corner of the wall –

Searching for them –

Vic crouching over Nova, bending and coming up under the black-clad arm and firing into the balaclava'd face –

Screams and bursts of smoke –

No, not smoke – CS –

Stinging glass needles in his eyes, nose, throat –

Everybody coughing, retching –

More shouts – and the black-clad bodies pulling back –

Vic head down below the window ledge, firing blind into the body of the van – men screaming and yelling –

The van pulling away – lumping along on its shot-up offside wheels – inertia sliding and slamming its centre door shut – the van lumbering blind into the white halogen blur of fog, smoke and gas –

Long, low stabs of orange flame pursuing it from number 25 –

Then – sudden as it started – silence.

And Opal, walking in from the back room, holding herself stiffly, leaning slightly backwards, a hand behind her hip pressing against the small of her back, eyes wide, mouth open: 'Help me –' Starting to fall, staying upright by holding on to the mantelpiece with her right hand, turning towards the wall, her left hand pressed against the kidney area, dark wetness spreading round it. Nova rushing to her, holding her as she collapses –

Nova saying, 'All right love, all right.' Turning her head to Cromer: 'John!' Nova spreading her sleeping bag over Opal, pressing a part of it to the small of Opal's back, staring at the dark stain spreading –

Cromer on the radio screaming, 'Casevac! Casevac! Oh-one-two Casevac! Twelve Palmer Street.' Repeat, Casevac one-two Palmer Street!'

A woman's voice, calm: 'Oh-one-two received. Casevac assist –'

Cromer looking at Vic, mic in one hand, Glock in the other.

Vic, eyes and nose streaming, pouring mineral

water down his face, trying to see: 'Stay with her, John.'

Cromer nodding, sinking to his knees, cradling her head in his hands, looking down on her calm, stricken face; her eyes closing. Nova putting her hand out to him. 'Get her sleeping bag as well, John.'

'What? Oh yes, right.'

Cromer moved into the back room, stood there a moment, mind gone blank, thinking what he had to do, what he had just been told. Then, as it came to him, he picked up Opal's sleeping bag, rolled its bulk into a pillow, took it into the front room and placed it under Opal's head. 'She's fainted has she?'

Nova looking at him, full of fear. 'I think so.'

Cromer nodded, moved towards the door between the two rooms. From somewhere outside the house, coming through the shattered window-panes of the back room, the pock-pock of a silenced automatic. Then another, slightly further away.

Pock-pock –

The thought emerging slow as a cloud: *They don't know it's finished – they've been left –*

Once Cromer had it figured out, where the shots were coming from, he moved into the room, stood beside the window.

Pock-Pock . . . Pock-pock-pock.

A punch hitting him in the chest. A hard punch. Then another. Knocking him back, but not hurting, not hurting at all –

Pock-pock-pock . . . Pock-pock-pock-pock.

This time he saw the small, flame-suppressed muzzle-flashes blinking orange through the fog: low down, left and right of a pile of bricks and a discarded cold-water tank. He moved down the passage into the

303

kitchen, then the scullery. He looked through the window down the length of the narrow back yard, sighted the flashes again, twisted the rusty key slowly, quietly, in the lock, opened the back door, and walked out firing.

The two black-clad men took a couple more shots at him through the fog and seeing him walk straight through them they panicked, got to their feet and started to run. Cromer fired low, counting his shots deliberately, his mind otherwise dull and anaesthetised, and got one by the back gate and the other as he tried to heave his partner out of the way. He went up to them. Towering over them, he emptied six shots into each of them by turn, the final ones into their heads. He told himself it seemed only fair.

29

Sam started off his early morning press conference by saying that those who had enjoyed a good night's kip last night should think themselves lucky because he hadn't, nor had the officers under his command. What, therefore, the ladies and gentlemen of the press and media should expect was no more than a brief statement of facts as at present known. More information would be released as and when, from the Press Office, throughout the day. Thank you, Mr Parnes.

Sam took two closely typed pages of notes from Parnes, put on the half-spectacles he used for press conferences and began: 'Now then, as a result of this force's activities over the last twenty-four hours, two black males, both armed, both with previous criminal records, one in his thirties, the other in his forties, names being withheld until this operation is fully terminated, yesterday afternoon opened fire with Ingram Mac 10 sub-machine-guns in the Fishponds Women's Refuge and declared their intention of taking the occupants, all of whom were women and children, hostage. When their intention was thwarted by a brave and, I stress, unarmed undercover police officer, they shot him dead. The undercover officer's name cannot be released for security reasons as I am sure you will appreciate. With their stolen vehicle crashed, the two black males ran into a nearby church. When negotiations failed they opened fire on police officers including myself who had been called to the scene. Subsequently the bodies of two black males were recovered from the church. Both had died as a result of injuries received in their confrontation with officers of Special Firearms Operations, SFO for short. Thanks to the bravery of the undercover officer none of the women or children present suffered physical harm; many of them will doubtless be in need of counselling for shock et cetera in consequence of the violent and dreadful nature of their experiences. Due largely to information received in connection with this incident, another attack, this time involving a large amount, namely seventy-three kilograms, of smuggled and stolen heroin of exceptional purity, was also thwarted. In the meantime, however, five white male youths aged between eighteen and twenty-four, had died of massive doses of this self-same killer heroin in a Feeder Canal squat. No names are being released until their parents have been informed. Also at this time, in connection with this batch of heroin, an older black male in his fifties was brutally and savagely murdered in a house in the St Pauls area of Bristol. Following police inquiries into the location of the heroin, a number of males of Turkish nationality or extraction, thought to be about fourteen in number, were lured into making a four a.m. attack on a house adjacent to that of the murdered man in the St Pauls area. Failing to heed police warnings, two of the armed raiders opened fire from the back yard on the occupants of the house. The two armed raiders and one other, also armed and riding in a stolen vehicle, were shot dead by detective police officers assigned for the protection of the occupants. All in all thanks to the dedicated bravery, efficiency and overall tactical and strategic coordination of all police units involved, nine armed criminals were detained, seven of whom were wounded; three more, as detailed, were shot dead and two are at present on the run in what is thought to be a stolen and badly damaged black Mercedes saloon. Attempts to trace them are being temporarily hindered by fog and so forth, but their identities and London whereabouts are known to our colleagues in the Metropolitan Force, airport watches et cetera are being maintained, and I have every expectation of a speedy and positive resolution of this operation.' Sam cleared his throat, adjusted his half-spectacles and turned over his notes. 'Sadly, a young woman whom I shall not identify except to say that she is the mother of a young child, was shot and injured by the armed raiders, and is as I speak fighting for her life. I am sure that all of your and my best wishes and prayers are with her. Thank you ladies and gentlemen, that's all.' Sam, escorted by Parnes and a uniformed inspector, left at speed before questions regarding the present whereabouts of the heroin could be put.

Cromer sat by her bedside all through the night and well into the morning. Long after she was dead he was still there holding her soft insensate hand.

Ellie came out of the brightly lit emergency operating theatre into the prep room, snapping off her gloves and pulling at the strings of her green shift; Vic was standing in the changing-room doorway. He looked across at the entrance to Intensive Care: 'I'm waiting for John.'

She said, 'She's gone, Vic.'

'Does he know?'

'I don't think so. He just sits there.'

'Poor kid.'

Vic sat on a wicker laundry skip, his head down and his hands clasped between his knees. He went deep into himself, and when he lifted his head he saw that Ellie had changed out of her theatre gown into her staff nurse uniform. When he spoke it was more to himself than her: 'What a fuck-up it all is, from fucking arsehole to fucking breakfast time, what a fucking fuck-up.'

'Vic.'

'What?'

'I'm pregnant.'

Vic felt as if he had just discovered America.

The glass tubes, drip stands, drains and monitors were quietly unhooked, unclipped and, lightly rattling, wheeled away. Vic moved the screens aside and went in. Cromer was sitting close to her, her hand in his. 'Come on, John.'

Cromer looked up, lost.

Vic took his hand, and Cromer allowed himself to be led away. Although the news was working inside him like yeast, Vic had neither the wish nor the heart to tell Cromer. In part it was because he did not know himself: it was too big to know, all you could do was experience it, live it, revel in it, worry like fuck about it –

Every minute, every second almost, something else either changed, or got marked down for change. All he knew was that somehow a big dark glass wall had been shattered, and there was something moving and

308

working away inside him, not the same as Ellie obviously, but something new was definitely happening, something that was going to change everything.

First Sam told them they were both being placed on immediate automatic suspension until the inquiry into the shootings had been completed, then he said he wanted to speak to each of them separately. 'You first, Cromer.'

Sam told Cromer he was overdue at least one commendation and that, after probation, promotion was also on the cards. 'You're a good copper, Cromer, you could become a very good copper, never mind Vic bloody Hallam.' He bent down to unlock his desk drawer. 'Unfortunately for us, lad, we do have the problem of this tape.'

Cromer, full of a heaviness he made no attempt to conceal, said, 'What tape?'

'This CCTV tape.' Sam put a white-jacketed VHS transfer on the desk between them. 'You blowing fuck out of these two guys in the fog. Anything to say, just between you and me?'

Cromer shrugged. 'They shot at me, sir. I've got the jackets to prove it.' Shrugging again. 'They asked for it.'

Sam nodded. 'And you gave it to them.'

'Yes sir.'

Still nodding, Sam said, 'That's the trouble.' He picked up a carved wooden paper knife he'd been given on a trip to Vancouver and turned it over in his fingers. 'Anything else to say?'

'Only –'

'Come on, son, get it off your chest. Never let things fester. You hear me?'

'Yes sir.'

'Well?'

'It's only that – it's only that at the time, you think one will cancel the other out – but it doesn't.'

'No.' Sam laid down the paper knife. 'It never does.'

To Vic, Sam said, 'Understand you're thinking of leaving us.'

'I was, yeah.'

But I'm fucked if I'm telling you everything –

'Fair enough,' said Sam. 'What you got in mind?'

'Not a lot.'

Not fucking much, you got a living to earn, family to keep –

'Just think about being a sleeper, will you?'

'What, like that kid got slotted?'

'Suspicious cunt aren't you?'

'Pays.'

'Does it? Well, as you ought to fucking know, sleeper's not the same as undercover, not the same at all. You don't get involved, for a start. All you do is keep your eyes and ears open. Same terms, same pay, only diff is you're on your own whether shit happens or not. Right up your alley –'

'Where?'

'South Coast if that's where you want to be.' Giving him the lipless smile.

Vic thinking, *The fuck you know that?*

Sam put his thick red hands palm down on his desk and pushed himself up. 'Think about it anyway. No rush. OK, mate? Take care.'

Maelee's procession and memorial service passed off without incident. The Church of the Lion of Judah was packed, hot, overflowing. In his address Rufus spoke first of Maelee, and her child, then of Opal, and her child. Vic saw Cromer starting to go, his face white and sweaty, and held him up by putting one arm round Cromer's shoulders and supporting him with the other. 'Love,' Rufus was saying, 'Love is what they tell us bring a child into this world – but if Love give life, you tell me is it Love that taketh that life away?'

'You tell it bro!'

'Yes it is!'

'Yes it is,' said Rufus, 'an' I got to stand here an' tell you yes it is: Love a God, Love a Lord Jesus, Love of Jah, brothers an' sisters –'

'You betta believe it!'

'Love eternal, Love everlasting, Love is where we come from, Love is where we go!' Then, quietening down, 'Love fools, my friends, Love lies, Love betrays and Love denies – don' we all know that kind a Love? Ain't we all met that kind a Love, my brothers and sisters? I know I have, I know you have, fact is I don't know anybody don't know that kind a Love, not in this countree –'

'Tell it, man!'

'Tell it like it is!'

Rufus held up a single index finger. 'Not in this countree, nor in any countree, only in one countree – in Jah's countree –'

'Hallelujah!'

'Praise the Lord!'

Leaning forward over the pulpit, eyes burning: 'Love wrecks, an Love kills – he can come in the door as Love, an' he can go out the door as Hate – and this is still Love, my friends, because this is the power a Love: it can wreck us an' burn us an' kill us, but in the

311

end, my friends, the hope for Love – the hope for Love – is all there is, the longed-for hurt that drives us on, on into Jah's arms an' Jah's Love, the last an' best of all, Love for ever, ever more. God bless an' love you all –'

Afterwards, at Maelee's graveside, Vic found himself standing next to Caroline. When he asked her how young Jamie's claim was going, she said she'd been talking to CORE's legal people and they thought Jamie had a good case and a real chance of compensation. Then she said, 'Steve thinks I should drop it.'

'He say why?'

'He reckons it could be a career-killer.'

'Yeah, well,' said Vic, 'don't listen to the rattle, look at the snake.'

'You bugger. You could just be right.'

'First time for everything.'

After Rufus had rattled a few silver shovelfuls of clayey earth on the coffin, Cromer and Nova stepped forward and each threw a single white rose in, and stood there, hands clasped, looking down into the grave.

Vic, finding all this hard to bear, moved to the back of the small crowd of mourners. In his jacket pocket his mobile began to vibrate. He moved a few paces further away, out of respect, and took it out.

'Vic Hallam.'

'Vic –' A woman's voice, stilted.

'Yes?'

'Vic – it's Louise – I'm – I'm down by the gates.'

Vic looked down the immaculate, new-mown slope to the avenue of cupressus leylandii and along the curve to the tall black wrought-iron gates. Parked

312

apart from the other cars was a white Mazda convertible.

'Vic?'

'Yes?'

'Is it possible to have a word with with John, d'you think?'

'You haven't seen him?'

'No – no – I called him at the hospital – but he was too –'

'Yeah.' Vic thought it over. 'OK, Louise, I'll try –'

'Thanks –'

'Might take a couple of minutes – he's still at the graveside.'

'Oh.'

Vic strolled back to the group of mourners, and when Cromer came away, his arm round Nova's shoulders, Vic held out his mobile. 'It's Louise, John.'

Cromer frowned, sighed, then held his hand out for the phone. 'Nova's pretty upset, Vic –'

'Course. Come here, love.' He put his arm round her and held her against him. Jesus, she was frail –

Cromer turned away from them. 'Hallo?'

'Hallo, John. How are you?'

'I'm all right. How about you?'

'Did Vic tell you?'

'What?'

'I've got my car, outside the – the grounds.'

'Oh.' Then, 'No, he didn't. He didn't mention it.'

'Oh.'

'You're not going to work, then?'

'What?'

'I said are you going to work?'

'No. John –'

'What?'

313

'Shall I –?'

'What?'

'Shall I take you home? John?'

Cromer looking round the striped green lawns and neat grey stones like a man bidding a last farewell. 'Yeah. All right. Thanks –'

'I'll come and get you, shall I?'

'What? No – no, it's all right, I'll walk –'

'I'm just outside the gates –'

'Yeah.' Cromer handed the mobile back to Vic. 'Thanks, Vic.'

Vic pocketed the mobile. 'I'll see you then, John.'

'Yeah.'

For a moment, neither knew whether to shake hands, then Cromer turned away. Vic watched him walking, stumbling, dog-tired and heavy-footed at first, as if his boots were thick with clay, then picking up his step and moving briskly down the slope towards the gates.

Rufus was helping the two council workers fill the grave. Vic went over to thank him and say goodbye. Rufus laid down his spade, wiped his brow and said, 'Man, this is hard work. Hard, hard work.' Then he said, 'Come an' have a glass a rum, say goodbye to an old friend.'

Vic looked round for Cromer and saw the little white Mazda indicating left and buzzing off down the dual carriageway. 'Why not? I'll see you there.'

'Fine.'

Rufus was waiting in his reception – neat and modern, with rubber plants and ceramic-potted palms – when Vic arrived at the funeral parlour. He led Vic through to the chapel of rest. It was a small windowless room to the left of the reception area: pale green walls, white cornices, two narrow occasional tables, a Yale-locked door at the back. On one table was a green vase with a fan of pale blue irises; on the other, a plain slate cross and an open Gideon bible. The room was cool, with a hum of ventilation, and when Rufus put his hand to the dimmer-switched concealed uplighting, soft organ music began to play. It was Bach's 'Jesu, Joy of Man's Desiring', just loud enough to mask the air-conditioning.

Between the tables, resting on dark oak trestles in the middle of the sage-green carpet, was a huge maplewood coffin with ornate brass handles and corner-pieces, its flecked ice-cream-coloured wood heavily moulded, fluted and bevelled to resemble glassily polished marble.

'Jesus, it's big.'

'Yeah,' said Rufus. 'That sort a thing important back 'ome. Big box, big guy. Everybody know is a lie but they impressed anyway. Show the man made an effort.'

In the massive bulk of the casket, resting on thickly padded white satin, in a dark suit, black polished shoes, arms folded across his chest, and with a dignified and statesman-like expression on his face, lay Julius.

Rufus said, 'They didn't mess too much with his face, excep' for round the mouth.' He took a bottle of pale Mount Hillaby rum from the drawer in one of the tables. 'This was the one he liked, the Bajan.' He poured two small gold-rimmed shot-glasses full to the brim. 'To Julius.'

'To Julius.'

'May the Lord forgive him.'

They downed the glasses in one, and Rufus refilled them.

'Fierce stuff,' said Vic.

'Yeah, he used to like his rum, Julius. Used to like to come an' sit in the back room when this casket arrive, sit with it, all on his own, lookin' at it, runnin' his hands along it, hours at a time. Sometime I go out to a service, come back an' he still there, inspectin' it, mekking sure everythin' just so.' Shaking his head in memory: 'Julius could be a very stubborn, fussy, cussed man, y' know —' In reception a phone softly rang. 'Excuse me.'

Vic, glass in hand, looked down on Julius. He raised the shot-glass silently, and took a sip. For a while nothing happened but the Bach, the hum of the air-conditioning and the muted sound of Rufus's voice next door. Usually the presence of death affected him, weighed him down; now he felt light, almost neutral —

Hang about —

There was a tear, a slit, in the thickly padded white satin: one of the diamond-shaped cushionings looked as if it had been torn or slit close to the seam and then resewn. Looking more closely, he found other resewn slits.

When Rufus came back, Vic pointed out the first tear. 'He wouldn't have liked this much. Or that —'

Rufus bending low, putting on his thick horn-rims, taking a good look. 'Was never like that, never. Julius never be doin' with somethin' like that — man, every time he come here he examine every damn speck I tell you —'

'Got a sharp knife, pair of scissors?'

Rufus went out through the locked door into the embalming room and came back with a hooked

316

scalpel: 'Sharpest ting I got –'

Vic took the scalpel and carefully slit up one of the resewn seams. White powder sifted out through a mass of brown parcel tape on to Julius' dark sleeve. Vic wet his finger, dabbed it in the powder, tasted it. Rufus did the same. They looked at each other.

'Man call himself a friend. What a rass, man –'

Ellie said, 'What did you do?' Half past eight and after her double shifts they were in their sag-in-the-middle bed in Bishopston.

'Wasn't going to tell Sam was I? Not straight off –'

'Why not?'

'He'd have Rufus straight down the slammer.'

'You going to tell him?'

'Look, Ellie, Rufus would never have shown me if he'd known the stuff was there –'

'All I said was are you going to tell Sam –'

'Oh yeah. He'll give me all kinds of grief but basically I couldn't give a fuck.'

'You're an awkward bugger aren't you?'

'Yeah. That's why he'll believe me.'

'You and him . . .'

'I know.'

'Then what?'

'We took Julius out, ripped out the lining, there it was. Seventy-two parcel-taped packs of it, size and shape of housebricks. Some in the sides, some underneath him.'

'What did you do?'

'Tipped the stuff down the embalming sink.'

'What, all of it?'

'Yeah, apart from the one that bust open, went missing.'

'Three and a half million pounds worth?'

'Yeah. More or less.'

She was looking at him quizzically.

'I phoned BWIA. Found out Julius was only hanging about here waiting for the carrier to collect it. He was going to have it flown out separately. If he'd have gone without waiting, he'd have got away with it.'

Ellie thought about it. 'You think he would?

'Probably. Anyway I cancelled the collection. End of story.'

She pulled him towards her. 'Come on, then.'

'What about the baby?'

'Oh come on, Vic. It's only a quarter of an inch long.'

'What is?'

'The baby, you daft haddock.'

Afterwards, lying there, breathing in her closeness, and awash in the rich satisfaction of her body and the new life it held, Vic fell asleep convinced that with a bit of luck, you could go on discovering Americas for ever.

About 3.15 a.m. Vic woke up thinking about Cromer.

You discovered yours, didn't you, John?

But what you found, you could also lose –

Vic turned over, folded himself against Ellie's warm naked back, and held on.

**READ ON FOR A CHAPTER FROM
DAVID RALPH MARTIN'S**
ARM AND A LEG

1

A soft tap at the bedroom door and Joe came in murmuring his apologies to the Macmillan nurse. He handed Baz a black plastic binliner, stood back and waited. Baz turned his back on the nurse and took two padded Jiffy bags out of the binliner. One contained the short-barrel Smith & Wesson .38, the other the Browning 9mm automatic. Baz paid Joe for keeping them with three fifties from a thick roll and Joe left saying he was sorry for the disturbance.

Baz packed the Jiffy bags inside his leather jacket and said if God was to stand before him now, he'd shoot the Rass. The Macmillan nurse, who was as black as he was, looked at him askance. 'Forty years a life,' said Baz, 'and my Sis, she the only one ever nice – why shouldn' I? He bad, man, He worse than me.'

The nurse told Baz he should hold his sister Evelyn's hand, let her feel his life and try to be a good last companion.

Baz sat alone with his sister for an hour. It was a spacious first-floor room on a tree-lined street off the Finchley Road, north London. Evelyn, who was forty-seven and seamed up with cancer, had been carried there from her basement by Baz and her cousin Joe. Even with the camp bed and rubber mattress they used as a stretcher she had felt very light. Baz had fixed up a pair of split-cane roller-blinds to remind her of home. Thin winter sun shone through, striping the room with light but no heat. Her hand lay on top of his, skin translucent, blue veins showing. The previous night she had suffered a stroke which left her unconscious and Doctor

Rao said the cancer had reached her brain. The flesh on her oval face, once so calm and full, had melted like ice and the skin had tightened into concave curves around the sharpness of the bones. She was still beautiful, to Baz, but she was hardly there. He sat very still and upright, and although he did his best to love and mourn her he felt himself slowly filling with black volcanic rage.

Needing to move, he stood up, kissed his sister on her damp forehead, murmured 'Love you, Sis' and left. Once out in the street his pent-up rage erupted like a fireball. When it had passed, and nothing had changed, he felt both weak and free. He walked along the winter streets, fighting the ache in his bad leg, and let the cold air clear his head.

That afternoon he collected five kilos of cocaine for delivery to Bristol. At eleven o'clock that night, sitting with Evelyn, holding her hand, he felt her slip away. There was no rage now, just loss and cold disbelief in the way people said things were. Things had never been the way people said they were. During the long night's wake he kept for Evelyn, Baz figured he had always known how things were. Pitiless. What happen, happen. All there was to it.

Because he was chief mourner, he said he should postpone the delivery a week or so, and the North London brothers agreed. The delay gave him time to make his moves. First off was a call to Chingola, his contact in Bristol. Chingola was a musician kid, white but from Africa, one of them Z-places, Zambia, Zamibia, seriously into smack.

Baz said, 'How you doin', man?'

Chingola said he'd call him back off the street.

The phonebox outside Belsize Park Tube was ringing when Baz walked in.

'Where the fuck is it, man?' said Chingola. 'I got people's tongues hanging out down here, you said five fucking keys, man—'

'Family business,' said Baz. 'I got bad family business.'

2

'Oh right,' said Chingola. 'When then?'

'What our situation?'

'Viz-a-vee what?'

'Your cop fren',' said Baz.

'Oh, right.' There was a silence. Baz could hear Chingola's breath wheezing in and out. Then Chingola said, 'I think he's nobbing her.'

'Who that?'

'The widow.'

'What you talkin' about, man?'

'You know, I told you, that other cop, got killed. What's his name, Webber, Inspector Webber.' Chingola was toking down long and hard on a joint now, and when his voice came on again he was half laughing, half choking. 'Well, our guy, Detective Chief Inspector Barnard—'

'That fucker, put me in the fuckin' hellhole—'

'Yeah-yeah-yeah,' said Chingola. 'Well, he's not only investigating her case, he's sniffin' her snatch, man.'

'How you know?'

'I'm in this Watershed joint waiting for our weekly meet and he's only buying her fucking lunch, isn't he? Nodding and smiling and patting the back of her hand and going tut-tut-fucking-tut and all the time his eyeballs have got fucking hard-ons.'

'Heh-heh-heh.'

'So if he's not got it yet, he's gagging for it. He's fucking grey-haired, man—'

'We all got weakness, y'know?'

'Don't tell me.'

Baz said, 'You don' tell 'im me an' 'im, we know one another?'

'Fuck you think I am, Baz?'

'What else he say?'

'Wants to know the ins and outs of the cat's arse, man. How much coke, where to, packed in what, where we going to stash it on the night—'

'An' you tell 'im?'

'I don't fucking know, do I?' said Chingola. 'Not yet.'

'That right,' said Baz. 'You don', not yet.'

3

'I reckon he's got his own little private fucking mojo working—'

'Who ain't? Tek care now—'

'Baz.' Chingola sounding urgent.

'Yah?'

'Bring some fucking smack, man. Because it's fucking thin on the ground down here, and I'm pretty fucking strung out—'

'Heh-heh-heh. Talk to you soon.' Baz put the phone down.

Outside a thin-legged, blue-lipped white girl was glaring at him, smoking furiously. He held the door open for her. She walked past him saying nothing, not even looking at him.

Back home in the eighty-degree heat of his basement flat Baz took a glass of pale gold rum and picked away at the deal. The way Baz saw it, him and Chingola and DCI Barnard were supposed to be pulling on the same end of the rope, supposed to be setting up a sting on the local dealers to get them off the streets and into jail. That way DCI Barnard got the credit and Baz and the North London brothers got Bristol . . .

Was life like that?

Was it *shit*.

Everybody always had their own deal going. Chingola did. DCI Barnard did. Either one could put Baz inside for ten, fifteen years. On the other hand, as Evelyn used to say, 'All you got to do is watch which way the fish swim.'

In between talking to the undertakers and the minister and the ladies from the choir Baz was talking to the Turks. Jesus, it was hard work. Every time you asked for Shabbahatin they said Sabbahatin. You say OK, Sabbahatin, they say Who? He ain't here, he gone back, nobody seen him in months. Then some big, dark blue BMW 7-series would follow him round all day, not hiding, just showing him, three guys in the back, one guy in the front. Shit man, like crawling through one macca thorn-bush into another. But Baz kept on because he knew Sabbahatin and he knew it was Christmas and he knew they'd have a shipment coming through Bristol or Southampton or somewhere. He also knew the Turks never liked to stick their heads up out the trench driver-wise when they could watch and pay somebody else to do it for them. So he was seriously pissed off when finally Sabbahatin did come on and say, 'Sorry, Baz, you're the wrong colour.'

'Heh-heh-heh.' Baz taking his time.

'We need a white guy.'

'Whiter than you, you mean?' Knowing Sabbahatin had that dirty newspaper-yellow look.

Now Sabbahatin took his time. These Turk guys could pass it out but they couldn't pick it up. 'Yes, Baz. Whiter than me.'

'OK. Why?'

Sabbahatin ignored that and said, 'Somebody who can drive, looks clean, not like some chip-fed shavehead Millwall shit.'

Baz said he'd see what he could do, and by the time the funeral had come and gone, everything was set, all fruit ripe, and apart from Evelyn, Baz was feeling pretty good.

It was a mother of a deal. Deliver and collect. And the collection was awesome. Was a pension, no more, no less, and Chingola and the cop Barnard were dispos-able.

Yah.

Baz swirled the rum round the stubby little shot-glass and looked at what he knew about Chingola. First off, the kid was a smackhead, so he got no loyalty to nobody but the needle. Second, he was a musician, and all dem come feckless as shit. And third, he was white and in the cop's pocket, so the only way to work him was keep him in the dark until the last minute.

And then he'd be disposable.

The cop, Barnard, was a different matter. Ever since the guy had got him sectioned to that psychiatric fuck-ing hellhole name of Hillside, Baz had been figuring

5

ways to mash and juke the fucker the way the fucker had done him. Yah, Barnard, you got it comin'. Thinking about it, about it happening soon, made the juices run in Baz's mouth.

Heh-heh-heh.

Baz raised a last thimble of pale gold rum to his dead sister. It was a mother of a deal, justice and profit all the way. Yah. *All you got to do is watch which way the fish swim.*

Only thing he needed was a cyar and a white-kid driver. Also disposable.

On a fine, bright late-December Friday morning Baz Baxter stepped up into a hired blue Land-Rover driven by a fair-haired English ex-public schoolboy and set off for Bristol to deliver, collect, maim, burn and kill.

Also available in paperback

Frank Lean

NINE LIVES

Christmas morning greets Dave Cunane sourly. Manchester's most intrepid private eye is in jail. Often known to take the law into his own hands, he now finds himself in the hands of the law.

Framed and arrested for a cold-blooded murder he hasn't commited, Cunane turns to the ever-tricky Delise, his parttime lover and full-time assistant, to save his neck and find the murderer. But as the plot thickens and the corpses pile up, Cunane realises that more than one party wants him out of the way, for good.

'Sharp, hip-shooting prose with a refreshingly nasty twist'
Arena

'Sparse, authentic and entertaining'
Manchester Evening News

RED FOR RACHEL

David Cunane is Manchester's most off-beat private eye. Fond of the booze, fatally attracted to the wrong women, champion of the lost cause, he walks a thin line ...

Rachel Elsworth is missing. Nineteen years old, she has vanished into the city's seamy underworld. Her father employs Cunane to find her. Rachel's trail leads Cunane into the maze of Manchester's criminal fraternity; and right to the heart of police corruption.

As Cunane finds himself drawn further and further into a web of deceit and danger, he realises that someone will stop at nothing to find Rachel before he does. Even murder.

'This is the kind of stuff the English thriller has been begging for'
GQ

'Wicked as they say ... the author should give up his day job'
Time Out

James Ellroy

MY DARK PLACES

An L.A. Crime Memoir

America's greatest crime novelist turns to non-fiction, and the 38-year-old mystery of his mother's murder.

On the night of 21 Juni 1958, Geneva Hilliker Ellroy left her home in El Monte, California. She was found strangled the next day. Her ten-year-old son James had been away with Jean's estranged husband all weekend and was confronted with the news on his return.

Jean's murderer was never found, but her death had an enduring legacy on her son who spent his teen and early adult years as a wino, petty burglar and derelict. Only later, through his obsession with crime fiction, an obsession triggerd by his mother's murder, did Ellroy begin to delve into his past. Shortly after the publication of his ground-breaking novel *White Jazz,* Ellroy determined to return to Los Angeles and, with the help of veteran detective Bill Stoner, attempt to solve the 38-year-old crime.

The result is one of the few classics of crime non-fiction and autobiography to appear in the last decades, a hypnotic trip to America's underbelly and one man's tortured soul.

'One of the most important popular fiction writers in America, whose best books take their readers to the darkest places of the human condition – a Tinseltown Dostoyevsky'
Time Out

AMERICAN TABLOID

1958 – America is about to emerge into a bright new age – an age that will last until the 1000 days of John F. Kennedy's presidency.

Three men move beneath the glossy surface of power; men allied to the makers and shakers of the era. Pete Bondurant – Howard Hughes's right-hand man, Jimmy Hoffa's hitman. Kemper Boyd – employed by J. Edgar Hoover to infiltrate the Kennedy clan. Ward Littell, a man seeking redemption in Bobby Kennedy's drive against organised crime.

The festering discontent of the age that burns brightly in these men's hearts will go into supernova as the Bay of Pigs ends in calamity, the Mob clamours for payback and the 1000 days ends in brutal quietus in 1963.

'Intense and flamboyant ... excellent. The plot runs on high-octane violence ... a powerful book ... one emerges breathless, shaken and ready to change one's view of recent American history'
Savkar Altinel, *Sunday Telegraph*

'Brilliant and appalling. It is deeply repelling portraiture, yet mesmerising'
Marcel Berlins, *Times*

'Laconic violence, terse, slang-driven sentences, and a gleeful blurring of the moral line between good guys and bad guys ... Seven hundred pages of this stuff left me feeling punch-drunk and dizzy, but then it sure beats the hell out of Anita Brookner'
Jonathan Coe, *Mail on Sunday*

THE BLACK DAHLIA

A chilling novel based on Hollywood's most notorious murder case.

Los Angeles, 10th January 1947: a beautiful young woman walked into the night and met her horrific destiny.

Five days later, her tortured body was found drained of blood and cut in half. The newspapers called her 'The Black Dahlia'. Two cops are caught up in the investigation and embark on a hellish journey that takes them to the core of the dead girl's twisted life ...

'One of those rare, brilliantly written books you want to press on other people'

Time Out

'A wonderful tale of ambition, insanity, passion and deceit'

Publishers Weekly

CRIME FICTION BESTSELLERS
AVAILABLE IN ARROW

☐ Arm and a Leg	David Ralph Martin	£ 5.99
☐ Nine Lives	Frank Lean	£ 5.99
☐ Red for Rachel	Frank Lean	£ 5.99
☐ Kingdom Gone	Frank Lean	£ 5.99
☐ Boiling Point	Frank Lean	£ 5.99
☐ My Dark Places	James Ellroy	£ 6.99
☐ American Tabloid	James Ellroy	£ 6.99
☐ Black Dahlia	James Ellroy	£ 6.99
☐ L.A. Confidential	James Ellroy	£ 6.99
☐ White Jazz	James Ellroy	£ 6.99

ALL ARROW BOOKS ARE AVAILABLE THROUGH MAIL ORDER OR FROM YOUR LOCAL BOOKSHOP.

PAYMENT MAY BE MADE USING ACCESS, VISA, MASTER-CARD, DINERS CLUB, SWITCH AND AMEX, OR CHEQUE, EUROCHEQUE AND POSTAL ORDER (STERLING ONLY).

EXPIRY DATE .... SWITCH ISSUE NO.

SIGNATURE ....

PLEASE ALLOW £2.50 FOR POST AND PACKING FOR THE FIRST BOOK AND £1.00 PER BOOK THEREAFTER.

ORDER TOTAL: £................................ (INCLUDING P&P)

ALL ORDERS TO:
ARROW BOOKS, BOOKS BY POST, TBS LIMITED, THE BOOK SERVICE, COLCHESTER ROAD, FRATING GREEN, COLCHESTER, ESSEX, CO7 7 DW, UK.

TELEPHONE: (01206) 256 000
FAX: (01206) 255 914

NAME ....

ADDRESS...

....

Please allow 28 days for delivery. Please tick box if you do not wish to receive any additional information. ☐
Prices and availability subject to change without notice.